INTRIGUE AND ELEGANCE

Also by Jean Morley:

Black Pearls

Talley Girl

Cotton Candy

Walking the Imp's Path

Intrigue and Elegance

A Novel

Jean Morley

iUniverse, Inc.
New York Bloomington Shanghai

Intrigue and Elegance

iUniverse books may be ordered through booksellers or by contacting:

iUniverse
1663 Liberty Drive
Bloomington, IN 47403
www.iuniverse.com
1-800-Authors (1-800-288-4677)

Because of the dynamic nature of the Internet, any Web addresses or links contained in this book may have changed since publication and may no longer be valid.

This is a work of fiction. All of the characters, names, incidents, organizations, and dialogue in this novel are either the products of the author's imagination or are used fictitiously.

ISBN: 978-0-595-50463-3 (pbk)
ISBN: 978-0-595-61522-3 (ebk)

Printed in the United States of America

Acknowledgements

My thanks go to Charles Muller for all his help and advice over the years in the writing of my books. And to my daughter Helen, a big thank you for her help in so many ways and continued love and support. Finally, thank you to all those who buy and read my books and enjoy them.

CHAPTER 1

━━━━━━━━━━━━━ ▼ ━━━━━━━━━━━━━

With a satisfied smile the Reverend Stephen Brooke stood looking out of his dining room window at the view beyond the rolling Wiltshire downs and blue sky. He drew up his tall frame and threw out his chest and pulled in his stomach muscles in an effort to disguise the paunch that was threatening to develop. He gave a sigh of contentment as he thought how fortunate he was. It hadn't always been like it, of course, especially when he had been a young padre in the army, but luck had smiled on him when he had caught the eye of General Peabody-Brown. Perhaps this was because of Stephen's physical features. He had been tall and good-looking with a head of very fair hair, now sadly turning grey, and eyelashes to match. But whatever it had been, when the General had retired from the army to settle in his large house in the village of Kingsbury, he awarded Stephen, as a favour, the living of St Martin's nearby as a piece of patronage. In due course the General had become godfather to Stephen and his wife's children.

Stephen had been lucky, he knew, but in all the time he had been at the Rectory he had never taken anything for granted and every day he thanked his Maker for his life and good fortune. To add to this he had inherited a serious amount of money from his father, which enabled him to furnish his rambling Rectory with comfortable chairs and sofas and good oak tables. Tasteful objects such as an engraving by Durer and a charming landscape by Claude Lorrain and others were set off to good advantage by attractive curtains and hangings. Now, in his late fifties, Stephen was a happy man.

He turned as his rumbling stomach reminded him he hadn't broken his fast that morning, so he went in search of breakfast and his wife. He found Eliza bustling to and from the kitchen, her skirts rustling, as she helped Cook to bring in the hot dishes. Her comely face broke into a smile when she saw her husband enter.

'Here we are, dear, everything you like to start your day. Potage of oats thickened with eggs, cured boiled ham, fresh baked bread and butter. What would you like to drink with it, dear?'

'A little ale, perhaps,' Stephen said as he sat down.

'Right,' said Eliza, then, calling out as she disappeared once more into the kitchen: 'Joanna will be with us in a moment but we needn't wait.'

Stephen was, or had been, a stickler for time keeping especially at meal times when the boys had been at home. Now only his daughter lived with them, he wasn't so particular and left Eliza to organise most things in the household including Joanna, the youngest of the family. They had been lucky enough to have had three sons born to them, Matthew, Mark and Luke. Mark had studied for the priesthood like his father and was now secure in a reasonable living near Exeter and married to Lavinia. He kept in touch with home and saw his father frequently. Luke, again like his father, went into the army and was progressing well in a cavalry regiment. He wrote home when he could, explaining how he was enjoying himself and waiting to go abroad to fight in the war. But it was Matthew, the eldest, who caused his father some concern.

Now as Stephen sat and helped himself to the food in front of him he asked his wife if she had heard from Matthew.

'No, but then Matthew never bothered to write a lot, did he? I expect he's busy,' replied Eliza unconcernedly. Her mind wandered temporarily to the boys' rooms where she often went when she was alone in the house and all was quiet. The rooms looked forlorn and as always, she missed her sons as she fingered Luke's toy soldiers or Mark's rocking horse. In Matthew's room there were only a few books to remind her of her eldest son. Then she would sigh and close the doors once more, wondering if any of them would return one day to stay. She came back to the present to hear Stephen answering her last remark.

'Yes, I suppose so. He never talked or told us much when he was young, did he? A bit of a slow-top I always thought him. You disagreed, though, didn't you?'

'Matt was a good boy,' said Eliza firmly, sticking up for her first born. 'I always said he couldn't grow in stature and brain at the same time. I'm sure he's fine now.'

'Mm. He always liked going to see the General, didn't he? It was Peabody-Brown who convinced me to send him to London.'

They were interrupted by Joanna, who rushed through the door. 'Sorry to be late, Papa. I had to write a note to my friend, Emily.'

Stephen's daughter, a petite and pretty girl of twenty years, favoured her mother in looks. She dimpled as she smiled across the table. Her father nodded vaguely. 'I don't suppose you've heard from Matthew, have you, Joanna, and forgot to tell us?'

'No, Papa. Why, is anything wrong?'

'No, but we've heard from your other brothers recently but not Matthew.'

'There's no need to worry about Matt, Papa,' said Joanna confidently. 'He's a giant of a fellow and heavy with it. I don't suppose anything has happened to him, even in London.'

'I wish I knew what he did exactly,' said Stephen thickly, with a mouth full of warm buttered bread.

'He has told us, dear,' said Eliza. 'He has a nice steady job in an office in the City of Westminster and he had to learn French and German. So perhaps he is translating papers but I don't really know what he does, of course, as I don't understand these things. As long as he's happy I don't mind. And he seems to be doing all right as he doesn't ask us for money or anything.'

'He's lucky living in London,' piped up Joanna. 'I wish I did.'

Her father looked at her. 'It's the most sinful place in which to live, Joanna, and the most ungodly. You are far better living at home.'

'But Papa, how do I know it is sinful and ungodly if I've never been to see for myself?' wheedled his daughter.

'You'll have to take my word for it,' said Stephen in such a way that showed, as far as he was concerned, the matter was closed.

Joanna made a face then opened her mouth to pursue the subject but her mother hurriedly interrupted. 'Are you seeing Emily today, dear? Would you have time to help me in the village? I have to take some food which Cook is preparing at the moment, for Mrs Tindley. She is quite ill so I shall have to stay awhile to help her. Could you take the soup to Mrs Henson for her children and a cake for a treat to old Mrs Perkins?'

'Yes, Mama, of course. Have you any cake for the Henson children? I'm sure they would rather have that than the soup?'

'Soup is better for them, but I expect Cook has some more cake somewhere if you ask her. We'll take the cart. It is a fine day and we shall have time to visit the shops. Are you going out, dear?'

Stephen, his breakfast finished, shook his head. 'I have my sermon for Sunday to write but I shall visit the General for a game of chess this afternoon. But if anyone wishes to see me, let me know and I'll visit later.'

'That's all right then. Everyone is happy. And don't worry over Matthew, my dear. After all, he is twenty-eight years old and I'm sure he can look after himself.'

'Mm. That's just what worries me. Someone like him just sitting in an office all day, pushing paper; why, there's no future in it. If that is what he does do,' Stephen said as an afterthought. 'I'm wondering if he's ashamed of what he does and doesn't want to tell us. And,' he went on as though he couldn't stop his grievances, 'he isn't even married yet. But then he always was lazy.' And with that remark he pushed away his plate and left the table.

Joanna made a face at his retreating back. 'I don't know why he is so hard on poor Matt. He was my favourite brother, after all, and I love him.'

Eliza nodded and just smiled.

Later, after they had finished their visits in the village, Eliza said she must go to the Shambles in Marlborough for some succulent beef, as the General would be dining with them later in the week. There were also a few other things Cook had requested them to buy. Joanna made a face.

Her Mama said: 'I know it is difficult for you, dear, and perhaps boring when the General comes, but we are so much indebted to him, you know, and you're quite used to his visits. You could go and visit Emily for once, though, don't you think? I could make your excuses.'

'No, Mama, she is away, you know. I wrote a note to her this morning and took it round to her house. I asked her to let me know the minute she returns how she went on.'

'That's nice,' said Eliza, as she negotiated the horse and cart through the crowds in the High Street. 'Where has she gone?'

'To Bath, to stay with her Grandmama. It's the second time. She's been before but this is the first time on her own. She was looking forward to the gatherings when her Grandmama would take the waters and hoped to attend some dances at the Assembly Rooms. I'm so looking forward to hearing all about it.'

'Yes,' said Eliza, 'you must be. Unfortunately, we have no-one we know in Bath.'

'But we do know someone in London,' said Joanna innocently.

'Yes, well, I will think about that,' said her Mother. 'I hope Matthew will be home sometime; then I will have a little talk with him.'

'Oh, Mama, thank you,' said Joanna, giving Eliza's arm a squeeze.

'I can't promise anything and you will keep quiet about it.'

'Of course, Mama,' replied her dutiful daughter.

'After all,' said Eliza meaningfully, 'we don't want to worry your Father, do we?'

'No, Mama,' said Joanna meekly, but with a grin.

'Oh, look, there's John Powell bowing to us.'

'Who?'

'The Mayor,' hissed Eliza. Both ladies acknowledged him with a smile and a bow in return.

While the shopping and visits were taking place, Stephen was hard at work preparing his sermon as he had said. The house was quiet so he had no excuse not to produce something suitable for Sunday morning. As his sermons were like literary exercises because they had to appeal to both the General and the lowliest person in the congregation, it took considerable thought to get everything just as it should be. His theme this week was tolerance. Eventually, after writing for some time, he produced something that would last for his customary half hour and was of reasonable interest to all. He looked up with a sigh and decided to come back to it again the next day, so that he could read it afresh and amend anything that needed to be done.

He gathered the sheets of paper together and he thought once more of his eldest son. Did he have to write as much, he wondered, and was his paperwork as important as the sermon he had just written? Thinking of the subject of it, he decided that perhaps it was after all, and not just some mundane routine work as he was wont to think.

CHAPTER 2

▼

Perhaps if Stephen had seen his son at that very moment he would have revised his thoughts, as Matthew had just rolled a piece of paper into a ball and thrown it at his secretary saying: 'Why so glum, oh worthy Hugh?'

Hugh Fenton skilfully caught the missile aimed at him and deposited it into the brass coalscuttle by the fireplace. He looked at the man behind the large oak desk and met his lazy smile. 'I'm not glum, sir,' said Hugh, 'just thinking.'

'Ah, but what are you thinking about? Do I give you too much work? Does Mr Oakley give you too much work? Or, could it be that your latest conquest has refused to …'

'No, sir, nothing like that,' interrupted Hugh hurriedly.

'I think perhaps you answered me a little too quickly there, my Hugh,' said Matthew, raising his eyebrows.

Hugh grinned sheepishly. 'Well, it is only that Miss Bush isn't interested in me any more, worse luck.'

'But that is not the end of the world, is it? There are many more young ladies who would vie for your attention, I shouldn't wonder, a handsome young man like you. Now let's see. There's Miss Hope, but she has a squint and hope is all she can do. There's Miss Smythe, she's the bossy type, but then you are used to taking orders from me, so she is a possible; there is also …' Seeing Hugh's expression he grinned saying, 'You are permitted to throw that ball of paper back at me, you know.'

'Certainly not sir.'

'In that case I had better go to lunch.'

Hugh gave a sigh. He was a pleasant looking young man of twenty-three years, medium height and rather sedate, but an ideal secretary to Matthew and Mr Timothy Oakley. Now, looking across at Matthew, he couldn't help but think if only he had his good looks he might fare better with the ladies. To Hugh's mind, any of them would die for that fair hair and those thick, long eyelashes, even if blond wasn't the fashion of the day. The eyes, though, were a different matter. Light blue in colour, they could sparkle like sunlight on the sea when Matthew was in a funning mood, as now. But if he was angry, or displeased, those same blue eyes resembled shards of flint, which sent shivers down the spine. Also, being a large gentleman in height as well as build, he would be a useful member in a fight, but only, of course, if he was on your side, as it was well known he had a "punishing right".

Hugh looked up from gathering the quill pens for sharpening and said: 'I believe Mr Oakley is already out at lunch, sir.'

Matthew, deep in thought, said nothing for a moment, then nodded. 'Let me know when he returns,' he said.

It was over an hour later when Tim Oakley appeared. He sauntered into the room, saying: 'Hugh said he thought you wanted to see me, Matthew.'

Matthew looked at the debonair Tim. He was tall and slim with a charming smile which showed his white teeth, added to which he had a face browned by the sun and topped by black curly hair. He was certainly one for the ladies.

'It's just that I didn't want to leave Hugh on his own in case Harry called. If you're staying I'll go and eat.'

'I'll go with you. It will be all right.'

'But I thought you had eaten.' Matthew looked up quickly.

'Ah … yes. No. I just had to see someone, that's all.'

'Who?' asked Matthew, abruptly. 'Anyone I should know about?'

'No, no,' said Tim carelessly, 'no-one really of import, just a personal thing.'

'Well, I'll take Hugh out with me now. You can eat later, dear Tim.' Matthew smiled sweetly at him.

Tim shrugged. 'Anything you say,' he said offhandedly, but Matthew could tell he wasn't pleased.

He put on a black coat, which had seen better days, and a hat, then felt in his pocket to check if his pistol was there. Swords, of course, were worn, especially in such an area. Matthew was particularly pleased with his, as it had been made by the swordsmith from Matthew's own specification. The Toledo blade was ornately worked in a fine manner. He knew how to use it too, of course, but preferred the science of bareknuckle fighting to duelling with a sword. However it was always preferable to be over cautious than take a risk. 'Come along, Hugh, let us eat.' Hugh hurriedly put on his well-worn coat.

They descended the stairs, which were in striking contrast to the rooms they had just left. Timothy and Matthew had a large room each, Hugh a smaller one and the fourth was for books and files. There was also a safe for special documents. They were not luxuriously furnished but they had everything of good quality and comfort. The worst thing was that the windows were small and the only view was of a run-down building next door.

The stairs then came as a surprise to anyone who did not know the building. They were safe but were undecorated and without polish on them, only dust. At the bottom of the narrow flight the heavy oak door was locked. Matthew now opened it and locked it again behind them. They were then faced with a pair of decrepit doors that opened easily and were in keeping with the outside of the building, which looked unused and seedy. There was a sign on the top of the building but it was so badly worn that it couldn't be read. In fact, the whole area around was dismal, dirty and derelict.

As they emerged into the street the wind blew the odour from the Fleet, a stream that led down to the river and where people living nearby emptied everything, from refuse, night slops and even unwanted babies. The prison wasn't too far away, either. Walking through the various alleyways where the dwellers scuttled out of their way, their pale thin faces showing their poverty and pain which they coped with by drinking gin, Matthew and Hugh came to a more salubrious area of Blackfriars. Here they entered "The Shoulder o' Mutton", a tavern that was reasonably clean. The landlord hurriedly showed them to a table, bowing as he did so. Matthew and Hugh sat with their backs to the wall so that they could view the rest of the inhabitants and also feel safe from a possible stab in the back from some drunken bedlamite. They ordered a meal of cold meat, fresh bread and ale.

'Thank you for buying me lunch, sir,' Hugh said as he wrestled with a stubborn piece of meat. 'I could have waited, you know.'

'I know, but Mr Oakley said he was out on personal business. He should have had his lunch then. Next time, perhaps he will think that others must eat and not just fit in with him.'

'Yes, sir,' was all Hugh managed to say. He was surprised, as Mr Brooke was usually so good-natured. Now, as Matthew finished his food, he looked round the room and noticed a scruffy individual who had just entered. He saw Matthew, who raised a finger and so he stepped over to their table. 'Sit down, my friend,' said Matthew. 'Ale?' The man nodded. The order given, Matthew asked: 'Any news?'

'Well,' the man whetted his lips, 'we've heard that Prussia had heavy losses at Zorndorf when the Russians attacked them. They say that Lieutenant General Seydlitz was surprised, but he and his cavalry restored the situation.'

Matthew nodded. 'How is Prussia coping, do you think? They have our help and our navy is keeping back the French in the Channel.'

'As far as we can make out, all sides have heavy losses. We have to report to our contact in Whitehall who decides what to publish in the daily sheets for the public to read.' He continued to inform Matthew further of news he had learnt until Matthew stood up. 'We must get back,' he said, dropping a coin into his informer's hand. 'Let me know anything of import. Oh, by the way, have you seen Mr Oakley at all recently?'

The man shook his head. 'No, sir.'

Matthew nodded and thanked the man. When he and Hugh returned to the office they found that Lord Harold Anstruther had arrived and was talking to Timothy and awaiting patiently their return.

'Sir,' said Matthew, shaking hands, 'I'm sorry I was out.'

'Good to see you, Matt,' said Harry with a smile, 'Tim and I are having an interesting chat.'

Lord Harry was in his early fifties, plump and friendly with a great sense of humour. He was happily married to an elegant wife and they lived with their children near Green Park, a more salubrious area than Blackfriars. He and Tim were drinking claret and now Matthew helped himself to a glass.

'Tim was saying he hadn't learnt anything new. Have you, Matt?'

'Evidently Prussia is having its trials and tribulations and has lost many men at Zorndorf. But perhaps you've heard that?' asked Matthew. When Harry nodded, he continued: 'Also I've just learnt that there are only a few French officers fighting in Prussia, so the rank and file have few leaders. Therefore discipline is practically nil and there has been much sickness. French troops are deserting and for good or bad, coming over to us to fight.'

Harry frowned. 'Mmm, could be useful. The trouble is we seem to have lost contact with one of our agents over there. Whether he's dead or not I don't know. The French are attacking our navy in the Channel and we can't afford to lose any of the ships. We have a fleet in North America and India too, and new ships aren't quickly made. Those in the Channel are doing a good job and holding off the French and the Prussians are trying to help us, but I want some first-hand knowledge. I think I shall have to send one of you two over there. How do you feel about that?' He looked at both the men.

'When would be the best time to go?' asked Tim eagerly.

'As soon as possible, I should think, but after the Ambassador's Ball in two weeks' time. We might learn something useful there and I want both of you to attend. Also by then we shall either have heard from our contact in France or if not, one of you will definitely have to go.' He felt deep within his coat pocket and produced two elegant gilt edged cards with their names written on them. 'I shall expect you both to be present although I suppose the company will be thin on the ground as the season is just beginning.'

'So which one of us do you wish to send over to France, sir?' asked Matthew.

Harry looked from one to the other. 'How's your French?' This was said to both of them.

'We're both proficient in that respect,' answered Tim quickly, 'but I think I have the edge on Matthew.' He smiled good-naturedly at his friend.

'I agree,' said Matthew, 'but I am prepared to go if necessary.'

'Well,' said Harry, 'I think I shall send Tim, not only regarding the language but he would blend in better. He looks like a Frenchman. With your looks and build, Matthew, you would be too well remembered. You did well in Austria, I know, and were taken for an Austrian easily enough, but this time I think it's Tim's turn.'

'I am quite happy to go,' grinned Tim, 'even if it's only to get away from the unsavoury stink of the river for a while. I fancy a bit of activity and you never know—maybe I shall find some balls to go to in Paris. The French ladies are particularly attractive, aren't they?'

Harry laughed. 'Be that as it may, you would be well advised to watch yourself. A safe place to stay will be supplied by someone known to me and if necessary I'll have further words with both of you after the ball. Now I must go but it was good to see you.' He shook hands with them and the bell was rung for Hugh to show him out.

After he had departed Matthew and Timothy were left to discuss what he had said, in French, and to finish the claret.

CHAPTER 3

▼

The long, oak dining table was beautifully set with the best wine glasses and silver cutlery on a damask cloth and the epergne in the centre held blooms of late flowering pink roses and greenery. Eliza, in the kitchen with Cook, was checking that the food was just right and placed on china dishes ready to serve as soon as Stephen brought General Peabody-Brown into the dining room. At the moment they were talking together in the library.

Joanna, too, waited for the men to appear. She was bored and hungry. She missed her friend Emily and their girlish heart to hearts, also their shopping together and their walks by the river. She had helped by seeing that the servants had tidied the rooms properly earlier, and she had prepared some of the vegetables for Cook. Then, not knowing what else to do, she had wandered into the garden and most annoyingly her feet became wet, as the grass was still damp on this autumn day. So slippers had to be replaced and then her dress changed as the hem was damp too. Now with her stomach groaning, Joanna said: 'Shall we place the food on the table, Mama? I can go and tell Papa we are ready or I can sound the gong.'

'No, don't do that,' said Eliza hastily, 'your Father doesn't like to be summoned. But, yes, we'll place everything in dishes on the table, then you can go and ask them to come in. When your Father gets talking, time stands still.'

Eliza and Cook brought in steaming dishes of roast beef and roast potatoes, plump partridges and a steamed carp, a vegetable soup, a dish of carrots and parsnips, a variety of sauces, apple pies and creams. When all was just as it should be Joanna hurried along to the library. She knocked on the door and entered and curtseyed.

'I am to tell you, gentlemen, that dinner is served.' She smiled demurely at the General.

He was an elderly man, tall but still straight of bearing. His grizzled hair was hidden by a neat wig, and his keen grey eyes now looked down at Joanna with amusement. 'Well, well,' he smiled, 'how charmingly you look, Jo—Joan …?'

'Joanna, sir.'

'Of course, I never remember, do I?' He stood up and offered her his arm. 'Make an old man happy, my dear, and let me take you into dinner.'

'It would be an honour, sir,' Joanna dimpled up at him.

'You can also show me which way to go as I never remember that either.' He smiled down at her and patted her hand as she led him along the passageway to the dining room, her father following. As he approached the table the General said:

'Well, well, Mrs Brooke, how wonderful all this looks, as usual.' He sat beaming at his hostess as he viewed the good food on display while Stephen poured him a glass of burgundy. Then grace having been said, they all began to eat. There was no talking for a while, but later when their appetites had been appeased, conversation was continued.

The General smiled at Joanna. 'How I enjoyed that. And what do pretty young ladies like yourself do for entertainment?'

'Well,' said Joanna, thinking hard. 'I help in the house and visit people in the village with Mama. When my friend Emily is home we walk together and talk either here or at her home. And we shop in Marlborough, of course.'

'Mm, your days seem filled with great excitement,' the General said dryly.

'I—I am happy, sir.' She smiled briefly at the General.

'And how old are you now?'

'I am aged twenty, sir.'

It was then that Matthew's name was mentioned by Stephen.

'Matthew?' said the General. 'I hear he is doing very well.'

'That is more than we know,' said Stephen.

'Yes, well, I hear more in my line of business than you do.' His tone brooked no argument and was rather dismissive, Stephen thought. He only said: 'I suppose so,' not really understanding why the General heard more about his son than they did.

'Is he well, General?' persisted Eliza, the worried mother. 'We hardly ever hear from him.'

'Good Lord, yes. I don't know a fitter man than Matthew.'

'I miss him,' said Joanna in a small voice.

'Do you, my dear?'

'Yes, he was great fun to be with.'

'Well, why don't you visit him? I expect you know someone in London who would look after you, don't you?'

'No, no, we don't,' Stephen broke in quickly, 'and I would be pleased if you didn't encourage my daughter, sir.' His expression showed he wasn't pleased.

The General said nothing but surreptitiously winked at Joanna. She suddenly felt elated and hurriedly looked down at her plate. The General was proving not so stuffy after all.

The conversation changed to other matters until they rose from the table. Afterwards, Stephen apologised for leaving them to say Evening Prayers in church, saying he would be back shortly. Eliza, Joanna and the General retired to the withdrawing room, breaking the custom of leaving the men to drink their brandy alone while the ladies withdrew. But Stephen had promised the General that they would drink their brandy later on. 'I shall look forward to it,' the General had said. 'I know you acquire it from the same source as I do so I know it is good.'

'That was a lovely meal, Mrs Brooke,' he said now. 'Thank you for inviting me. I always enjoy myself when I come.' The General coughed slightly as he sat down. 'Mm, yes. Now, while Stephen is out, tell me, why does he not want this young lady here to go to London, Mrs Brooke? You know, I do think that a pretty girl should show herself a little further afield than around here. I know this area is very pleasant but it is a little limiting for the young.'

'Well,' said Eliza thoughtfully, 'we have no-one we know in London and Joanna must be chaperoned. She couldn't live with Matthew, could she?'

'I think it a good thing for a young girl to see something of life before she is married,' mused the General. 'Anyone on the horizon, my dear, mm-mm?'

'No sir,' said Joanna. 'I don't meet many suitable gentlemen, unfortunately.'

'Now, if I was younger,' began the General with a twinkle in his eye, 'but regrettably I'm not. However, if we can talk your Father round to my way of thinking, I believe I know of a way we can accomplish a little trip to London. I feel as I am Joanna's godfather, I should put myself out for her. After all, I helped the boys.'

'Oh, sir, how wonderful!' Joanna's eyes shone.

'You have been very good to us all,' said Eliza, 'but General, tell me frankly, is it dangerous in London? I mean because of the war. London is much nearer to it all, isn't it?'

The General smiled gently. 'Well, it isn't really but there is no fighting in London, it is all on the Continent and further afield.'

Eliza nodded, relieved a little. Like a mother hen she wanted her chicks round her to protect them. Her boys, she could do nothing about unfortunately and she feared daily for Luke in his cavalry regiment, but Joanna she could protect. However, if the General said it would be all right for her to go, she would be guided by him.

'Let me tell you both quickly before Stephen comes back and then I'll have a word with him. My youngest sister, Dolly, had a daughter, and as far as I remember she was the youngest of a large family. Her name is Melanie Shaw and she lives in Chippenham with a companion. She is a widow, you know. Her husband was killed at the start of the war in France. A fine fellow, he was, and had risen to the rank of Colonel. He was forty-five years old, I believe. Very sad. However, she will be going to London for the start of the season and hiring a house there. It will be the first time she has been back since Shaw was killed. So it would be good for her to have Joanna with her and to look after her. It would take away the loss of her husband a little, you know. If Joanna is with Mrs Shaw she will come to no harm. She will probably take her usual house in Curzon Street, which is a very genteel area of London. And she has a companion, too, a Mrs er—er somebody or other. So you need not worry. She usually calls to see me on the way. I am sure she would take your daughter, Mrs Brooke, and look after her well. If you agree, I can arrange for you to meet her and her companion when she visits and I can write to her before that, of course.'

'When will she be travelling to London, General?' asked Eliza warily, wondering what her husband might say.

'In a week or two, I expect.'

Eliza gasped. 'Gracious, so soon?'

'So you see, we have to persuade your husband tonight, if this young lady is to go at all.'

Joanna's heart stopped. Papa would never agree so quickly, if at all.

The next morning Eliza came bustling into the library where Joanna was trying to find a suitable book to read on this wet day. 'Your father wants to talk to you. He's in his study. Hurry.'

'Is he angry or …?' began Joanna.

'Just go,' said her Mother.

With trepidation Joanna swallowed hard as she knocked on her father's study door. When he bade her enter she said: 'Mama said you wished to see me, Papa?'

Stephen looked at her and smiled. 'There's no need to look so anxious. Come and sit down. I will put this briefly. The General thinks it would be a good thing for you to have a season in London with a Mrs Shaw to look after you and act as chaperone. I must tell you I'm not too happy about it but your Mother agrees with the General that it would be a good experience for you to see a little of a different life. So, against my better judgement, I have said you may go if you wish.'

'Papa, oh! Papa, thank you, thank you!' and Stephen found himself enveloped in a big hug.

'Yes, well,' Papa said when he was able, 'You're a good girl, but you will behave yourself, won't you?' He frowned at her.

'Yes, of course, I shall.'

'You see I know you can be a bit wild at times and there are many people out there that are not, shall we say, nice to know. And if you are taken to assemblies and such you will wear decorous dresses and take care to whom you speak, won't you?'

'Of course,' she said again. 'I will see Matthew too and I can write and let you know how he goes on and I will do exactly as Mrs Shaw says, Papa.'

Stephen nodded. 'I will let you have some extra money, of course, but you must be sensible with it. We can't expect Mrs Shaw to pay for everything.'

'No, Papa, of course not.'

'Very well, then. I hope you enjoy yourself, my dear, and give our love to Matthew.'

Outside the study door Joanna danced a very unladylike hornpipe!

CHAPTER 4

▼

Matthew left the office at last with Tim and Hugh as the evening light was fading. He took Hugh up with him in a hackney while Tim quietly disappeared along the back streets and alleyways of Blackfriars. Obviously he knew where he was going and was able to look after himself, as he was quick to draw his sword or snatch his pistol from his pocket at the first sign of any danger. All three of them understood what went on in this place after dark and they were always careful and on their guard. They knew the risks involved when working for Lord Harry Anstruther.

Sometimes Matthew's manservant, Ned, would wait for him with his horse and carriage at a convenient place in a more wholesome area, if Matthew had asked him to, but that was only if he knew he was leaving early and in the daylight. Ned was quite handy in using his whip if necessary, which could be useful. Then he would drive Matthew home to his suite of rooms in the quiet square in Bloomsbury. But Matthew, usually not knowing the time when he would be leaving, would catch a hackney rather than walk and run the risk of being molested or worse, after a tiring day. He was also concerned for Hugh, of course.

The hackney now stopped and they both alighted at the corner of Bloomsbury Street where they could easily walk to their respective homes.

'Goodnight, Hugh. I shall be late in tomorrow. I did tell Mr Oakley but remind him.'

'Very well. Fisticuffs, sir?' Matthew just grinned and left with a wave of his hand.

His rooms were comfortable and pleasantly light, and furnished with good solid oak. Anything delicate and ornate was Matthew's nightmare, being such a large gentleman. He had been lucky to find his rooms and Ned, after the demise of their previous owner.

Ned was in his late forties, a dark haired man with a lined face. He had been invalided out of the army when he had been shot accidentally in the knee in a skirmish during the war in Spain in 1739, which resulted in a stiff leg and a limp. When Matthew had taken the rooms he asked Ned to stay on, much to Ned's relief. Finding another similar position would have been difficult at his age and with his affliction. He found Matthew an easy master to work for, as he was usually good-natured and treated Ned as an equal, which was a new experience as his last employer was old and crabby and liked ordering him about. Ned respected Matthew and tried to be helpful when called upon for his opinion, whether it was advising him on the cut of a new waistcoat or discussing the problems of the war. He also acted as valet, cook, coachman and anything else required of him. He found life with Matthew was never dull.

Now as he opened the door for his master, he caught the smell of the sewers on his clothes. Matthew, as usual, discarded hat and coat for Ned to hang out in the air. The rest of his clothes were deposited on the floor once he was in his bedroom. After Matthew had washed and changed he began to feel a different person and entered the dining room ready to eat the large dinner that had been prepared. Sirloin of beef, vegetables and more sat on the table before him.

Later, when not much food remained, Matthew stretched out in front of the fire, drinking his brandy and talking to Ned. He suddenly remembered the invitation he had left in his pocket.

'That's taken care of, sir. I placed it on your dressing table.'

'Do you usually go through my pockets, then?' asked Matthew with that lazy smile.

'Of course I do. It's no good me cleaning your clothes with things in your pockets,' complained Ned. 'I expect you will let me know what you'll be wearing to this ball in good time, so I can get it all pressed ready, won't you? Or are you buying something new?'

'I don't know. I haven't thought about it. I suppose I shall have to look and see what I have but I'm too tired tonight, I don't know why.'

'You think too much, that's what,' said Ned, nodding his head wisely. 'I'll get out your coats and things tomorrow and you can tell me what you want to do. If you're going to order something new, you'll have to hurry up and do it *tout de suite*.'

'Yes, Ned, I know.'

Ned discreetly left the room, closing the door quietly behind him.

Matthew stared into the fire. Yes, he was tired but that wasn't the whole problem. Something niggled at the back of his brain. He went through the day's happenings in his mind, the talk with Harry and then with Tim, his contact in the tavern, even his chats with Hugh. And he still couldn't place a finger on the problem. He finally came to the conclusion that he was indeed more tired than usual, and eventually he took himself off to bed.

Next morning, up bright and early, Matthew ate his usual hearty breakfast consisting of ham and pie washed down with ale. At the same time Ned had been sorting out Matthew's clothes and then requested him to look at the coats and waistcoats, which he thought suitable for the prospective ball.

'Mm,' frowned Matthew, 'I cannot hope to look inconspicuous but …' He fingered a dull wine velvet coat and a deep purple one and shook his head. 'I'll find a new one. Dark blue, perhaps. What do you think, Ned?'

'Very dark blue would be good, sir. Will you wear a wig?'

'No,' said Matthew, who found wigs itchy. 'While I have enough hair I'll stay as I am.'

'Then you'll have to have it powdered. And you'll need a new waistcoat, too, don't forget.'

'Yes, yes, Ned, I know.'

'There will be many beautiful ladies there, I shouldn't wonder,' said Ned airily.

'I expect so,' said Matthew sourly, 'but there are always pretty ladies around, all of them spending too much money on themselves.'

'Oh, we are in a mood, aren't we?' teased Ned.

'I don't go there looking for beautiful ladies, I have work to do by looking and listening to what is said.'

'It hasn't stopped you before. What about that Miss Fanshawe and Miss Cullen and Miss …'

'All right, all right but …'

'And don't tell me they were all in your line of duty because I don't believe you. Sir.' Ned added as an afterthought.

Matthew ignored him.

'And Mr Oakley, sir, is he going as well? He likes the ladies too and …'

'Yes Ned, Mr Oakley is invited too, but we usually keep away from each other unless we have to pass a message on urgently. But no doubt I shall drink and eat and dance as well. What more could I wish for?'

'An evening without trouble, that's what,' muttered Ned.

Ignoring him Matthew said: 'I'll go to the tailors now, then on to Jack's for a little exercise.'

'And don't forget to wrap something round your hands. You don't want to alarm the ladies with all them cuts and bruises.' Then, as he saw Matthew pick up his working coat: 'You're not wearing *that* coat to visit your tailor, are you sir? He won't let you in and I don't blame him.' Ned sniffed disgustedly. 'It isn't respectable.' He referred to the hat and coat that Matthew wore to the office in Blackfriars.

'But I shall be going to work afterwards,' complained Matthew.

'Perhaps you will sir, but think of my pride. After you've been to the tailors and that nasty fighting place, you come back here for this 'orrible old hat and coat and I'll take you in the carriage.'

'Yes, Ned,' said Matthew meekly.

So Matthew, looking smart enough to please Ned in a coat of dark mulberry and with his tricorne sedately placed on his head, strode out to his favourite tailors to submit to being measured and to choose and discuss a suitable material and style for his coat and to agree on a date for the earliest delivery. Then Matthew walked on to Jack's Academy for some bare knuckle fighting to keep him in practice and literally on his toes.

Matthew wondered if Jack Broughton would be there as these days he served in the Yeomen of the Guard as well as running his Academy. Matthew liked Jack. He had brought in simple guidelines and rules, which ensured fair play where none had existed before, and fights had been conducted previously with more brawn than brain. In his heyday he had been a Champion and in the seventeen thirties earned the reputation of never losing a fight. He was popular and greatly loved.

Matthew was of a similar build to Jack, nearly six feet tall and heavy with it. Both of them looked down on most men who were usually less in stature. Matthew, now stripped to the waist, entered the hall. He had a powerful chest and muscles. His only drawback, if it was one, was that his skin was pale as befitted someone with such blond hair. Therefore he was easily marked. This did not deter him in the slightest as he had always said that 'he was used to what he'd been born with.'

He was pleased that Jack was there to greet him. 'Welcome,' he said, 'we haven't seen you for some time, Mr Brooke. I have someone new for you to meet today. This is Silas.'

Silas had originally come over to England as a slave but for some years now had been freed. When Jack had found him, Silas was trying to earn money by prize fighting but Jack had soon seen his potential and offered him work in his Academy. After a while, liking the man for his own sake, he had asked Silas to stay permanently.

Now Matthew saw before him a gigantic black man who grinned at him, showing a set of beautiful white teeth. They shook hands and Silas said in a soft voice that he was pleased to meet Matthew and especially one who stripped to such good advantage. Meanwhile Jack called for muffles to be brought. These were thin gloves for his visitors to protect their knuckles. No one wanted to leave with bloodied or bandaged hands.

Matthew and Silas climbed into the ring, which was elevated on a stage and surrounded by wooden rails to form the enclosure. In the centre a square of a yard was marked with chalk and Matthew faced Silas on opposite sides of this. At a call from Jack they began sparring, fists clenched, moving lightly on their feet. Jack kept a sharp eye out for faults in Matthew's movements and Silas issued breathless comments like "good" and "more, more," when Matthew wasn't punching hard enough. In Prize Ring rules, aiming at the face and eyes were permitted as were short spikes on the shoes, but in the Academy, where clients came only to keep supple or use techniques for self defence, these were not allowed.

Matthew and Silas parried, struck out on retreat, stopped and rained blows mercilessly on each other, trying to bring the other down to their knees. The rules stated that when this happened, the man had to move to the side of the chalked square in half a minute, if the fight was to continue, otherwise it finished. This was known as the scratch line. In a real fight, when a man could not come "to scratch", he would be declared the loser and the fight would be brought to a halt. However, Matthew and Silas were merely practising and Jack did not allow the men to go that far. He would stop them to show Matthew a new move and shouted encouragement when he was pleased with what he saw. After half an hour they finished. Matthew thanked Silas, who complimented him on being light on his feet, and shook hands with Jack who told him not to be so long in returning.

Matthew went to swill his face and torso in cold water. No doubt bruises would show on his body the next day, but no one would see them. Then, donning his clothes, he sallied out into the London streets once more. He felt pleased with his progress and Jack's encouraging remarks but more than anything he felt fit enough to win any fight outside the Academy if he had to.

He returned home to change his coat and hat ready for Ned to take him to Blackfriars. It was only then that he remembered the thought which had been evading him.

CHAPTER 5

▼

Since the General's visit, Joanna had walked around with her head in the clouds. She went through the motions of visiting the sick and poor with her mother, and although she did what was right, those who knew her well realised her heart and mind were elsewhere. Eliza caught her daydreaming many times when she should have been working and she would reprimand her daughter and tell her not to let her father see her like that. Then Joanna would try and focus on the matter in hand. She wouldn't like Papa to refuse his permission for her to go to London now. The most difficult thing of all was when she was expected to keep her mind on her father's sermon in church on the last Sunday before she travelled. Did anyone listen to him, she wondered? She looked up at him fleetingly and saw him glance down at her briefly from the pulpit. Did he smile?

Later he said to her: 'I'm pleased you were listening to my sermon, Joanna. You're a good girl and I shall miss you.' Joanna felt a little guilty but consoled herself that at least she had made her father happy.

She visited her friend Emily, who had returned from Bath. There was much to discuss and tell each other so they met frequently to thoroughly exhaust the topics of Bath and Joanna's impending trip. There was also much giggling. Joanna began to wonder as to what kind of ladies were Mrs Shaw and her companion. If Mrs Shaw's husband had been forty-five years of age when he had been killed, as the General had said, would Mrs Shaw be around the same age? Emily had suggested that she would be no younger than thirty-five. Would she be a staid person and still grieving, even after two years? Well, whatever she was like, it was kind of Mrs Shaw to agree to have her to stay. Apart from seeing London, would they go to social gatherings and perhaps a ball, she wondered? And would she meet some handsome young men? And so Joanna's thoughts went on and on.

It was Wednesday morning at last and they were all up early as usual. Joanna could hardly eat any breakfast for excitement, as it was today that the General would send his coach over for them at ten o'clock. He had said they would be able to meet Mrs Shaw before she and Joanna took their leave for London. Joanna's bags were packed. Eliza had seen she had new petticoats and two new dresses for daytime. They were plain but of good quality. Joanna had asked her Mama what she would wear in an evening. Eliza had said she thought the usual dress she wore when visitors came to dinner would be suitable. She didn't think Mrs Shaw would go to any frivolous social occasions, so there was no need to buy clothes that wouldn't be worn. Joanna had privately not agreed with her mama but decided, if she did need another dress and her money had run out, that she would ask Matthew if he could help her. It would be lovely to see him again, she mused. As far as she knew, no one had seen fit to apprise him of her visit which, she hoped, would be a lovely surprise.

Then there was an interruption. A parishioner had called to ask if Mr Brooke would visit old Mrs Hammond urgently as she was very ill. Stephen, in one way relieved at not having to be at his daughter's departure but annoyed that he couldn't meet Mrs Shaw, said of course he would visit Mrs Hammond at once. He said his farewell to Joanna, kissed her quickly, told her to be good and hurriedly went out.

'Well,' said Eliza, 'just when I wanted him with me, he has to go. It's always been the case, of course, but I had hoped …' Her voice trailed off unhappily.

Joanna, privately pleased that Papa was not to go with them, as he could be a little pompous at times, said: 'Never mind, Mama, you can tell him all about the ladies on your return.' Eliza nodded but had no time to say anything more as the General's coach arrived.

Fortunately, they didn't have far to travel. They were soon being welcomed by the General. Eliza apologised for her husband not being with them, but he said it was of no moment and took them into the morning room where an older lady, in a brown dress, was sitting near the fire. 'Oh, thank goodness,' Eliza thought, 'just the kind of person I had hoped for. She looks kind and motherly but above all sensible. A brown dress for travelling, too, and her appearance, while not showy, looks clean and well groomed.' Eliza relaxed at once. A smile came to her lips as she waited to be introduced. The lady stood up, her eyes vaguely looking at the visitors.

'Ah, yes, mm,' said the General. 'This is Mrs Dobie. She's a relation of Mrs Shaw's. I don't know where Melanie is, do you?'

Mrs Dobie gave Eliza and Joanna a small curtsey and a smile, saying in a soft voice: 'I believe she went to see the coachman. Shall I …?'

'No, no,' said the General, 'she will be here in a moment, I expect.'

Eliza and Joanna sat down. Eliza was a little disappointed that the softly spoken lady wasn't Mrs Shaw, as she thought she would be just the kind of person she would like to look after her daughter. Joanna's thoughts were just the opposite.

The General had just asked her if she was excited about her forthcoming visit to the Capital, when the door burst open and a tall, fashionably dressed young lady entered. Her dark curly hair was simply styled and her keen blue eyes quickly surveyed the visitors. She now said in a pleasant husky voice: 'Forgive me for not being here when you arrived. I had to see the coachman about the journey.' She looked used to giving orders and capably organising things, thought Eliza.

The General stood up. 'Let me present Mrs Shaw to you, Mrs Brooke.'

The ladies curtseyed. 'And this is Joanna.'

As Joanna curtseyed she saw before her no 'very much older lady' but one not too far from her own age.

'May I call you Joanna? If we are to be friends it will be much nicer, don't you think? And you must call me Melanie.' She smiled as she took Joanna's hand in both of hers. 'I've been looking forward to meeting you so much. You will be able to tell us all about yourself on the journey. It will be so good to have someone with us, won't it, Lily?' She turned to Mrs Dobie, who smiled and nodded.

As they were talking Eliza looked at this attractive young lady. Young she may be but with such an air. It was amazing to Eliza how one so young could behave with such confidence. Still, she supposed, being married to an older man, and one who had been in the army, she would have had to show composure and mature quickly.

Melanie went on: 'We have a lovely house to go to, you know, and everything will be comfortable and just as you would like it, I am sure. It's in a quiet street near a park, so we can relax. You mustn't worry, Mrs Brooke, we will take the greatest care of your daughter. Do you have my London address for Mrs Brooke, General? Then she will feel more comfortable if she knows where her daughter is living.'

The General hunted in his pocket and brought forth a card, which he handed to Eliza.

'I'm sorry not to have met your husband but I hope to rectify that at a later date. So now I think we should be on our way, as we want to be in Speenhamland before it is dark. Goodbye, Mrs Brooke, do not worry.' She curtseyed once more and went out with Mrs Dobie and the General followed them. He reminded Mrs Shaw of the important commission she had promised to undertake for him when in London for his friend Harry Anstruther. She nodded and said he wasn't to worry and she would supply the address.

Mother and daughter were left alone to make their farewells. Eliza kissed Joanna and said if she wasn't happy she was to ask Matthew to bring her back home. Joanna nodded and they both hurriedly joined the General and the ladies outside. He turned, kissed Joanna and handed her into the coach, which Eliza noticed was piled high with bags and boxes of all shapes and sizes. Gracious! How long was Mrs Shaw planning to stay in London? Eliza would have been more perturbed if she had known that another coach with abigails and more boxes had already travelled the previous day. The door was closed, the coachman gave the horses a command and they were away. Eliza was left waving and dabbing her eyes. The General took her arm in his and led her back indoors. He gave her a sweet sherry and talked soothingly to her.

'You know,' he said, 'there is no need to worry. Melanie is a very capable young lady and sensible.' Eliza nodded. 'Good. May I suggest something to you, Mrs Brooke?' She nodded again. 'I cannot help seeing how hard you work. You brought up four children and you still worry about them, which proves what a good mother you are. You look after Stephen well and support him in everything he does, which shows what a good wife you are. You also are concerned for others in the village. When do you go or do something *you* wish to do?'

Eliza looked at him. 'I—I don't know, General. I've never thought about it.'

'Mm. Well, I think you and Stephen should go away together. Perhaps travel to the sea? Would you like that?'

'Well, yes, it—it would be lovely. I've never been away before.'

'I shall talk to Stephen, then. You deserve some attention.'

A rather dazed Eliza thanked the General. He sent for his coach once more to take her back to the rectory and, holding her hand in both his, promised to do what he could for her.

On her journey home Eliza worried what she would say to Stephen if he asked her to describe Mrs Shaw. She was pleasant enough but so much younger than they had imagined she would be, and everything from the dresses and cloaks to the coach and horses seemed to be in the highest fashion. Eliza decided not to say anything of this to her husband, except that the ladies were well mannered and charming and pleased to have their daughter with them and that she would be well looked after. She wondered what he would say to the General's suggestion of staying near the sea. Eliza crossed her fingers.

CHAPTER 6

▼

The road from Marlborough was deep and rough. The coach in which the three ladies travelled, although solid and well upholstered, shook and rattled. After a while Joanna learnt to let her body sway with the coach's movements rather than keep taut and upright. Melanie decided that she and Joanna would take it in turns to sit with their backs to the horses, as travelling that way always made Mrs Dobie ill. Joanna didn't mind at all as she would see a different view of the countryside and there was much laughing as the two young ladies endeavoured to change places while the coach was moving. Melanie asked Joanna about her life in Marlborough and after Joanna had told her, which didn't seem to be very interesting to Joanna's ears, Melanie considered what she had heard.

'You know, in London there is so much to do and see,' said Melanie. 'We can visit places of interest like the Tower of London and Westminster Abbey and …'

'If I visited the Abbey,' broke in Joanna eagerly, 'I could let Papa know all about it. He only let me come with you because he didn't want to upset the General. He has a very poor opinion of London, you know. He said it was a "den of iniquity" whatever that means. So if I told him about our visit it would make him feel happier, I think.'

Melanie looked at her, amusement on her face. 'You are either a very kind person or a devious one,' she said. 'But for all that your Papa was probably right. But it is a very lovely city and an exciting one.'

Joanna laughed. 'What else is there to see?'

'There is the River Thames. It is so busy with all the ships from abroad and seeing them unloading their cargoes is fascinating. That would be a good outing for one day when the weather is fine but we would need a gentleman's escort to go there. We must think about that one. Then there is Kensington Palace where King George and Queen Caroline reside. And, of course,' Melanie paused and looked at Joanna with a twinkle in her eyes, 'we will be going to some social events, too. Do you dance, Joanna?'

'I—I do a little, but ...'

'Well, we must hire a dancing master to give you a few lessons before you attend those functions and then you will feel more confident. Also we have to shop in London, don't we, Lily?'

'Oh, yes,' murmured Mrs Dobie. 'I love to shop. There's nothing like the London shops, Joanna. I know exactly where to go for the best clothes and all the necessities ladies need. You can rely on me to take you to the smartest places, can't she, Melanie?'

'Certainly,' said Melanie. 'I rely on your good taste, don't I, dear?'

'Oh, yes. And Joanna, there will be many invitations to dances and musical evenings to attend as dear Melanie is very popular, you know, and she is invited everywhere.'

'Now, now, Lily, you are making me sound like a sad romp.'

'Please don't do anything differently to what you usually do because of me. I can stay home, you know, if it's not convenient for you to take me with you,' said Joanna.

'I thought you wished to see some life,' smiled Melanie.

'Oh yes, I do, but please don't ...'

Melanie placed a hand fleetingly on Joanna's. 'It's all right. I was only teasing but thank you for being so thoughtful. I think we shall get along famously and have some fun,' she nodded.

'Yes, indeed,' broke in Mrs Dobie, 'there's always fun with dear Melanie around. And, you know, there are exhibitions to see and we go to the theatre. I do so love a good tragedy but there are lighter plays if you prefer.'

'We shall have to have a gentleman or two with us when we go to the theatre, though, Lily.'

'Well, that will be no problem, dear, you know so many.'

'Lily,' laughed Melanie, 'Joanna will wonder what kind of person I am. I am quite respectable, I promise you.'

'Oh, I'm sure you are. I'm sure you both are,' instantly replied Joanna, but she did wonder at Mrs Dobie. She had seemed such a quiet and sombre creature when she and her Mama had first met her. Now she seemed as gay and lively as Melanie. And although Joanna smiled back happily, it did cross her mind, however, that she might have to ask for some more money from Matthew. She also wondered if she should broach the subject of meeting him to Melanie but perhaps it was too early in their relationship to ask. There would be plenty of time when they reached London.

'Oh, yes,' continued Mrs Dobie, breaking in on Joanna's thoughts, 'there will be many invitations to dine with friends and you will be included, Joanna, of course. Yes, yes, when they know Melanie is back in London we will have such a gay time. Do you know we are sometimes out every evening? We play cards, you know, and gamble. Nothing too terrible, just a little to make it interesting. I like silver loo the best.'

Melanie, seeing the doubt on Joanna's face, laughed. 'How you do run on, dear Lily. But Joanna is a clergyman's daughter, perhaps she wouldn't like to gamble.'

Joanna smiled a 'thank you' at Melanie. 'Well, I'm sure he wouldn't like me to, but I don't mind watching if I'm allowed.'

'Of course you could,' said Mrs Dobie immediately, 'but there are other things like soirees with poems read by the gentlemen or there are singers, which can be pleasant as long as it's not those castrati. I like a deep voice best.' She gazed dreamily out of the window, remembering certain handsome gentlemen from the past.

Melanie smiled at Joanna and winked. Joanna had been sitting and listening with her lips apart. 'Gracious,' she said now, 'I didn't realise there was so much to do. I—I shall be exhausted.'

'Nonsense,' said Mrs Dobie, now back in the real world again. She had enjoyed telling this little country girl of all the delights in store for her. She now smiled kindly at her.

'You will love it all. Don't worry, we will take good care of you, won't we, Melanie?'

'Of course. Lily and I go most places together, although as a widowed lady I am allowed a little more freedom. But you, Joanna, must always have one of us with you or a maid, when you go out. There are many, er—gentlemen and even ladies who are not as they should be, you know. You will remember to take care, won't you?'

'Yes, yes, of course.'

Now, looking out of the window, Joanna could see the land was quite marshy. 'Ah,' said Melanie, 'I see we are near to Hungerford.'

'Have you been along here many times?' Joanna ventured to ask.

'Oh, yes,' said Melanie blithely, 'we went to London for the season every year, you know, before I was married and after. In fact, we had to stay longer sometimes. It depended on my husband. He was in the army. It will be good to be back again and lovely to have you with me, Joanna, to take around.'

Joanna smiled to herself, thinking how brave and worldly wise her new friend was and so different to herself.

By the time they rode into Speenhamland the sun was setting. The horses were reined in outside the George and Pelican. 'We are staying here tonight,' Melanie informed Joanna. 'We shall continue early tomorrow. It would be too dangerous to go further when it's dark. Besides, the horses need to be fed and watered, you know, and we need to dine too.'

The inn was popular and said to be the best conducted one on the London to Bath road. It was patronised by statesmen, generals and even royalty. Now the coach door was opened, the steps let down and the three ladies descended. They shook out their crumpled skirts and Melanie confidently led the way to the door, where the landlord came forward with a large smile on his round face. Bowing low, he said: 'Welcome, Mrs Shaw, welcome.'

Joanna was surprised at how capable Melanie was and only a few years older than herself. But Melanie, married to an older man, had learnt quickly what was expected of her and she prided herself that she was able to deal with servants and the gentry equally well. Charles, her husband, had always told her to keep her temper in check, be fair, especially when dealing with servants, and always be her charming self. She was lively and enjoyed life. Although much older, Charles had been a kind man and very patient. Deep down, Melanie hadn't really loved him but she had admired him and liked him. He had found her affectionate and sweet. When she had learned he had been killed, she felt a great sadness, as if the "rock" behind her had disappeared. But in time, and with the help of her friends and family, she recovered and was able to view the past with pleasant memories. She now thought she could face London life again and having Joanna to take around and introduce to the sights and entertainments, would be fun, like having a younger sister to show around. The General's suggestion had been a good idea in more ways than one. She wondered if Joanna realised the pace in London was a lot faster than around Marlborough. Melanie thought her a sweet little thing and it would be a joy to show her a different world. The General had also mentioned a brother, so no doubt she would wish to visit him sometime although there was no hurry for that yet. There would probably be an occasion when Joanna didn't wish to accompany them for some reason, so then would be the time to arrange a visit.

Now they dined on a sustaining meal, which included a fine oxtail soup, roasted chickens, dishes of different vegetables and, of course, fruit and pastries.

As all this was taken with a variety of wines, which Melanie chose, it was a sleepy and happy Joanna who retired to bed a short time later.

They were up early the following morning and after eating a light breakfast continued their journey. It was slow as the roads were narrow and much time was lost when meeting a conveyance travelling the opposite way. This entailed Melanie's coachman leading the horses as near to the hedge as possible while the other carriage did the same, so that between them, they were able to pass each other safely with the minimum of space. Also at the turnpikes where tolls were paid, the keeper of the gate wasn't always as speedy as he should have been in opening up, although the assistant coachman had blown on his yard of tin in good time. They made a short stop at Reading for cakes and ale then travelled on to Maidenhead where they stayed the night at the Bear Inn.

'We daren't go any further when the light fades,' said Melanie. 'You see, highwaymen abound in the thicket from here on so we must travel our final stretch in daylight. But do not worry, I have ordered outriders to accompany us tomorrow even though it will be daylight. I like to feel safe.'

They were ready the following morning in good time and with the outriders accompanying them they set off for the final part of their journey. Joanna was excited and couldn't wait to see London. Melanie pointed out Windsor Castle to her as they passed and then the horses made an extra effort to gallop across Hounslow Heath, which pleased Melanie and Mrs Dobie as it had been known that highwaymen had been active during the daytime here. However all went well and in no time at all they were on the outskirts of the great city.

The coach threaded its way through the streets and Joanna saw changing areas from dirty impoverished places to open spaces of parks and trees. It was as they came to a quiet, tree-lined street that at last the tired horses brought the coach to a standstill outside a large house in Curzon Street. They had arrived.

CHAPTER 7

▼

While Joanna was travelling to London, her brother Matthew was working, as usual, at his office in Blackfriars. He hadn't seen Tim for a while but no doubt he was preparing for his journey to France. This, of course, was a serious business, as even all preparations that were perfected and seemingly foolproof could always go awry. Matthew knew this from experience on his last trip to Austria when he had to find out where the enemy were to strike next and he had to extricate himself from a few tight corners. But on Friday morning Tim appeared looking relaxed and pleased with himself. Hugh opened the door for him and was surprised at how cheerful he looked. Hugh thought if he were in Mr Oakley's shoes he wouldn't sound so happy.

'Well,' said Tim with a grin, 'everything is in place and I shall be leaving these shores after the ball tomorrow night.'

Matthew looked at him, a glimmer of a smile on his face. 'I hope you'll be dressed differently,' he said.

'I don't think so,' mused Tim. 'I shall turn up at the ball dressed in fisherman's clothes and boots. The ladies might think how wonderful I am, especially when I dance on their toes.'

'I doubt it,' said Matthew, 'you wouldn't be allowed to enter, anyway.'

'How stuffy,' Tim said.

Matthew was pleased Tim was in such an optimistic mood but as he was busy he didn't really have time to waste on pleasantries.

'Care to talk through your journey with me?' he asked.

'That's why I came in, actually,' said Tim. 'Everything is in order as far as it can be. I went down to the coast and organised things there well enough, I think.'

'Right. Let us begin at the beginning. You go to the ball dressed suitably. Now go on from there.'

'I leave sometime after midnight.'

'That's a bit vague.'

'Well, you can't walk out in the middle of a minuet or if you're deep in conversation with someone.'

'So what do you do next?'

'I go home, change into some dark clothes suitable for travelling. I ride to the coast, near Dover, where there is a tavern by the original name of "The Ship". I can leave the horse there, change into fisherman's clothes and also meet the men who will take me across the Channel. I shall take my own clothes with me, of course.'

'Who are these men? Are they trustworthy?'

'Who can tell? But I shall have to risk it. I promised them enough money, which seemed to please the captain. They're smugglers and they will pull into a cove on a lonely beach near Calais. Evidently they use more than one—it depends on the tides.'

'Do they smuggle the usual whisky and woollens?'

'Yes, and trade them for brandy and tobacco, I expect.'

'Don't drink the whisky!'

'Only enough to keep out the cold,' grinned Tim.

'What about the tides? Did you check those and the times?'

'Yes, the captain said they should be just right on the Sunday night, which will give me a day to travel down.'

'What happens if ships challenge your craft in the Channel? You're likely to be stopped by both British and French, you know.'

'The captain says he knows how to handle both, he's done it before.'

'Have you money for your journey and papers?'

'Yes, Harry Anstruther saw to that.'

'So,' said Matthew, 'you're in France and you're aiming to go where?'

'Paris. I shall go by the name of Andre de Noyons. At the ball, Harry said I had to contact a Mrs Shaw and give her a letter from him introducing me. In return she will give me a name and address where I can stay safely. We seem to have used up all our safe houses recently.'

Matthew looked at his friend. 'Have you told me everything?' he asked gently. 'Who was "the someone you had to see" the other day?'

'Someone I …? Oh, that. Trust you to remember.'

'That's my job,' Matthew said smoothly.

Tim turned and looked out of the window at the filthy street below and thought how good it would be to get away from it all.

'Tim?' Matthew broke in on his thoughts.

'Oh, it was nothing, nothing at all.'

Matthew didn't believe him and after waiting to see if he said any more let the matter drop.

'How will you get information to us? Any idea?'

Tim shrugged. 'Smugglers, perhaps, or I'll try and locate our previous agent. What was his name again?'

'Something like Jim Worcester, no—um—Webster.'

'That's right. His name in France was Henri Bernard.'

'Well, I'll see you on Saturday night when you will let me know the address where you are to stay in Paris.'

Tim turned to go. 'Thanks for your help, Matt.'

Matthew inclined his head. 'We'll have a drink to wish you luck. Hugh,' he called, 'bring three glasses and the wine.'

'Yes, sir,' answered Hugh delightedly.

Joanna was happy. After arriving in Curzon Street she had been shown to a large bedroom with pretty, pink flowered curtains at the window and around the bed. The furniture was all she could wish for with more than enough space for her new dresses and undergarments. The view from the window was mainly of trees, which at this time of year were covered with bronze leaves. Melanie had come in to see if she was happy with her room and told her to ask for anything she couldn't find. There was a bell-pull to summon a maid. Joanna had met three of the staff, a footman, the housekeeper and the butler by the name of Bayliss. Those in the kitchen she had yet to meet if she met them at all.

When they had arrived on the Friday, it was only to see to the unpacking, which didn't take long, eat a meal, which was excellent, and go to bed. Joanna thought it was a lovely feeling to stretch out on the cosy feather mattress and think she had, at last, made the trip to London, something she had always wanted to do. She couldn't wait to see all the sights they had planned to visit. In the middle of thinking of these, she fell into a sound sleep, which lasted until eleven o'clock on Saturday morning. She was awakened by a young girl of about twelve years of age, entering the room. 'Good morning, Miss,' she said.

'Oh, good morning,' said Joanna. 'Who are you?'

'I'm Tilly, Miss. I've brung your hot chocolate. Shall I draw the curtains?'

'Yes please,' said Joanna, sitting up and reaching for her drink. 'Is it a nice morning?'

'Oh yes, Miss.'

By the time Joanna went downstairs, Melanie and Mrs Dobie were already having breakfast. Melanie was opening a pile of letters and sorting through them. 'Did you sleep well?' she smiled. 'Come and join us. As you can see we have some invitations here already. Isn't it exciting? But I'm afraid Lily and I will have to leave you tonight, which is a bore. I do hope you don't mind, especially on your first evening.'

Joanna said immediately: 'That is quite all right. I am sure I can find something to do. For one thing, I have to write up my diary about our journey. So that will amuse me very well. Are you going somewhere exciting?'

'What a treasure you are,' observed Melanie with a smile. 'We have invitations to a ball given by the Prussian Ambassador. I am expected to attend because of my late husband's position, you know. But Lily and I will have dinner with you before we go and then we shall be home soon after midnight, I hope, unless it's particularly interesting.'

She finished sorting through her letters, handing those of interest to Mrs Dobie. 'Well, we seem to be free on Wednesday evening; would you like to invite your brother over to dine with us? I'm sure you wish to see him soon.' Melanie thought this would give something for Joanna to look forward to, apart from making herself feel better about leaving her young friend the first evening.

'Oh, I would love to write to him. He will be so amazed to know that I am here in London.'

'Good. That's settled then. Give your letter to Bayliss when you've finished, make sure to write the address on the outside and then someone will deliver it for you. Now shall we visit some shops this morning? Would you like that?'

'Oh, yes,' said Joanna, 'I would love to shop.'

'Good. And I must decide on my dress for this evening so that it can be hung and pressed to make it respectable after travelling. Which one do you think, Lily?'

Mrs Dobie thought for a while. 'We have to remember this is the first time you've attended the ball since dear Charles died. I think the dark red one. It looks rich because of the colour but it isn't bright, which will befit the occasion. It has ecru lace which is not so showy as white and you can wear some black on the underskirt.'

'Black?' Melanie wrinkled her nose. 'Oh no, Lily.'

'Yes, my dear, black. You will find the effect quite stunning, believe me, with your dark hair.'

'But my hair will be powdered. It is a grand ball, you know.'

'Oh, yes, of course it will, I forgot. If you wear your diamond and ruby neck-lace and the clasp to match in your hair, you will look very distinguished.'

'Mm,' said Melanie, nodding, 'I expect you're right. You usually are.'

'And what will you wear, Mrs Dobie?' asked Joanna with a smile.

'Me, child? Oh, something blue, I expect.'

'Lily always looks just as she should,' said Melanie.

'May I see you both before you go? I've never seen anyone dressed for a ball before.'

'Of course. And you can tell us if there's anything wrong with our appearances.'

But when Joanna saw them later, she could see there wasn't anything wrong. It did cross her mind though, that Papa might not approve entirely of Melanie's dress as it was cut low over her bosom with the bodice fitting quite tightly. The deep colour of the silk showed off her creamy skin and the jewellery glistened as she moved. Her powdered hair was dressed high with two long ringlets over one shoulder. 'What a beautiful person she is,' thought Joanna enviously. Mrs Dobie's dress was more sedate but still very elegant in a shade of grey-blue. It wasn't cut so low but it had soft white lace at the neck and elbows. Her hair was powdered grey and dressed high so that she seemed taller.

'I—I think you both are—are beautiful,' gasped Joanna.

The ladies laughed and thanked her, donned their cloaks, and kissed her in a cloud of perfume before stepping outside and into the carriage.

With a sigh and wondering if ever she would be dressed for a ball, Joanna went to write her letter. After seeing the end of the quill pen was sharp and giving a few moments thought as to the content, she dipped her pen into the ink and began to write:

Dear Matthew,

You will be surprised, I know, to learn that I am in London. I travelled here with two ladies yesterday and I am staying with them in Curzon Street. They said I could invite you to dine with us all next Wednesday. I do hope you are free to come. The ladies are very kind and I am so looking forward to seeing you.

Your loving sister,
Joanna.

After shaking the sand from the pounce box over it, the letter was dry. She folded and sealed it with a wafer and wrote Matthew's name and address on the outside. That done she sat down happily in front of the fire and became engrossed in writing up her diary. Eventually, with the heat from the fire and tiredness from walking round the shops in town that morning, she just sat staring into space. How wonderful it would be if she had a house like this one, she thought dreamily, and was married to a man she loved and he would open the door and ... She heard a tap and the door opened revealing Bayliss. Her dreams were shattered.

'Do you require anything more before bedtime, Miss?' he asked.

'Goodness, is it that late? I'm sorry, I've been busy.'

'That's all right, Miss, only Cook has to be up early in the morning and ...'

'Yes, yes, of course. No, I don't require anything, thank you. But could you arrange for this to be delivered tomorrow, please?' She handed her letter to him as she passed.

'Yes, of course, Miss.'

Joanna smiled at him. 'Thank you. Goodnight.'

'Goodnight, Miss. We hope you enjoy your stay.'

As she mounted the stairs Joanna couldn't help adding to herself, 'So do I, oh! so do I.'

CHAPTER 8

▼

'Now the finishing touch, sir,' said Ned as he held the new blue coat ready for Matthew. 'And it fits a treat,' he finished as he smoothed the brocade across the broad shoulders. 'The tailor has made it well.'

Matthew surveyed himself in the mirror, pulling down the rich cream waistcoat beneath and shaking out the lace ruffles at his wrists. 'It looks well enough, I agree,' he said.

'The ladies will be delighted,' Ned continued, a twinkle in his eye.

'Maybe, but I am not going to delight the ladies. I have work to do. Unfortunately,' he added.

'I'm sure you'll manage to meet some, though,' Ned persisted.

'Mm. I'm supposed to be in the background, looking and listening.'

'With all due respect, sir, with your height and build, you still will be noticed whether in the background or not.'

'Thank you, Ned, you are a great comfort. What do you suggest I do, stand around like a statue?' He placed his handkerchief, snuffbox and invitation card in his pocket and left the room.

Ned followed. 'I'll have the carriage round in a jiffy, sir.'

While Matthew waited, he picked up his tricorne and cloak and checked that his pistol was in the pocket. Even if travelling from door to door, it was always desirable to have some form of weapon, apart from fists.

It wasn't long before Matthew arrived at the Embassy. As he alighted he saw others with whom he was acquainted and they walked in together. He, like everyone else, was announced and he trod down the stairs to the large ballroom below.

He was greeted by the Prussian Ambassador and his wife and Matthew uttered the pleasantries that were expected. He was conscious of the lady's eyes following him as he moved away.

The music from the orchestra added to the chatter and greetings of the guests and made a welcoming background sound to set the pulses racing. But Matthew was impervious to this, like others who, being invited, only came for politeness' sake and removed themselves as soon as was permissible. The large room was chilly and no doubt some ladies in their low cut dresses were cold but when everyone had arrived and the dancing was well under way, the temperature would rise. Added to this was, of course, the heat from the many candles lit in the chandeliers and in the sconces on the walls. In turn their light caught the sparkle of the jewellery adorning the gentlemen and ladies present. All in all it was a romantic and enchanting scene.

Matthew nodded slightly to Harry Anstruther who, with his wife, was chatting to another couple, but he moved on, helping himself to a glass of wine from a tray held by a powder-wigged lackey who stood by the wall. 'Now,' thought Matthew, 'why didn't I think of that? He is able to see and hear everything without anyone noticing him. But perhaps it wouldn't be such a good idea. After all, he only stares into space, not seeing anyone or saying anything.'

Someone spoke to Matthew and he stopped to chat and all the time his keen eyes, hidden by those long eyelashes, viewed the room. He circulated more, bowing to acquaintances but all the time keeping a sharp eye on those descending the stairs. He noted the retired military men and admirals present and those in government. William Pitt, Earl of Chatham, was talking to his friend the Duke of Newcastle and standing quietly in a corner was William Whitehead, the Poet Laureate and his lady. He was a nice enough fellow, Matthew always thought but he wasn't keen on his protracted periods.

Eventually Tim arrived looking as debonair as usual and no one would guess he was about to leave for dangerous and foreign shores later that night. There were many interested eyes of young and not so young ladies turning his way, as his dark good looks and slim figure were just made for dancing. And it wasn't long before he was leading an attractive partner into the centre of the room to dance the minuet. Matthew's eyes followed him. Something irked him about his colleague but he didn't know why. He shrugged it off and moved on but his eyes still went back to that elegant figure. One thing, Tim earned full marks, in Matthew's opinion, for looking as carefree as a bird, knowing what was to come. He wondered if it was that which bothered him—Tim's 'don't care' attitude. It wouldn't bode well for his safety if that was his way of thinking. Matthew shook his head. Perhaps, after all, it was Tim's safety that worried him. He dismissed all thoughts about him and concentrated on circulating more but still keeping a low profile.

There was a stir as Mrs Shaw and Mrs Dobie were announced and the two ladies descended the stairs. It had taken Melanie a great deal of effort to control her nerves and to look cool and calm, as this was the first time she had been invited since the death of her husband and she was conscious that many eyes were upon her, especially those who had known Charles. However, those who were watching, including Matthew, saw nothing more than two elegant ladies, one young and one older, both dressed in the height of fashion, curtseying to the Ambassador and his wife. They looked delighted to welcome them and Melanie was kissed on both cheeks. After that, a group of ladies who evidently had known them in the past, took them to sit on gilded chairs to catch up with the latest gossip.

Inevitably, young men gradually gravitated towards the beautiful and young Mrs Shaw, especially when they found she was a natural and graceful dancer. Melanie began to enjoy herself. It was good to move to the music again and mix with people around her own age after what seemed a long time. She was, therefore, able to smile and laugh and feel what it was like to be young again and to forget she was a widow.

Matthew watched her from afar. She certainly cast all the other ladies into the shade as far as he was concerned and he wondered what kind of person she was underneath all her laughing charm. He wished he could dance with her himself and find out but unfortunately he had work to do. He was just turning to move on again when out of the corner of his eye he saw Tim approach Mrs Shaw. Of course, Matthew might have known he would do so as he would certainly be attracted to the lady. In fact, they looked a handsome couple. Although Matthew envied Tim at the moment, at least it would be something pleasant for Tim to think about when he was riding to the south coast later that night.

They were dancing the cotillion, quite a difficult dance that involved changing partners and the giving of favours. For some reason Matthew stopped to watch them. He saw Mrs Shaw look quickly up at Tim, a startled look in her eyes. It affected her so much that she missed a step at which time he handed her what appeared to be a billet doux. Was that Harry's letter of introduction? Matthew was alerted, although he looked just as relaxed as ever. Only his eyes were keener. He saw Mrs Shaw hastily tuck the note into her sleeve as Tim whispered quickly in her ear.

The dance finished and Tim escorted Melanie to one side. She said something to him, he nodded and began to move away as she disappeared from the ballroom. Matthew followed discreetly. He had decided to see this Mrs Shaw for himself and learn the Paris address. If Tim left without letting them know his destination, which he was very likely to do with other things on his mind, they had nowhere to contact him. Of course, they could always find out from Mrs Shaw afterwards but it didn't look very professional and besides, Matthew felt like meeting the attractive lady himself. He was allowed a little fun, wasn't he?

Melanie saw a lackey hovering by the door and she asked him if there was a private room where she could write a note. He bowed and showed her to a pleasant anteroom decorated in crimson and gold. He smiled to himself as he was used to seeing notes passed from one to another requesting assignations. As he came out he saw Matthew standing there and his inward smile became a smirk.

Melanie, meanwhile, had lost no time in finding pen and ink. She looked at the note she had been given. It read:

Dear Mrs Shaw,

May I introduce Andre de Noyons to you? Please be kind enough to furnish him with a letter of introduction to your friend in Paris.

Yours sincerely,
Harry Anstruther.

She hadn't expected to be contacted so soon or by such a personable gentleman, and it had come as a shock when she had been given the note. Consequently, as she settled down to write, she was breathing a little quicker and her hands were trembling. Her first attempt to write resulted in the pen making scratchy marks and blots. She had to stop and trim the quill to a finer point. Eventually, she was ready to try again. She took a deep breath and this time, because her hand was steadier, her note was completed satisfactorily. She read it through twice and then folded it. She searched for a wafer to seal it but could find none. Well, it would have to go without! She stood up, tidied the desk, turned and saw a large gentleman leaning against the fireplace watching her.

'Sir?' she looked at him frostily.

'Madam,' he answered with just a faint nod of his head.

'Well, why have you come in here? I wished to be private. You should leave.'

He looked at her and smiled. 'I don't think so,' he said.

Melanie tried not to panic. His reply was harmless enough but the way he stood, as though he was a fixture and not offering to move, unnerved her, especially as he was between her and the door.

'Why are you here, then? Your manners are ungentlemanly and I would like to leave. Please stand aside.'

Again came the same answer: 'I don't think so.'

Melanie frowned. 'You can stay there and—and I shall leave.' She made a step towards the door. The only move the man made was to hold up a key.

Melanie opened her eyes wide. 'You've locked the door? Well, of all the ...' She didn't finish the sentence; she only just managed to bite back the very rude word that came to her lips.

The large gentleman grinned. 'Tut—tut,' he said.

'We can't stay like this all night.' Melanie was a little frightened but also annoyed. Why didn't he go away? 'What do you want?' she blurted out.

'Ah, that sounds more promising, although not a very ladylike utterance.'

Melanie's colour rose at the reprimand. How dare he! 'Well,' she repeated, holding on to her temper as best she could. 'What *do* you want?'

Matthew thought she looked magnificent, the lovely face now stormy with flashing eyes, and heaving bosom. 'Only a glimpse of the notes you have there,' he said pathetically.

'They are nothing to do with you,' said Melanie and to emphasise the point, she folded them and placed them down her cleavage.

The gentleman laughed. 'That won't deter me,' he said.

'You—you mean you would molest me to—to ...' she couldn't continue.

'It would be nice.'

'You are insulting, sir.'

'On the contrary, I'm being complimentary. It's not every lady's ...'

'Go away—you are disgusting,' she snapped, placing her hands over her ears. 'I won't hear any more.' She turned away.

'There are other ways, of course,' he went on conversationally. 'I could easily turn you upside down, you know, and shake you like a pounce box so that the notes fall out.'

Automatically her hands went to hold down her skirts. She turned and looked at him in horror. She could well believe he would do it too as he looked strong enough. As much as she hated doing it, she would have to give in. To try and fight him would be unladylike and ridiculous. She turned and threw the notes onto a nearby table. 'There you are. Read them if you are able and much good will they do you.' She turned her back on him. She heard a sigh.

'Life's full of disappointments,' he said.

She lashed at him with her tongue. 'You are the most insensitive man I have ever met and I hope I never meet you again. I shall report you for harassment and—and being rude to me.' She was near to tears and vexed at having been treated so badly and made to feel so helpless. In all her life she had never known anything like it. And she continued to rail at him until at last running out of words she turned round. She stood still. He had gone. The notes were on the table where she had left them. Was she going mad? Had she dreamt it all? On looking closer she saw the key was there. Thank goodness for that. She read the notes again, tore into shreds the one from Harry Anstruther and refolded the other.

She picked up the key. At least she wasn't locked in. Then she frowned. If the key was on the table how had the man left the room? She went to the door and put the key in the lock. It didn't fit. It wasn't the right key and the door, therefore, hadn't been locked after all. Angrily, she threw it across the room.

As she entered the ballroom once more, Tim was waiting and she silently gave him her note. She wished him well and gave him a tight little smile as he led her back to Mrs Dobie. Meanwhile, she looked all round the ballroom, her eyes searching for that tall figure but she couldn't see him anywhere.

It wasn't long before Melanie and Mrs Dobie returned home.

CHAPTER 9

———————— ▼ ————————

It was Sunday morning and the ladies had decided to attend the service in Westminster Abbey. Joanna was particularly happy to do so as she would be able to make mental notes about the building and the service and include the information in a letter home. She hoped Papa would be pleased. She had wondered when she woke up, if they would be going, as she thought that perhaps Melanie and Mrs Dobie might be too tired after the ball but they were breakfasting as usual when Joanna joined them.

'Good morning,' she smiled, as she sat down and took a piece of toast. 'Did you enjoy your evening?'

'Oh, gracious, yes,' said Mrs Dobie. 'It is a pity you were not invited last night as you would have loved the spectacle immensely. It was a sight to see, I can tell you. The room was lit with a myriad of candles that was very flattering to the complexion, you know, that is, those of us who don't use maquillage. And some of the hairstyles! You could never imagine them. Some ladies' coiffures were at least two feet high and decorated with flowers, feathers and birds. Do you think they suffered with headaches, Melanie dear?' She didn't wait for an answer but went on: 'The dresses were wonderful, though. You would have enjoyed seeing them, Joanna. Some ladies wore beautiful silks and satins in gorgeous rich colours and embroidered lavishly on the underskirt but I must say ours were just as lovely. But some, oh, my dear, they had panniers that stretched across so far that they had to walk sideways when entering through a doorway. It was so funny when they danced. The gentlemen had a long walk round them. It's a good thing they are forbidden to dance with the same lady all night, otherwise they would have been tired out.'

Joanna laughed. 'I would have loved to have seen that,' she said.

Melanie smiled briefly. 'How you do go on, Lily. You are a bad influence on our guest.'

Joanna thought this was said automatically, as though Melanie's thoughts were far away.

'Did you enjoy yourself, Melanie?' Joanna asked tentatively. She thought it would be rude not to ask. But Melanie only said she had liked dancing again and on the following day they must see about lessons for Joanna. Otherwise, she was quieter than usual and Joanna saw her frowning to herself, so perhaps something was bothering her. Joanna knew from experience that when people were bothered, it was best to leave them alone.

Later they took the carriage to Westminster Abbey and Melanie seemed herself once more, as she pointed out people and places of interest on the way and chatted as usual. When Joanna saw the Abbey she gasped, it looked so large. Sitting inside, she found it hard not to stare all around her and to look upward but consoled herself that perhaps she may do so on the way out. The service was long and the Abbey cold, so the ladies were pleased when their visit was over. As Melanie said: 'We did our best to keep warm by saying our prayers and singing, but now we need a hot drink and food.' Although Melanie talked to her friend, Joanna still thought something worried her or perhaps she was just tired.

After lunch Joanna was able to write a page about her morning's visit, so that she could include it in a letter home when she had a chance to write it. She thought it would be kind to tell Mama that she would see Matthew and hoped she would hear from him soon and that he would accept the invitation to dine.

Melanie had much to think about. Mrs Dobie sensed something was wrong and taxed her with it. 'Is it something that happened last evening, dear? Would you like to discuss it with me? I can keep a secret you know. Or do you just have a wretched headache?'

Melanie smiled briefly. 'I know you can keep a secret, Lily, and you're always kind and helpful, but this is something I have to work out for myself. But thank you dear and no, I haven't a headache.' A large frown appeared and her breathing quickened as she thought of that detestable giant who had read her note. Who was he? Should she contact someone and tell him what had happened, like this Mr Anstruther? Did the giant understand French? Probably not, she thought and dismissed the idea. She had written it in French so that "Andre" would have no difficulty, if he were stopped and searched and the authorities were suspicious of him when he was in France. It looked just like any note written to a friend. But why was that large man so desperate to read it? Perhaps she was making too much of it all and he was hoping to come upon a romantic assignation and was reporting it to a jealous wife for money. Her lip curled. Or on second thoughts was he someone important and working for the French? But perhaps the incident wasn't worth thinking about after all and he was just trying to be clever and he fancied her! If that was the case he could look elsewhere. And so the thoughts went round and round in poor Melanie's head.

She wasn't the only one who sat pondering. Matthew sat frowning, wondering about Tim. Matthew had written down the contents of the letter and the address in his notebook as soon as he arrived home and now he looked at them again. He translated it from the French to:

My dear Adele,

This is to introduce you to my cousin, Andre de Noyons, who is visiting Paris for a few days. Perhaps you will be kind enough to let him stay with you until he can find his own accommodation.

Your ever loving,
Estelle.

It was addressed to: *Madame de Marne, 16 Rue de Honore, Paris.*

Matthew wrote down the following points:

1. Tim was Andre de Noyons. Fact.

2. Why hadn't he stopped to tell Matthew of his Paris destination as arranged? If Matthew hadn't taken it upon himself to obtain the information from Mrs Shaw, Harry and he would have no means of contacting Tim other than finding where Mrs Shaw lived etc. which didn't look very professional. Is this what Tim had wanted and he was going to disappear once in France?

3. Was "Estelle" Mrs Shaw's name and was the address of "Adele" real or was Tim walking into a trap?

4. There was still the question of the contact who Tim "had to see" some days ago. Who was this and was this something to do with Mrs Shaw?

One thing he should do, Matthew thought, is to enquire as to Mrs Shaw's whereabouts. Matthew smiled to himself. That could be an interesting meeting. He grinned even wider. Would she deign to see him? The words that had tripped off her tongue were really something and he had wished he could have stayed to hear her finish. Was she annoyed when she had discovered he had left? He felt she might have been. What a pity he couldn't have met her socially, she was really a most attractive woman and one with spirit. A smile came to his lips. Bless her, but she had looked magnificent when she had been angry.

A knock on the door interrupted his thoughts. Ned appeared. 'A letter for you, sir,' he said. 'Looks like a lady's handwriting. Someone you met last night, was it? I told you, you would.'

Matthew said nothing. He was used to his manservant's banter. The writing looked familiar but he couldn't quite place it. Frowning, he opened it and then, having read it, laughed. 'It's from my little sister. The minx. How did she persuade my Father to let her come, I wonder? She is in London with two ladies and I am invited to dine with them on Wednesday. I don't have an appointment then, do I, Ned?'

'Not to my knowledge, you don't. Oh, and if you want to send back a reply now, a young fellow is waiting in the kitchen to take it.'

Matthew wrote his acceptance.

The ladies were sitting in the withdrawing room, quietly looking through some fashion magazines and Joanna had found on one of the pages, a dress with large panniers like the ones Mrs Dobie had remarked upon. They were laughing, as Joanna had said she would look as wide as she was tall if she wore that fashion. In the middle of their chatting Bayliss knocked on the door.

'A missive for Miss Brooke,' he said as he entered.

'Oh, thank you,' said Joanna, her face wreathed in smiles as she opened her letter. 'Listen, ladies,' she said.

'Dear Jo, my brother writes.

Thank you for the invitation. I look forward to dining with you and your friends on Wednesday next. I hope you will tell me all the news from home and how you persuaded Papa to let you come to London, you minx.

Love Matt.

I'm so pleased he can come. He is great fun, you know.'
'That is good news, Joanna, isn't it Melanie?' said Mrs Dobie
'Yes, yes, of course it is,' Melanie replied. 'We shall look forward to it.'

CHAPTER 10

▼

By the time Monday morning came Melanie had ceased to worry. She had slept well, consequently her head was clearer. All the problems of the previous day would work themselves out and at the moment there was nothing she could do about them anyway. So it was a cheerful Melanie who suggested, tactfully, that perhaps Joanna would like to buy a new dress for the occasion of her brother's visit. Melanie had seen the limitations of Joanna's wardrobe and thought a few more modern and luxurious clothes would be necessary. If money was a problem Melanie was quite happy to supply it, considering it a worthwhile cause.

Joanna was very willing to be the centre of attention and buy a new dress, so the three ladies sallied forth to the shops in high spirits. After much laughing and also serious consideration of the material, colour and style suitable for a young lady, Joanna became a proud possessor of an emerald green gown, not cut too low, ('we don't want to shock your brother,' Melanie had said,) and trimmed with lace. It became her colouring beautifully and enhanced the glow of her dark brown eyes. They also visited a dancing master who gave Joanna more confidence in the steps and it was fun too. So Monday passed pleasantly enough.

As the weather was still fine on Tuesday they went walking in the park and spent the evening dining with friends whom Melanie had known for some years but she hadn't seen since her last visit to London, which seemed a long time ago.

Wednesday came and Joanna couldn't wait for the evening.

'You must be very fond of your brother,' said Mrs Dobie.

'What is he like?' asked Melanie. 'What does he do?'

'I don't really know what he does.' Joanna frowned. 'I don't think any of us knew at home either, to be honest.'

'Oh, a mystery then,' Melanie laughed.

'Although I loved my other brothers too, Matthew was the one who was always kind to me and he would help me out of scrapes before Papa knew. I think Mama pretended not to notice or he asked her not to. Mama had a soft spot for Matt too, I think.'

'He sounds a paragon, indeed,' said Melanie.

'Now leave the poor child alone, Melanie,' rebuked Mrs Dobie. 'You'll find out all about him when you see him. Now I'm going to borrow a tin of buttons from the housekeeper. I thought we'd teach Joanna how to play silver loo. No one can object if she gambles with buttons.'

'No indeed,' laughed Joanna.

The "paragon" had arrived home early from the office. Ned had laid out clean clothes ready for him and a coat the colour of dark claret with a waistcoat to match trimmed with gold braid.

'Do you think a box of confectionary is suitable to take, Ned? The two ladies will be much older than my sister otherwise I can't see that my Father would have given his permission for Joanna to accompany them.'

'Why ever not, sir?'

'Because London is a barbarous place and no well brought up young lady should live here. It is in some parts, of course,' Matthew added as an after-thought.

'What about men, then? Doesn't he like you working and living here?'

'Ah, well, that is a different matter. I am dull and only fit for pushing paper in an office, so London won't harm me.'

'But—but, sir, you are no such thing. How can anyone believe that? Good gracious, you are necessary to the—the country and your job can be dangerous. Why, look how you went over to Austria earlier this year and—and you speak French and ...'

'Yes, Ned, I know,' interrupted Matthew. 'But my parents don't know any-thing about all that. It is far too dangerous to tell them these things anyway, and Joanna must not be told either. The least said and all that, you know.'

'Well, I think you should tell them something different. They probably think you're work shy.'

'I live with it.'

'But you're just the opposite.'

Matthew shrugged.

'What do your other brothers do then that's so wonderful?'

'Mark is a good priest in Exeter and Luke is doing well in the army. And before you say anything more, you should know that they are great fellows and we always were good friends. Now can we change the subject?'

Ned said no more but Matthew could tell what he was thinking by his looks.

'Now let us concentrate on the matter in hand. Do you think I look well enough to charm two elderly ladies?'

'You'd charm the ducks off a pond, sir. And I'd like you to know that I'm proud of you and what you do, if no-one else is.'

Matthew looked at Ned and placed a friendly hand on his shoulder, giving him a smile. 'Thank you,' he said. 'I appreciate that.'

The three ladies were sitting chatting and waiting for their visitor. Eventually, there was a knock on the door and Bayliss entered and announced: 'Mr Brooke, ladies.'

The ladies stood as Matthew entered. Their reactions were mixed. Mrs Dobie's face was wreathed in smiles of welcome as she curtsied, Melanie stood frozen to the spot, her mouth open as she saw who had entered and Joanna, all decorum forgotten, ran forward with arms outstretched.

'Matt, how good to see you,' she called, laughing up at him.

Matthew caught her up in his arms and heartily kissed her. 'Little Jo, how are you, love? You're looking as beautiful as ever.'

'Oh, Matt,' she grinned, 'it is lovely to see you after all this time.' Taking him by the hand she led him forward. 'Let me introduce you to my very kind friends. This is Mrs Dobie.'

'Mrs Dobie.' Matthew returned that lady's smile and bowed.

'And this is Mrs Shaw, who has been kind enough to let me stay with her.'

Melanie who had partially recovered from the shock of seeing the last person she wished to see present in her withdrawing room managed a curtsey, although she still looked pale. On the other hand, Matthew had been able to glance briefly at those who were present on entering the room and although it was a great surprise to discover Mrs Shaw standing there, by the time he'd given Joanna a hug, he was in control again. So it was with a very correct bow and impassive face that he was able to say: 'Mrs Shaw, how kind of you to invite me.'

Melanie for once in her life was tongue-tied. It was Mrs Dobie who, looking at her frozen face, answered for her. 'You are very welcome, Mr Brooke. We are so pleased to meet Joanna's brother and she has been looking forward to seeing you so much. Do come and sit down, it won't be long before we dine.' She frowned across at Melanie wondering why her manners had left her.

Melanie mentally shook herself. She must behave as though she had never met Mr Brooke before, she thought. After all, that is what he seemed to be doing. She was pleased he hadn't blurted out about their meeting on the previous Saturday. Of course, he could still do so but she hoped he would not. She found herself saying: 'No, no, indeed, dinner won't be long but Bayliss should be bringing drinks anytime. Ah, here he is now.'

Bayliss entered with a tray and served sherry and Madeira. Conversation was general and mainly about what Joanna had been doing. Matthew thought the situation amusing but he dared not smile at Mrs Shaw. He didn't wish to antagonise her and spoil Joanna's evening.

Melanie encouraged Joanna to talk, so she told her brother how she had had help from the General to travel to London and how he had persuaded their father. All the while Matthew was listening, his keen eyes were watching the others. To Melanie's relief it wasn't long before dinner was announced.

The meal was good and there was plenty of choice, ragout of beef and a dish of anchovies, boiled mutton with a caper sauce and duck served with turnips. There were potatoes and parsnips and various dishes of creams, all to be tasted or rejected as each diner pleased. But Melanie, being confused in her thoughts, took and ate very little. Joanna chatted happily enough as did Mrs Dobie. Matthew played his part in the conversation too but his eyes continually flickered towards Melanie, noticing her lack of appetite. Surely something more was bothering her other than their last meeting. He decided he would have to find out later what it was.

When they had finished Matthew said: 'Thank you, ladies, for a very enjoyable dinner.' He stood as they left the room and Bayliss brought in the port wine. He felt sorry for Mr Brooke's solitary state so he hovered around the sideboard and the wine glasses.

Matthew asked him how long he had worked for Mrs Shaw. 'All her married life, sir, and before, I had the privilege of serving her husband. She is a very nice and kind lady, sir.'

Matthew nodded, finished his wine and shook his head when Bayliss suggested more. 'I believe I must join the ladies,' he said.

In the withdrawing room again, he said: 'Will you let me repay your kindness by inviting you to the theatre one evening? As I don't know your taste, may I leave it to you to choose?'

'Oh, how wonderful,' said Joanna, her eyes shining.

'That would be delightful,' said Mrs Dobie, 'wouldn't it, Melanie?'

She had to agree, of course. She didn't really wish to spend an evening at the theatre in Mr Brooke's company but it would sound churlish not to accept. After all, there were only the intervals in which to talk.

'With your permission,' said Matthew, 'I will bring along a young friend of mine, Hugh Fenton, whom I'm sure you will like.'

'Oh, yes,' said Mrs Dobie, 'two gentlemen will be very nice.'

Melanie said not a word and Joanna was beginning to notice that her friend wasn't the usual laughing person she knew. Did she not like Matt? However, some time was spent in discussing possible plays. Mrs Dobie said although she preferred tragedies, she thought perhaps, as it was Joanna's first visit to the theatre, that it would be better to see something lighter. 'I think Shakespeare's "Twelfth Night" is playing somewhere and there's one of Congreve's Restoration plays, "Love for Love" I think it's called, but …'

'Oh, that sounds nice,' said Joanna, the romantic.

'Yes, but I don't think it suitable for you,' said Matthew.

Joanna looked about to argue but Matthew just pointed a finger at her and shook his head.

Melanie, seeing Joanna's puzzled face, couldn't help but say something at this point. 'Congreve isn't really nice, you know, but I do think there is a light comedy on at the Playhouse called "The Lost Fan." I think the author is unknown but it could be amusing to see.' She hid a smile as she hoped it would bore Mr Brooke and his friend to death.

But Matthew took the wind out of her sails by saying: 'Oh, yes, the very one. I was just going to suggest it.'

Melanie bit back a sharp retort.

Arrangements were made after which conversation became general until Matthew said to Joanna: 'Have you written home yet, Jo?'

'Not yet. I have some notes to include about our visit to Westminster Abbey and a few general topics but I was waiting until I had seen you before I sent the letter. Why?'

'I wondered if it would be convenient to all of you if you could finish it now and then I will see to the posting of it.'

'It would be easier for me but …' She looked at the others. It was Mrs Dobie who answered.

'That is a good idea as long as you don't take hours to write it, Joanna,' she laughed.

'Oh, no indeed,' Joanna said, rising from her chair.

Matthew rose with her and accompanied her to the door. As he opened it he whispered: 'Make it about half an hour, please.'

She nodded, giving him a roguish smile.

Mrs Dobie rose too. 'I'll come and show you where to find the best paper, Joanna. Then it will be time for tea.'

'You don't have to go yet, Lily, Joanna knows where ...' Melanie's voice trailed off. Why did she have to entertain this man all by herself? It wasn't fair.

Matthew came back to his chair and sat down. 'I think you and I have some talking to do, don't you?' he said.

CHAPTER 11

▼

Melanie decided she had to stand up to this man. 'Mr Brooke,' she said without preamble, 'do you usually organise everyone, even in their own homes to which you have been invited?'

Matthew, appreciating the situation, lowered his head on to his steepled fingers and looked across at her, noting her raised eyebrows and straight look. His eyes laughed and Melanie hurriedly viewed her hands in her lap.

'I apologise,' said Matthew, 'but I had to see you alone somehow and I knew you wouldn't agree if I had just asked.'

'So, why do you wish to see me?'

'Well, the main reason is that something is worrying you; otherwise you would have eaten more of that excellent dinner which was supplied. I realise it was a shock to see me but I had a shock too, you know. So if we talk, some problems might be solved?'

'But why would I have problems?' She pulled herself together and thought she must be on the attack otherwise Mr Brooke would probably ask all the questions which she didn't like the idea of at all. 'So who are you really?'

Matthew raised his eyebrows, looking perplexed. 'Why, I am Joanna's brother, Matthew, who else did you think I was?'

'Yes, yes, I know that. What puzzles me is, why you of all people were at that ball on Saturday?'

'Well it was because I was invited. I hope you were invited too or did you just decide you would like to be present?'

'You know that isn't true and you should know I wouldn't do that kind of thing. Can we stop beating around the bush and will you tell me why did you have to be so unpleasant about those letters last Saturday and why were you so interested in them?'

'M-mm. Was I unpleasant? Let's just say they concerned a colleague of mine.'

'You mean the one calling himself Andre de Noyons? The man I danced with?'

'The same.'

Melanie looked puzzled. 'But if he was a colleague of yours, couldn't you have just asked him?'

'I suppose I could but then I preferred to ask you.'

Melanie frowned. The answer sounded plausible but on second thoughts something wasn't right. She supposed Mr Brooke, like most men, had enjoyed being obnoxious when they met. 'I—I see,' was all she could think of saying and so lost the chance to continue her questioning.

Matthew noticed her flushed cheeks and how she avoided his gaze. 'What I would like to know,' he said, 'is why you are involved in the writing of letters for an unknown gentleman and how does Joanna come into all this?'

Melanie looked up quickly. 'Oh, she doesn't. She is not involved at all. Honestly. I was only called upon to supply the address of my friend. That is all.'

'Why is Joanna here?'

'Oh, that was General Peabody-Brown's idea.'

'Ah! I might have known he would be involved. Do you know why?'

Melanie wished she hadn't to explain to this man of all people but she couldn't see she had any alternative; she felt Mr Brooke had a right to some explanation, being Joanna's brother. Trying to be matter of fact, she said: 'You probably know that my husband was killed nearly three years ago. This is my first time back in London without him and to take away the pain of remembering happier times the General thought it a good idea to have someone other than Mrs Dobie with me to take around and show the sights to, and he suggested Joanna. I think he thought it would be good for her to see a little more of life than—than where she lives, I think, although I am sure she is happy at home. I met Mrs Brooke and I liked her. She looks to be a very hard working lady. Mr Brooke I didn't meet as he had been called away to someone who was sick, I believe. But Joanna is a charming girl and I like her very much.'

'Thank you for the explanation. You know, I wondered why my Father had agreed to Joanna accompanying you, especially under the eye of yourself only. If he had seen you, he would have said you were far too young.'

'Really? I'm not all that young and I do have a position.'

'I realise that.' Matthew smiled charmingly at her. 'But twenty four is still young.'

Melanie opened her eyes wide. 'How did you know that?' she asked.

Matthew laughed. 'I didn't. I just guessed.'

Melanie frowned at him. 'You really are the most annoying person,' she said.

Matthew became serious again. 'Why did the General want you to supply an address in Paris?'

'He said his friend Harry Anstruther had mentioned he needed a safe place to go to in Paris and did he know of one. The General asked me, that is all, as he knows I have a friend living there. Do you know this Mr Anstruther?'

Matthew ignored the question. 'Is Adele and Estelle your real names?' he asked with a smile.

'No. My friend and I went to the same finishing school, you see, and in French lessons we chose our French names. My friend and I always signed our letters with those when we wrote anything secret. That is why I used them this time.'

'So that's all there is to it?'

Melanie looked at him. 'I think there's a lot more to it, only you won't tell me.'

'My dear girl, you can't expect me to tell you all my secrets.'

'Oh, you have some, do you? And I'm not your dear girl, I'm a widowed lady.'

'Right. My dear widowed lady, all I'm concerned about is that you and my sister are not involved in anything dangerous, that is all.'

'No, Joanna and I are not involved in anything and please don't address me as ...'

'There's no pleasing you,' sighed Matthew.

Melanie's lips twitched. 'I think it's time Joanna and Mrs Dobie returned, don't you?'

'They should do so in precisely two minutes,' said Matthew, looking at the clock on the mantelpiece.

Melanie gasped. 'How do you know?'

'I told Joanna to be away half an hour and ... ah! Here she is now, I believe.'

A small knock had sounded on the door and it opened a fraction to reveal Joanna's smiling face. 'May I come in, Melanie? My letter is finished and Mrs Dobie is coming with Bayliss and the tea tray.'

'Yes, yes, do come in, dear,' said Melanie, forcing a smile.

Joanna danced over to Matthew. 'Here it is,' she said. 'I've told them what we have been seeing and doing and how you both were enjoying each other's company while I was writing this.'

A small choking sound came from Melanie. 'Oh, I expect your throat is dry with talking, dear,' said Mrs Dobie kindly. 'Tea will set it to rights, I'm sure.'

Melanie didn't bother to explain.

After a general chat, mainly about what Joanna was going to see and do and arrangements for the theatre visit on the following Saturday, Matthew took his leave. He held out his hand to Melanie who had no choice but to place hers in his and was surprised when he gently kissed it. Before releasing it, he said: 'Your name suits you. It is very pretty.' He gave her a brief smile before turning quickly to take his leave of Mrs Dobie.

Joanna put her arm through his and went with him to the front door. He gave her a small bag of money, told her if she needed him to send a note to his address but above all to behave herself. He kissed her on the cheek and left.

Joanna thanked Melanie and Mrs Dobie for an evening which she had enjoyed immensely, after which they all retired, each one's thoughts on the evening differing but as they did not compare them, they weren't aware of this.

It had been delightful to see Matt again, Joanna thought. She found he was the same kindly brother she had always known. He still had that twinkle in his eye. She was a little surprised that Melanie wasn't quite her usual charming self but perhaps she had been overwhelmed by Matthew's large figure. Joanna had always thought him a gentle giant. She wondered why he wanted to be private with Melanie but expected he wished to know a few details regarding the length of time they were to be in London and what they intended doing. But why couldn't he have asked while Joanna was present? She shrugged. What did it matter? She was looking forward to the theatre visit on Saturday. It was the first time she had ever been to a proper play. Little plays had been acted at home and a Nativity Play was always performed at Christmastime in the church, but that was the limit of her knowledge. She hoped it would be fun and looked forward to meeting Matt's friend. With these thoughts she drifted off into a relaxed sleep.

Mrs Dobie had also enjoyed the evening and thought Matthew a kind and considerate guest. She was delighted with his manners and attitude towards herself and the prospect of the coming theatre trip pleased her greatly. Perhaps "The Lost Fan" by an unknown author might not be her own choice but there were acquaintances to see and wave to and no doubt Mr Brooke's company and that of his friend would be pleasant. Mr Brooke had wanted to see Melanie alone, she could tell, and he had glanced at her continually over the meal. Perhaps he wanted to know how she knew Joanna? She had been concerned about Melanie, though, and wondered why she hadn't been quite her sunny self. Bearing in mind Melanie's preoccupation with her own thoughts earlier in the week, she had asked her if anything was wrong when on their way to bed. Melanie had only said her stomach didn't feel too comfortable, that was all. Mrs Dobie wondered if this was true but had not pursued the matter further. She had kissed her goodnight as usual before seeking her own bed.

But Melanie's thoughts were in a whirl. She had been amazed to see Joanna's brother was that particular person she had met last Saturday. She wouldn't have guessed in a thousand years that they were closely related. She must remember to ask how it came about that Mr Brooke was so fair while Joanna and her mama were dark haired. She also wondered what his work was exactly. Joanna didn't seem to know and he didn't say. Was it something to do with the Foreign Office and was the General involved in some way? Otherwise, why had Mr Brooke attended the ball? What was the connection between him and "Andre", whoever he was? She frowned. Or, here her eyes opened wide, were these men spies? No, they couldn't be, surely nothing so dangerous. She could understand his being concerned for Joanna's welfare but why did he wonder about her, Melanie's, part in it? As she had told him, she had only supplied an address. Did he believe her? Was she bothered whether he did or not? He certainly liked his fun at her expense and, here she frowned, he seemed genuinely kind and gentle when he had taken his leave and kissed her hand. She quickly turned her thoughts to the coming the-atre trip. It was a kind gesture for him to suggest it but probably it was for Joanna's benefit really. She frowned and was conscious of feeling ungenerous. Her stomach rumbled. Now things were clearer in her mind she could have eaten. Mr Brooke had said it was an "excellent dinner" and she had been too uptight to eat hardly anything. Oh! damn Mr Brooke. She would go to bed, put the evening out of mind and make up for her lack of food tomorrow.

CHAPTER 12

Matthew sat at his desk the next day, looked at the pile of papers upon it and rubbed a hand over his face. He had been late to bed the previous evening after sorting out facts in his mind. He had enjoyed his visit to Mrs Shaw's house and seeing Joanna again. She looked happy and Matthew felt quite sure that she wasn't involved in any of the General's schemes other than he thought her a suitable companion for Mrs Shaw and also it was a treat for Joanna to be away from home for a while to broaden her outlook a little. Matthew had been very surprised to see Mrs Shaw, though, and thought he had hidden the fact well. Apart from passing on the address of her friend in Paris, he didn't think she was involved in any way and he was satisfied that Tim was not walking into a trap. Something still worried him about his colleague but, after all, he could look after himself as he had done so before when on a similar mission. That was what the job was all about. Now Matthew's mind went back to last evening. He was sorry Mrs Shaw hadn't been able to eat her dinner. She must have been shocked to see him. He hoped on Saturday she would, somehow, be able to enjoy it all. He thought her a remarkable woman and beautiful with it.

Hugh came in with a cup of coffee. 'Pleasant thoughts, sir?' he asked as he saw the smile on Matthew's face.

'Mm. Ah! Yes. I wanted to see you.'

'Yes, sir?'

'Are you free to visit the theatre next Saturday evening, Hugh?'

'To—to visit the theatre, sir? I expect I could. I have no other arrangements made. May I ask why and what am I to see?'

'Why? Because I am taking three ladies and need another gentleman present as it would be nicer. And ...'

Hugh interrupted. 'Nicer for whom, sir, if I may ask?'

'For all of us, of course, and me especially,' Matthew replied blandly. Then he relented. 'I visited a Mrs Shaw and her companion last evening for dinner. My little sister is staying with them so I thought I should do my duty and return their hospitality with a visit to the theatre, that is all. Your presence would help.'

'Oh, I see, sir. I would like to join you. Thank you for asking me.'

'I'm afraid what we are to see will be a most frippery production, I wouldn't wonder. It is called "The Lost Fan".'

'And you wish to see it, sir?' asked Hugh, opening his eyes wide.

'Not really but it is my sister's first theatre visit, you see, and it has to be something suitable.'

'Oh, yes, of course, I see. How young is she, sir, if I may ask?' Hugh had visions of a dumpy twelve-year-old that he would have to take under his wing.

'You may, Hugh, you may. If I remember correctly I think she is twenty.'

Did Hugh's eyes brighten?

Harry Anstruther came in later bringing with him an older man called Arnold Kent to replace Tim temporarily. He was a middle-aged man, thin and studious but pleasant enough and his sole purpose was to help with the paperwork. Harry knew him well as he worked in his office. Matthew took the opportunity to have a private talk with Harry to see if anything was taking place between him and the General that Matthew should know about. But as Harry said, the previous agent had been lost to them, he needed another safe house for Tim and the General had found one for him from Mrs Shaw. He had known Peabody-Brown from a long time ago and he was reliable, as Matthew should know. Matthew was content for the moment, at least.

'Melanie,' said Joanna at breakfast the next morning, 'which of my dresses should I wear on Saturday evening? Would the one I wore last evening be suitable?'

'No dear, I think something a little more lavish in style would be better. It doesn't want to be overdone, of course. If you haven't one perhaps we should shop.'

'I don't think I have anything that will do,' said Joanna.

'Would you like me to check with you after breakfast and then we could go shopping this morning if you do not want us for anything, Melanie. I know you have writing to do,' said Mrs Dobie.

'Would you like Lily to go with you, Joanna? I can let you have some money if there's a problem.'

'As a matter of fact,' said Joanna, 'Matt gave me some when he left last night but thank you for offering. And Mrs Dobie will know just what I need, I'm sure.'

So Joanna and Mrs Dobie visited the shops, much to both ladies' delight while Melanie sat down to write invitations to a dinner party. It was not to be a large affair but now she was established back in London once more she must play her part and return hospitality. She had a list of close friends to invite but should she invite Mr Brooke for Joanna's sake? It was all a little uncomfortable and he wasn't a close friend anyway, so perhaps she could refrain from including him. Of course, he had invited them to the theatre but that was because of Joanna, really, wasn't it?

Saturday evening arrived and the two gentlemen, smartly arrayed in velvet coats, waited in the foyer of the Playhouse Theatre. It was a busy scene against the background of the dark crimson walls and decorations of gold. What it looked like in daylight Matthew didn't like to think but in the candlelight it looked sumptuous and rich. Hugh was a little nervous but hoped it didn't show. Matthew had briefed him beforehand not to call him "sir" but "Matthew" and also reminded him not to talk about where they worked. If asked, he was just to say "in an office".

Although it was an unknown play, many people arrived so it looked as though the actors would have a large audience. Ladies and gentlemen were powdered and patched and it seemed as if they were all trying to outdo each other in the height of their elaborate coiffures. Dresses in some cases were quietly elegant, others over-decorated with ribbons and a clash of colours. Men as well as ladies carried fans and others had eyeglasses in order to view the actors on the stage and the occupants of other boxes. All was mayhem with laughter and the shouting of greetings. Flunkeys were holding open the doors and there were more at the foot of the broad opulent staircase.

The ladies arrived. Joanna looked around her with wide eyes and smiling mouth. Mrs Dobie looked pleased to be there and Melanie looked happy enough but a little anxious, Matthew thought. He stepped forward, bowing and welcoming them and introduced Hugh before escorting them up the staircase to their box. The ladies sat in the front with the gentlemen sitting behind them but all could see the stage, which at the moment was curtained, of course. Joanna was enthralled by everything. It all looked so rich and pretty and she hadn't imagined so many people. She turned to ask about the gentlemen walking around in the pit and instead of her brother, it was Hugh who bent forward to answer her questions. Matthew smiled and immediately conversed with Melanie and Mrs Dobie.

The play was better than they thought. It was light and nonsensical but amusing and fairly well acted. Matthew watched Melanie and she was able to smile and even laugh at some parts. When she did this she held up her fan to hide her amusement so that Matthew wouldn't, she thought, see her. Mrs Dobie, for all her talk of preferring tragedies, joined in the laughter and turned to Matthew saying how enjoyable it all was. Joanna confided to Hugh that this was her first visit to the theatre and would he explain all to her and tell her how to go on, as she didn't wish to let Matthew down by saying the wrong thing. Hugh smiled sweetly at her and said as she looked as pretty as she did no-one would be embarrassed by her at all. Indeed her new dress suited her to perfection, as it was in a deep shell pink with an underskirt of quilted ivory silk.

The first interval came and more gentlemen arrived. They came mainly to pay their respects to Melanie who they hadn't seen for some time. Most of them were older gentlemen and couples who had known her husband. Matthew and Hugh were introduced, of course, and also the ladies. Hugh took the opportunity to take Joanna into the corridor at the back of the box for a little exercise, as he put it. Matthew noticed, smiled slightly and left them alone. He knew he could trust Hugh.

When the bell sounded for the second act their visitors left and Melanie thought it only good manners to apologise to Matthew for the surge of gentlemen. Matthew said he was honoured to have invited such a popular lady. Melanie thought he sounded a little piqued so she tried to placate him by saying she was enjoying the play, the box was just in the right position and she thought inviting Hugh along had been a good idea.

Matthew's lips twitched. 'Thank you, it is good of you to say so,' was all that he said.

'You're laughing at me,' Melanie accused him, tapping him with her fan.

'Now would I do that?'

'Yes, you would do whatever you pleased, I think,' Melanie said.

'I wish I could,' Matthew said gently.

Melanie turned round in her seat quickly, her colour high. Thank goodness the curtains were being drawn back ready for the next act.

During the next interval supper was served in a small room set aside for the purpose. This was a light meal consisting of small savoury biscuits with toppings of cheese and fish followed by elegant dishes of jellies and creams, and sweet little cakes. All was accompanied by whatever wines were required.

The room was crowded but as Matthew had the forethought to request chairs and a table for his guests they were quite comfortable. They discussed the play and Matthew was pleased to see Melanie relaxed and charming as she talked to Joanna and Hugh. Matthew found Mrs Dobie a likeable and intelligent companion but he did keep an ear on the other conversation too. So he was able to smile slightly when he heard Melanie say: 'Mr Fenton, do you work with Mr Brooke?'

'I do, ma'am,' said Hugh.

'And what kind of work do you do?'

Hugh looked at her and obedient to Matthew's instructions said: 'Unfortunately, nothing very interesting. Like, er—Matthew, we write and sort out papers for other people.'

'Is it interesting? Can you explain a little more?' asked Melanie with a sweet smile.

Hugh looked blank. 'Well, not really. It's all very boring.'

'And where do you do this boring work?'

'Why in an office, ma'am,' said Hugh raising his eyebrows.

'Where is this office?'

'Oh, to the north of the river.'

Melanie glanced at Matthew, who still conversed with Mrs Dobie but he gave Melanie a particular smile at the same time that told her that she would not succeed in finding out more. She frowned at him and refrained from questioning Hugh further as to persevere would be very bad manners.

Matthew stood up. 'If you have had sufficient, ladies, perhaps we should return to our seats?'

Melanie rose like the others. She would find out what it was these gentlemen did somehow.

CHAPTER 13

▼

It was Monday morning and Matthew and Hugh were back at work. Matthew had a long chat with Arnold and found him clever, quiet and pleasant. He could be relied upon, Matthew felt, to do a good job and no doubt Harry would be visiting to see how they were progressing. They should soon hear from Tim in some way, too, if only to say he had arrived safely in Paris.

When Hugh saw Matthew alone he said: 'I enjoyed the theatre visit very much, sir. Thank you for inviting me. The play was quite pleasing, wasn't it?'

'Mm. Not bad, Hugh, not bad,' said Matthew, looking up at the younger man, a smile lurking in his eyes.

'All the ladies were very friendly and nice, weren't they?'

Matthew nodded, thinking of one particular lady.

'Your—your sister is very pretty, sir.'

'Jo? Mm. I suppose so.'

'Sir, would you mind ... I mean could I see ... Could I ask Miss Brooke out sometime, do you think?' he finished in a rush.

'Why?' Matthew asked.

'Why? I thought she would like to go with me to walk in the gardens or visit an art gallery or whatever she would like to visit, that is all. We seemed to enjoy each other's company and I thought it would be a change for her to go with me and ...' Poor Hugh finished, his words trailing off as he caught the look of amusement on Matthew's face.

'You have my permission, Hugh, to ask her. I cannot vouch for her answer but I am quite happy for you to take her out. But a word of warning, she can be mischievous and naughty so bear that in mind.'

'Of course, sir, I'll look after her well. Thank you.'

'Oh Hugh?'

'Yes sir?'

'You did very well evading Mrs Shaw's questions. Well done.'

'Oh, were you listening? Thank you. Why did she want to know where I worked, do you think?'

'Well, she's a woman and curious. But still be on your guard in that respect, even with Joanna.'

'Yes, of course sir.' And Hugh turned and went back to his work with a smile on his face and a spring in his step.

But Joanna was the least of Matthew's worries. Ships were still being sunk in the Channel by the French, although he must admit that some French ones were sunk too. The situation there wasn't as good as it should be and in time Matthew hoped Tim would find out the reason and alert Harry here in Britain as to when the French attacks would take place. Of course, the navy knew what it was doing. Admiral Rodney was a great man, but Matthew was concerned for the men who would be killed or drowned; also those taken prisoner by the French. It had been known, though, that British smugglers had picked up a few lucky survivors and brought them back to England by night.

It had been arranged that Hugh would take Arnold to lunch with him at their usual tavern, "The Shoulder o' Mutton", as he did not know the area but they had to wait until Matthew was back before they left. Harry Anstruther was expected soon so the building could not be left empty. As usual, Matthew had gone out alone, a foolhardy thing to do in that area, as all manner of assault or surprise attacks from the criminals and desperate people living in such a place were likely at any time. They had been referred to as "the dregs of society" by the government. Matthew had sympathy for the inhabitants of Blackfriars. Life was hard. As he walked among them he wasn't worried but he had his wits about him, a pistol in his pocket and a sword at his side apart from his ability to punch someone to the ground within seconds.

But he arrived safely at the tavern and saw an empty table in a corner where he could view the rest of the clientele and also the door. The landlord, knowing him as a regular customer, personally came to serve him. 'We have an excellent meat pie on today, sir,' he suggested, 'if you feel like it or …'

'Thank you,' Matthew interrupted, 'that will do nicely, and some ale.'

'Yes sir, thank you, at once.' And he rushed away shouting the order to his wife who was in the kitchen.

The pie was reasonably good by Matthew's standards. While he ate it he appeared relaxed to anyone looking at him, but he was on the alert the whole time. He had always had this ability even when young, which had led his father to believe him either lazy or retarded in some way, but Matthew had never worried about that fact, he knew he could cope.

He was nearing the end of his lunch when a scruffy individual came through the door. He looked keenly round and Matthew, seeing him standing there, nodded. The man approached and was told to sit down.

'That smells good, guv'nor,' he said.

Matthew crooked a finger, which brought the landlord over. 'Same again for my friend, if you please.' The man nodded and rushed away.

The informant gave Matthew a sickly smile. 'Thanks. You'll find it's worth it.'

'I hope so,' said Matthew, 'so tell me.'

'Your man has arrived in France but where he is at the moment I haven't been told. He should be all right if he avoids large towns and is careful to keeping a low profile when he reaches Paris. The peasants work as usual and are not interested in the war. They don't hear much about it unless a visitor from outside brings the news. The British have made another push towards taking Fort Duquesne in America and also outside. In Madras the regiments have been reinforced. It's thought there will be lots more trouble there, though. Hochkirch will be the centre of a battle any time now and more Prussian naval troops have been sent over to help protect British shores. That was worth a pie, wasn't it?'

Matthew asked more questions but couldn't find out anything more of importance. He passed over the usual coin. The man looked at him and hesitated. 'What is it?' asked Matthew.

'It's nothing definite, just a feeling I have. But watch yourself, guv'nor.'

Matthew nodded, and getting up, patted the man's shoulder and left.

As he walked back along the dismal street he saw men sitting on doorsteps or lounging against the walls. Babies cried and frustrated mothers shouted. A group of older children were playing a singing game and a little girl detached herself from them to run over to Matthew holding out her hand. She was a poor little shrimp with a small body topped by an older face, which was now pink with the exertion of her singing. Matthew had met her before and given her a coin. He now placed another in her hand. She smiled and gripped his fingers. 'You're being followed,' she said and ran back to her group.

Matthew resumed his way back to the office at his usual pace. He turned the corner and backed quietly into a passageway and waited to see if anyone was indeed following him or whether his little informant was wrong. He didn't have to wait long. A figure in a voluminous cloak and large floppy hat turned the corner slowly. As soon as he stepped abreast of the passage Matthew shot out an arm and made a grab at the man and held him tightly by a fistful of cloak under his chin. The man, being surprised, gasped, but recovered quickly and said breathlessly: 'Sir, let me go at once.'

Matthew didn't and continued to hold him in a vicelike grip. 'Now my friend,' he said, 'why are you following me?'

'I—I wasn't.'

'If you weren't, why are you here?'

'I—I've lost my way.'

Matthew continued to hold him with one hand and tipped back the man's hat with the other. He was in his thirties and not a poor man or underfed as Matthew thought he might be. 'Who are you and why are you in Blackfriars?'

'I do not have to answer you,' said the man.

To Matthew's ear there was something different about the way he spoke, a slight accent perhaps? But, of course, that could be a regional one.

'Let me go, sir, I am lost. I would not hurt you. I thought …' All the time he was talking his hand was moving carefully to his sword. Matthew felt the movement and wasted no time. Suddenly he let the man go and brought up his fist, administering a stunning blow to the man's jaw. The man fell to the ground. Matthew picked him up without difficulty and carried him over his shoulder to the office.

He arrived in his room just as Hugh was taking in some papers. 'Why, sir, what has happened?'

'This individual was following me. I think we need to ask him some questions. Has Harry been in yet, by the way?'

'Not yet, no.'

'Good. Fetch Mr Kent, Hugh. Perhaps he would like to join us.'

Arnold came in and was surprised to see the man in the chair. 'Friend of yours?' he asked quietly.

'Hardly. You don't know him, I suppose?'

'Afraid not. Shall we search him?'

They took out his pistol from his pocket and relieved him of his sword. They found his purse but there was nothing inside, other than coins. A bundle of papers came next from an inner pocket. 'Keep an eye on him, while I go through these,' said Matthew. As he sorted through, he found a bill from a tailor that had to be paid, some cards of invitation to various evening functions, membership cards of some clubs and some general personal notes. All that came to light of any importance was that his name was Henry Fox and his address was in Kensington. Matthew made a note of the name and address and also wrote down the other information although it was nothing out of the ordinary. They searched every pocket and went through every stitch of his clothes but nothing else was found.

They were contemplating pouring water over him to assist him to wake up when they heard footsteps and Harry Anstruther appeared.

'Gentlemen,' he said as the other three stood up. Then noticing the inert figure in the chair said: 'Who have we here?'

Matthew explained briefly.

'I see,' said Harry. 'And do you think he is of importance even if he was following you and trying to pry?'

Matthew shrugged. 'I don't know but what I do know is that he was following me but wouldn't say why. And he tried to reach his sword.'

'So you—er—…' Harry made a fist and punched the air.

'Yes sir.'

Harry nodded. 'Well, I had better take him back with me to the Foreign Office and get him questioned further by our trained gentlemen. Everything else all right? Are you happy here, Arnold?'

Arnold laughed. 'Oh, yes sir, thank you. There's never a dull moment.'

The next few minutes were spent in bringing Henry Fox round and Hugh brought a glass of wine to aid his recovery. Still very dizzy, Henry managed to feel his jaw. 'It feels broken,' he said thickly.

'We'll have someone look at it,' said Harry. 'You are coming with me to answer a few questions and then if all is well you can go home. But I'm afraid we'll have to blindfold you until you arrive there.'

Mr Fox began to protest but Matthew had already tied his arms behind him and Arnold bound his eyes. Once more Matthew hoisted him on to his shoulder and following Harry downstairs deposited him on the seat of the carriage that waited outside. Harry entered, pistol in hand, and the bundle of the man's effects were placed next to him on the seat. The horses were given the order to start and they were away.

Back upstairs in the office again Matthew still thought there was something odd about Mr Henry Fox but couldn't place his finger on it. Just then he heard a noise. He looked up, a grin on his face. Hugh's stomach had just rumbled. 'You and Arnold had better go to lunch,' he said.

CHAPTER 14

▼

Hugh lost no time in going to see Joanna, and on the following Saturday morning he was knocking on the door in Curzon Street at the proper visiting hour. He was free this morning, which was not always the case. When there were important papers to be delivered to Harry Anstruther or other secret ones to be fetched, Matthew gave Hugh the rest of the day off after the task had been performed and then he was at leisure to do as he wished.

The ladies, who were about to prepare themselves for a visit to the shops, sat and waited to see who it was when they heard the knocker sound on their front door. It wasn't long before Hugh was announced, much to Joanna's delight.

'Oh, Mr Fenton, how nice of you to call,' she said. Hugh had no qualms that he had done the right thing when he saw Joanna's happy smiling face.

He bowed to the ladies, saying as he sat down: 'I came to see if Miss Brooke would do me the honour of walking with me in the park this morning. The weather is fine and I do not think too cold.'

'I would love to,' Joanna immediately replied clapping her hands. 'Oh, Melanie, I may go, mayn't I?'

'Of course you may. But you must take someone with you.' Joanna made a face. 'You know you must,' said Melanie but relented slightly by saying: 'How about little Tilly?'

Some minutes later Hugh and Joanna, with a highly delighted Tilly who was able to leave her jobs below stairs for someone else to finish, left the house. The park was not far away and they were soon walking along its paths. At first their conversation was a little stilted as they discussed the plants and trees they saw but eventually they both relaxed enough to be more at ease with one another. Joanna, eyeing the dried leaves below the trees, looked innocently up at Hugh. 'You know,' she said, 'at home we are not far away from Savernake Forest.'

'Really? I have heard of it. Do you go there often?'

'This time of year is best, you know, as all the leaves, like these, are dry and crunchy. We jump and run through them,' she finished innocently.

'Do you?' said Hugh, mindful of Matthew's warning about his sister. 'Well, you can't do it here, people would be horrified.'

Joanna sighed. 'How stuffy,' she remarked. She changed the subject then and asked airily: 'And what is my brother doing today?'

'Working.'

'Oh, how boring. Do you not work today, then?'

'Sometimes, it depends.' To forestall any more questions, Hugh said: 'Tell me about your life at home.'

Nothing loath, Joanna told him about her family, her friends and what she did. Hugh decided it wasn't a very exciting life but it could be very pleasant, no doubt.

By this time they were walking near the lake and the ducks and swans came to be fed. 'Next time, we must bring some bread, Tilly,' said Joanna.

'Oh yes Miss,' said her diminutive chaperone, for once her pale cheeks now pink with pleasure.

They wandered further until Hugh said: 'Perhaps it is time we returned.' They were nearing the gate when Hugh, having looked round and found no-one in sight, suddenly grabbed Joanna with one hand and Tilly with the other and ran with them through the mound of crunchy leaves below a beech tree. Laughing and out of breath, Joanna looked up at Hugh. 'Oh, Hugh,' she puffed, 'you cheat. I thought we weren't supposed to do that here.'

Hugh looked down at the laughing face turned up to him and grinned, although he would have liked to kiss her. But all he said was: 'And may I call you Joanna?' Without waiting for an answer he looked round at Tilly. 'All right?' he asked.

'Oh yes, sir,' she gasped. 'I haven't had so much fun for a long time.'

Hugh's heart was touched. He smiled and gave her a small coin.

'Oh, sir,' said Tilly, clutching it to her chest, 'thank you.'

Outside the house, Joanna thanked Hugh and said she had enjoyed his company and invited him inside to partake of lunch. He declined but said he hoped he might call again.

'Please do,' she said, extending her hand.

Hugh bowed and kissed it.

As Melanie had begun entertaining once more the house seemed always full of people and the knocker was never still. Joanna, being of an amiable disposition, made friends with the daughters and sometimes granddaughters of the ladies who visited Melanie. It wasn't long before she was invited to their homes or to an outing or a social function where she met other young men. Melanie tried to keep an eye on who she was with and where she was going but found it difficult owing to her own busy lifestyle. But Joanna told her not to worry, as the girls who accompanied her were known to Melanie, or she knew their mamas. So all of a sudden Joanna was pitched into a busy life of her own, attending more dances and dinners that she had ever thought possible, where she laughed and talked and blossomed.

Melanie noticed and so did Matthew. They met at a formal evening given by, evidently, mutual friends, a Mr and Mrs Weston, the occasion being the betrothal of their daughter. Joanna was invited too because of her association with Melanie.

Matthew had arrived later than Melanie so although she was surprised to see him there, she had an opportunity to watch him. This was done surreptitiously, of course, and she found his easy manners just as they should be. Also he seemed popular with the gentlemen who put themselves out to speak to him, and the ladies of all ages smiled upon him to which he responded with kind words and his lazy smile. True, he was an eligible bachelor, thought Melanie a trifle waspishly, so that would account for the attention of the mamas with daughters on the marriage market being particularly interested in him. One such lady introduced him to her daughter, a rather tall, gangly, red haired girl who looked conscious of her size and was dressed inappropriately in the wrong shade of yellow. Matthew immediately asked her to dance in the next set that was just forming. She smiled gratefully at him and as far as she was concerned, he had made her evening a success. Afterwards, escorting her back to her mother, he heard a voice he knew and trod over to a group of young ladies and gentlemen. Joanna looked up quickly, her eyes wide. 'Why, Matthew,' she gasped, 'you here? I didn't know.'

'Why should you? Introduce me, Jo.'

Joanna hurriedly introduced him to the group. Matthew was amused at the young men who straightened themselves after their bow, trying to catch his eye to be singled out, and the young ladies made much use of their fans as they curtseyed demurely. Matthew couldn't imagine why he had this effect on even young people and put it down to his size and unusual colouring. He extracted and escorted Joanna to a corner where there were chairs and somewhere on the way he managed to obtain two glasses of wine. 'You look blooming,' he said, 'enjoying yourself?'

'Very much. Did you—did you bring Hugh with you?'

'No. If he wasn't invited it was not for me to bring him. Why, do you need him? I thought you were happy enough with the circle of young bucks back there.'

'Well, yes, but he is so much nicer to be with, you know.'

'Oh, I see. Is Mrs Shaw with you?'

'Yes, although Mrs Dobie had another engagement. Melanie is dressed in a beautiful sea green coloured dress, over there talking to that gentleman. Did you wish to see her?'

'I should pay my respects, don't you think?'

'Is that all?'

'What more should there be?'

'I—I don't know,' Joanna shrugged. 'I thought perhaps ...'

'You think too much, Jo,' he said getting up. 'If you wish to dance with me now, come along.'

It wasn't until another hour had passed before Melanie found Matthew bowing before her. She had wondered whether he would approach her at all and thought that if he didn't it would be the shabbiest thing. In her heart of hearts she wished he had approached her earlier as the company, although very pleasant, consisted of older men or very young ones. Very few were around Melanie's age group.

'May I have the next dance, Mrs Shaw? Unless you are too tired,' he added.

Startled, she said: 'Sir, why should I be tired?'

'You have been dancing all evening, ma'am, and I thought ...' He left the sentence in mid-air.

'I may be twenty four, sir, but I am not in my dotage.' Melanie didn't know whether to be annoyed with Mr Brooke, as usual, or flattered that he had noticed her dancing all evening.

Then he disarmed her by giving her a sweet smile. 'Of course not,' he said. 'How unhandsome of me.' He offered his arm.

She gave him a measuring look. 'It is a cotillion, sir. A difficult dance.'

'I remember you dancing it beautifully at the Ambassador's Ball, you know. As you know it well, I hope I shall be able to muddle through somehow.'

Melanie bit her lip. Did he always have an answer? They took their places on the dance floor and it was soon clear to Melanie that Mr Brooke knew the dance very well indeed and what was more performed it most elegantly. Because of this, she enjoyed her part in it, of course, but why did he take pleasure in provoking her so? As soon as the dance was finished, she asked him.

'I provoke you? I humbly beg your pardon, ma'am.' Matthew looked at her in such a way that Melanie hurriedly looked down and busied herself in smoothing her already smooth dress.

'I would like to talk to you about Joanna, sometime, if I may,' said Matthew, changing the subject. 'It isn't convenient now, of course, but perhaps you are free sometime?'

'Yes, yes, of course,' Melanie said, 'She seems happy, though, doesn't she?' She looked anxiously up at him.

'Very much so. I am indebted to you for looking after her so well. Would it please you to drive out with me sometime? I'll be on my very best behaviour, I promise.'

A small smile came to Melanie's lips and was hastily repressed. She found herself saying: 'Yes, yes, of course. I believe I am free next Sunday afternoon, sir.' And so it was arranged that Matthew would call.

He walked away feeling pleased with himself, for he had noticed Melanie's smile, and took his leave of his hosts soon afterwards.

Melanie frowned and wondered why she had so easily said yes. She supposed it was because of the importance of the discussion as evidently Mr Brooke was worried for some reason about Joanna. It would be as well that they should soon meet and sort things out. That was what Melanie told herself, anyway.

CHAPTER 15

▼

It was Sunday and the three ladies were occupying the morning room, sitting around the fire as the weather was decidedly chilly and what was more, made worse by a light drizzle outside. As the previous evening's social event had proved to last longer than they had expected and they hadn't been in their beds before three o'clock, they had decided to relax this morning and forego their visit to church. Now, as Mrs Dobie turned the page of a fashion magazine, she looked at Joanna who was pretending to read a book. She knew she wasn't really reading it as she hadn't turned a page these last fifteen minutes. Mrs Dobie wondered if she had dozed off but her eyes were decidedly open so perhaps Joanna was enjoying some private thoughts and hopes as young girls were wont to do.

Mrs Dobie, of course, was right. Joanna was dwelling on the previous evening's dinner with music and a little dancing. Everyone had been pleasant and welcomed her and she had met some friendly young people too. But how much better it would have been if Hugh had been there, she thought. She imagined what it would have been like if he had sat next to her at dinner, making her smile. He was serious one minute and then would say something amusing the next. She would love to have danced with him and hoped he could dance. She sighed longingly and continued her reverie.

Mrs Dobie looked at Melanie next. She was just staring into the fire but she had a frown on her face. What was her problem, Mrs Dobie wondered? Was she worried about her house? Mrs Dobie wouldn't have thought so as anything really complicated she would have discussed with Mr Strong, her lawyer, and there were no staffing problems that she knew of. Was Joanna the problem? She couldn't think so as Joanna seemed to be no trouble and very compliant to whatever plans were made. Perhaps it was something connected with General Peabody-Brown as she still kept in touch with him even though Charles Shaw had been dead for a while now. Or, more interestingly, was it something to do with Joanna's brother? Did he bother her in more ways than one? She didn't wonder at it, he was attractive enough. No doubt it would all be made plain eventually. Mrs Dobie returned to her magazine.

Eventually luncheon was served and the ladies were a little more sociable with each other but Mrs Dobie could feel a certain amount of tension still in her younger companions. She didn't say anything though, and tried to take their minds off their worries or whatever they were, by regaling them with a few amusing happenings of the evening before.

The ladies went to change their dresses afterwards and Melanie took particular care in choosing an afternoon gown in a deep rose hue as she thought it might give her a little more colour. As she was expecting Mr Brooke, she wanted to feel she was looking her best as it gave her more confidence. She did wonder if he would call after all or would he use the inclement weather as an excuse not to. She felt now she had made the effort she would be disappointed if he didn't arrive. She wondered where they would go and hoped there wasn't much walking involved as for some reason she felt extra tired today. Usually, arriving home in the early hours of the morning was something she was used to and she was asleep as soon as her head touched the pillow. But last night it must have been nearer to five o'clock before she slept. And she knew why if she were honest with herself. It was, of course, the thought of going somewhere with Mr Brooke and wondering what was so important about Joanna for them to discuss. She felt in one way, although she could stand up to him, he frightened her a little. But he could be charming, amusing and he was accomplished in the social niceties, apart from their first meeting, of course. He certainly was a favourite with his sister. Melanie still felt that there was a layer of firmness and toughness about him and perhaps it was this that frightened her.

The ladies assembled once more but this time in the withdrawing room and each looking decidedly more sprightly. Was it the effects of lunch or what the afternoon promised to bring?

It was a little after two o'clock when Bayliss knocked, then opened the door announcing Mr Brooke. Matthew came in and bowed to the ladies.

'Matt,' exclaimed Joanna, 'I didn't expect you to call.'

He lifted his eyebrows. Obviously Mrs Shaw had not told her of their arrangement. 'Why should you?' he answered her.

Joanna pouted. 'Have you come for a special reason then or were you just passing?' She looked cheekily at him.

'No, minx, I came specially to take Mrs Shaw out.'

Joanna opened her eyes wide. 'Really?' She turned to Melanie.

Melanie, finding all the attention and inferences attached to the situation might lead to the wrong impression, said hurriedly: 'I daresay you could accompany us but as I don't know where your brother is planning to go …' She looked hopefully at Matthew.

Matthew ignored her. 'No, Joanna, you are not going with us. Mrs Shaw, shall we leave?'

Melanie hurriedly left the room while Matthew said goodbye to Mrs Dobie. He ignored Joanna as he shut the door and she stood there not believing her eyes that she had been ignored. 'Well!' was all she could say.

Then the door opened a fraction and Matthew put his head round. 'Oh, Joanna,' he said 'I forgot. Hugh is on his way.' He shut the door quickly and hoped none of Mrs Shaw's figurines would be thrown at it.

Outside the rain had stopped briefly which enabled them to enter the carriage without getting wet. Ned was driving and as soon as they were inside and the door closed they were off.

'Joanna could have come if you had …' began Melanie, not knowing what else to say.

'No. I said I would take you and giving her a set down now and again doesn't hurt. Besides,' his face softened as he turned to Melanie, 'Hugh is on his way and I really think she is better with him.'

'Oh yes. I liked him when we went to the theatre. I thought him a very kind and well brought up young man. He works with you, so you must know him well.'

'I do and I like him.'

'Would your parents approve if it became more serious?'

Matthew shrugged. 'I expect so. I would at all events.'

Melanie thought she had better change the subject. 'Where are we going?'

He turned his head and looked down at her. 'Oh, a trip to the river so we can walk a long way along its banks.'

'But—but it's raining again,' she protested. Nothing could be worse, thought Melanie, to become wet through and tired into the bargain.

'Well,' said Matthew, relenting, 'instead we'll go and visit Lady Eliot. She has some beautiful china, I believe.'

Melanie looked at him. 'You know, I can never tell when you are laughing at me.'

He looked down at her. 'Did you really think we'd walk near the river on a day like today? Besides, you're looking far too tired to walk anywhere.'

'Well, of all the charming things to say.' How was it he noticed everything?

'Do you want to tell me why you're so tired? Is Jo at the root of the matter?'

'You really do believe in the direct approach, don't you? And it's nothing to do with Joanna. I was out late and had little sleep. That is all. I shall be better tomorrow.'

'But I shan't be here tomorrow,' complained Matthew.

Melanie bit her lip. 'You know, you're making me as obnoxious as yourself. And you promised to be good.' She turned her head to look out of the window for a while.

Matthew watched her. Was it just lack of sleep or was something really worrying her? Well, he couldn't do anything about it unless she chose to confide in him and he didn't think she trusted him completely yet.

She turned back to him. 'What was it you wanted to ask me about Joanna?'

'You've really answered my question earlier. I just wondered if you thought Hugh suitable for her, that is all. I'm quite happy about it as I know him but I just wanted another opinion.'

'And—and did you invite me out just—just to ask me that?'

'No, but I didn't think you would come if I didn't have a good excuse.'

'Oh dear, now you're making me sound ungrateful.'

'Never,' he said gravely.

She looked up at him suspiciously but as he only smiled sweetly back at her, she said no more.

The road they were travelling on wound its way to Richmond but Ned brought the carriage to a halt long before. Melanie thought it a pity that it still rained as she would have liked to see more of this little hamlet and thought as it was near the river it would be as pretty as one could wish to see. To prove it they had stopped outside a thatched cottage surrounded by a well kept garden, except that there were many autumn leaves fallen on the ground from the plum, apple and pear trees there. Matthew had already opened the carriage door and had a word with Ned, telling him to go to the King George Tavern to see the horses rubbed down and to amuse himself for the next hour and a half. Then he turned back and let down the steps for Melanie. Fortunately she had a cloak and hood to protect her from the elements but as the pathway up to the cottage was quite a distance and it was still raining, Matthew placed his arm around her and quite easily lifted her off her feet and ran with her towards the house like a child carrying a doll.

The door opened very quickly and a maid stood there to welcome them.

'Come in, sir. Come in, madam. What a pity about the weather. Let me take your cloaks and you will find her Ladyship in the room at the back, sir.'

'Thank you, Carrie. How is her Ladyship today?'

'Well, sir, and looking forward to seeing you.'

Matthew led Melanie to the large and pleasant room at the back of the cottage. It overlooked the flower garden. Lady Eliot, a small and frail lady, was on her feet and walking slowly with the aid of her stick. She came towards them as they entered, a smile of pleasure on her face. 'Matthew, oh Matthew, it is good to see you.'

Matthew took her hand and kissed her cheek 'How are you, Bella? Here is Mrs Shaw whom I promised to bring.'

'Oh my dear, how nice of you to come.'

Melanie curtseyed and smiled. 'It is a pleasure to meet you, Lady Eliot.'

'Call me Bella, dear.'

'Then you must call me Melanie.'

'Thank you. Now do sit down and Carrie will bring in the tea things presently. Has Ned gone to the village, Matthew?'

'Yes, the horses needed a rub down and Ned does as well, I expect.'

Bella laughed. 'A nice fellow is Ned. You know, Melanie, Ned came to take me out one day and he was great fun and looked after me so well.'

Melanie didn't say anything but thought it odd that Lady Eliot would like the company of a manservant.

'Now are you warm enough there? Do move nearer to the fire if you would like, dear. Am I right in thinking you are the youngest of your family?'

Surprised, Melanie said: 'Yes, I am the youngest of six daughters.'

'My memory isn't very good but I feel you have a look of your mother. She was very pretty, you know.'

'Really?' said Melanie, avoiding Matthew's eye. 'Did you know my Mother?'

'Only a little. She was a kind and loving person, I seem to remember.'

Melanie nodded. 'From what I remember of her that was true. My older sisters looked after me when Mama died.'

'I expect you know General Peabody-Brown?'

'Yes, of course. He doesn't live too far away from my house in Chippenham.'

'And now you know Matthew. He is a great friend to have. I must tell you how he ...'

Matthew interrupted. 'If you're going to be a dead bore, Bella, I shall leave and go and talk to Carrie.'

'Well, she will be delighted, I expect. In fact she will be bringing in the tea any time now.'

'I'll go and see if she needs any help then.' And Matthew found his way to the kitchen.

Conversation became general after that and Melanie wondered what Bella was going to say about Matthew before he interrupted. But she didn't like to remind her.

Melanie asked a few questions about her Mother and Bella told her a little. She had been much older and Bella hadn't seen her often. She said that the General had suggested Matthew visited her from time to time as her youngest son had died of a lung disease and she was lonely.

'Did Mr Brooke know your son?' asked Melanie.

'Matthew? Oh no, Bertram was much older you see but Matthew keeps an eye on me.'

'I see,' was all Melanie could say although she didn't see at all.

There was no chance for further questions as Matthew appeared carrying a heavy silver tray complete with silver teapot, and cups and plates as delicate as eggshells, from China. Carrie followed with a plate of small cakes and scones. Everything was placed on a tea table and Carrie proceeded to pour out the tea while Matthew handed round the plate of cakes.

'Carrie makes these and they are delicious. She's a treasure,' said Bella. 'Are you not having any, Matthew?' she asked in surprise.

'No, I shan't want my dinner if I eat cakes,' he said virtuously.

Bella looked at him. 'Mm. I expect Carrie has already given you some.'

'Never mind what Carrie and I do in the kitchen,' he said.

Bella laughed. 'Ignore him, Melanie. I know for a fact that he loves Carrie's cooking.'

They talked on a variety of subjects after that and Melanie told Bella how she had come to London for the season and brought Joanna with her and explained she was Matthew's young sister.

'How wonderful,' said Bella, 'she must visit me too. Does she have a gentleman friend?'

'I believe so,' said Melanie.

Their tea finished, Melanie suggested she help Carrie, thereby giving time for Bella to talk to Matthew privately. Soon after, they left as Bella had begun to tire.

On the way home Melanie said politely: 'I learnt a little more about my mother, you know. And the china was beautiful. It was so delicate I hoped I wouldn't drop it or the handle come off. Thank you for taking me.'

'I enjoyed it too. Bella is so young in her mind and she hasn't had a great life. I believe her husband was a drunkard and died leaving her to bring up three young boys without much money. The General helps her now, of course.'

'I believe you do too,' said Melanie, having seen Matthew leave a slim package on the table just before they left. As he didn't acknowledge or deny the remark, she went on: 'And what was that all about Ned?'

'It was when I had to cancel my visit to her for some reason. Ned went in my place. He's a kind fellow and droll. I believe they enjoyed each other's company.'

Matthew was quiet after that and Melanie wondered what he was thinking. She ventured to remark: 'It is still raining but for all that it was very pleasant and just what I needed.'

Matthew looked down at her, his eyes glinting. 'Did it wake you up then or ...'

'Don't be unkind, sir. I—I might have been tired but as I say I ...'

'Enjoyed it. Yes, you told me. Seriously, though, I'm pleased you came. Would you like another theatre visit soon when you have a free evening? And shall we go alone or take your friend or the children with us?'

'That would be very agreeable. I—I suppose,' she said slowly, 'we have to take someone with us, though.'

Matthew was gratified to think that Melanie considered going with him on her own but realised protocol demanded otherwise, unfortunately.

CHAPTER 16

▼

Melanie had enjoyed her visit to see Bella in spite of the rainy afternoon and her tiredness. It had been much better and a lot less tiring than walking round an art gallery or museum. The length of the visit was just right for everyone concerned and the journey both ways was as pleasant as a wet day permitted. She came to the conclusion that Mr Brooke liked to tease her and she remembered how he had looked at her with those light blue eyes peering through those ridiculously long blond eyelashes. But she had liked his company if she were honest with herself, apart, of course, when he treated her like a little girl, picking her up so that her feet didn't become wet. He had done it so easily, too, and as she knew she was no lightweight like Joanna, she came to the conclusion that Mr Brooke was very strong. She decided there was a lot more to him than met the eye; his unexpected strength was not just physical, there was a mental toughness too. It had been kind and thoughtful of him to take her to meet Bella though, as she supposed he thought she would like to learn a little more about her mother. She found herself smiling and Mrs Dobie, seeing that smile as she came into the hall, enquired: 'A good afternoon, dear?'

'Yes, Lily, very pleasant. I'll tell you all about it later. Is Joanna back yet?'

'No, not yet. There is a lovely fire in here,' she pointed to the withdrawing room. 'Shall we spoil ourselves and ask for some tea?'

'Yes, do, dear, and I'll tell you where I've been when I come down,' and Melanie tripped up the stairs to her bedchamber.

Over the teacups Melanie was telling her friend where she had been taken and that Mr Brooke had been a considerate companion when there was a tap on the door and Joanna put her head round.

'Come in and have some tea,' said Mrs Dobie. 'And did you have a lovely time too?'

'Yes, yes. Of course.'

Did Melanie catch a note of uncertainty in her voice? She said: 'I was just telling Lily that your brother and I went to tea with Lady Eliot and I found she had known my mother.'

'Oh,' said Joanna, 'that's nice. Hugh took me to a gallery where there were pictures painted by new artists. Some were quite pretty.'

Melanie smiled at this naive remark but all she said was: 'Did you take Tilly or ...'

'No. Hugh said there was no need as we were to meet a friend and his wife. They haven't been married long and they were very kind to me, especially Rosie. She was from the country, you know, and very friendly. We had a hot drink afterwards at a little place nearby.'

'How delightful,' said Mrs Dobie. 'You both seem to have had a lovely time.'

'And what did you do, dear?' asked Melanie.

'Oh, I was very dull in comparison,' said Mrs Dobie. 'I just sat and looked at my magazines and I dozed a little by the fire.'

'A restful afternoon,' said Melanie.

'Very,' agreed her friend.

Joanna was quiet during the evening and Melanie came to the conclusion that she was either tired or that she and Hugh had had a slight disagreement, which often happened between two young people, and others too, Melanie thought wryly.

After she had retired that night Melanie turned to thoughts of Mr Brooke and herself. Why had he taken her out? Did he like her or was it that he thought he owed her some attention because of his treatment of her in the first place? But he didn't sound as if he was placating her when he spoke; in fact, he was just being friendly. He hadn't stepped over the line when in the carriage that afternoon when they had visited Lady Eliot and previously he had seen to her comfort at the theatre as any gentleman would. When she had met him at functions of mutual friends he had behaved just as he should do. She was pleased to think that another theatre visit had been suggested. But there was a glint in those eyes at times. Was he always to be trusted? Melanie frowned. Something told her he could be but there was that little doubt present. She sighed. Time would tell.

Joanna, too, lay awake in bed going over her argument with Hugh. Joanna's group of girl friends, whom she often visited and with whom she went on outings, and whose mamas were known to Melanie, had invited her to a party to be held in Upper Wimpole Street. The young lady holding the party was unknown to Joanna but she was told what exciting evenings they were. Joanna had asked Hugh if he would like to go with her. She had hoped he would as it sounded such fun with games, dancing and entertainment and to have Hugh there would be wonderful. But Hugh, without giving any reason, flatly refused the offer and what was worse told Joanna not to go either. There had been a little argument but Joanna, mindful of Hugh's kindness in taking her out that afternoon, said no more. If he wouldn't accompany her, she would go by herself, she thought. After all, they were girls she knew and it was true that Hugh hadn't been specifically invited, but as she told him, she would have preferred he was with her. However, he didn't want to go and she respected his choice but there was no need for him to say she shouldn't go. She had thought him highhanded. He didn't say why she shouldn't go or even suggest they went somewhere else together. Joanna mentally shrugged with a "see if I care" attitude and was more determined than ever to go to the party. She turned over in bed with a bounce, still annoyed.

Hugh was having trouble sleeping. Had he been too blunt in refusing to go to this party with Joanna? The district where it was to be held he didn't think was too desirable and Joanna did not know the girl so to serious minded Hugh this place was not somewhere that his Joanna should visit. He knew she was disappointed that he refused to go with her and he unfortunately couldn't offer her an alternative evening out as he had promised to accompany his parents to visit his married sister. All he felt he could do was to tell Joanna it wasn't a suitable place for her to be and hope that she would be guided by him. But for all his decision he wasn't happy and spent a restless night.

The following morning at work it was noticeable that Hugh was worried. Matthew, the only person who had plenty on his mind in more ways than one, had slept well. He didn't say anything to Hugh but kept an eye on him. However, finally, when he noticed Hugh sitting staring into space with a frown furrowing his brow, he said softly: 'Something wrong, Hugh?'

Hugh looked up with a rueful grin. 'No, not really sir.'

'No problem with the work?'

'No, of course not.'

Matthew said no more but later he asked gently: 'Did you have a good time on Sunday?'

Hugh smiled. 'Yes, thank you. We visited, that is Joanna and I visited a new art exhibition with friends.'

'Was it interesting?'

'Yes, sir, very. I think Joanna enjoyed it all.' He wondered if he'd mention the party but quickly decided that that would be unfair to Joanna. Besides, in one way it was his responsibility and Matthew should not be bothered by it. Also he hoped Joanna wouldn't go.

Matthew looked at him. Obviously something was worrying Hugh but he couldn't enquire further and after all, he was old enough to sort out his own problems.

Hugh, hoping to divert Matthew, as he knew that he missed nothing, said: 'And did you enjoy your day, sir? The weather wasn't too good, was it?'

Matthew's lips twitched. 'Thank you, Hugh. Yes I did enjoy my day and the weather could have been better.'

No more was said for some time.

The silence was broken by the opening of the outer doors. They heard footsteps on the stairs, and Matthew's office door opened and Harry Anstruther appeared. As he took off his coat he said: 'Where's Arnold? Fetch him, Hugh, please.'

The three men sat round Matthew's desk, Hugh having gone back to his own room. 'Gentlemen,' said Harry, 'let's not waste time. I will come straight to the point. I have problems. That Fox fellow is in hospital with a broken jaw. Why did you have to hit him so hard, Matthew? Now I can't get much out of him. But one thing, when he was delirious after the surgeon had seen him his words were in French, but he didn't say anything of importance. Also, we have had only one communication from Tim Oakley regarding our ships in the Channel and that is to tell us that the French were aiming to blow them up and that didn't reach us in time for us to do anything. Fortunately the British Navy are hard to beat and they turned the tables and every French ship was attacked successfully. So, what I want to know, who really is this Fox fellow and what is Tim playing at? Any ideas?'

Matthew said slowly: 'I know before Tim went away he met someone whom he wouldn't tell me about and I assumed it was a private matter. However, I kept an open mind but I did wonder about Fox. There was a slight, very slight edge to his words that wasn't quite right but I didn't necessarily connect it to French. Also he was definitely moving around to this building, so was he trying to get in touch with Tim not knowing he had gone to France?'

'Was he a French spy?' asked Arnold.

'If he was,' said Harry 'why was he contacting Tim?'

Matthew said: 'Tim was using him or Fox was using Tim.'

'Well, certainly we are not receiving anything from Tim. Has anything happened to him like the last fellow we sent over, or has he just disappeared from his own personal choice? I shall have to send someone else over to find out, I think.' Harry frowned and Matthew could tell he was annoyed as well as worried.

'Would you like me to go, sir?' he asked.

'No, I don't think so, Matt,' said Harry slowly. 'You would be quite capable, of course, but you would leave a trail of people with broken jaws!' A quick smile flashed across his face. 'No, Matt, you would be known to Tim and I must send someone he doesn't know. I have a man in mind and hopefully he will find out what Tim is doing or if he's dead. I can't think what else I can do but I must get results, which I am not getting at the moment, and Mr Pitt is waiting for them urgently and keeps sending me memoranda to that point. Can you think of anything, gentlemen?'

They discussed the problems in more detail and Matthew said they would know more when Fox was able to tell what he knew.

'If he will,' said Harry.

'Well, tell him if he doesn't co-operate, I'll come and break his jaw again,' grinned Matthew.

'Thank you,' said Harry dryly. 'I'm sure that would be a great help.' He then departed.

Matthew sat with a frown on his face. Why would Tim defect, if he had? He had acted strangely recently but surely nothing so extreme as that. But if that was what he had done, British secrets would be passed on to the French, and that was something that didn't bear thinking about.

CHAPTER 17

▼

Only Mrs Dobie and Joanna sat down to an early dinner that evening. Melanie was up in her bedchamber preparing herself, with the help of her maid, to attend a dinner given by General and Mrs Carew. Now retired, the General, having been wounded severely when fighting against the Jacobite rebellion, now, with his wife were often wining and dining friends who had connections with the army. The General liked to talk of old days to colleagues, while Mrs Carew enjoyed the social part of talking to the other ladies. They had known Charles Shaw slightly, but he and Melanie had often been invited to dinner when in London and now the invitation was still sent to her. She liked to go as it was a pleasant evening but she hoped that there would be someone younger whom she knew other than those older ladies who liked to talk to her about Charles. Although she had admired him and had been happily married to him up to a point and had her own pleasant memories of him, she would rather talk about other things. Nothing could bring Charles back and she had now moved on, becoming more mature and making a different life for herself.

Mrs Dobie was visiting people that evening whom she had known for some time and Joanna was partying, so it had been decided that as Mrs Dobie was being collected by a friend, there was no need for her to use the carriage. Melanie, therefore, would take Joanna and deliver her to her friend's house and then proceed to Mrs Carew's.

Both the ladies looked particularly attractive that evening. Mrs Dobie wore a dress of dark crimson with a chaste fichu of lace while Joanna had chosen a pretty green dress with an underskirt of pink with pink trimming on the bodice in the form of daisies. As usual it wasn't too low that Papa would dislike it, but she felt it a shame that Hugh wasn't there to admire it as it suited her dark eyes and pretty face admirably. When Melanie joined them she eclipsed them both by wearing a dress of rich blue silk, shining light and dark as she moved. Although the bodice wasn't very low it showed enough of her creamy skin, which was enhanced by her sapphire necklace. A quilted underskirt of the same material was contrast enough to be noticed but sedate enough for a dinner.

'Well, ladies,' she smiled after they had complimented each other, 'let us hope we all enjoy our evenings. At least we are all looking ravishing so no-one can fault us. Do we all have fans? Good,' She kissed Mrs Dobie then sent for the carriage while she and Joanna donned their cloaks. They travelled the short distance to the house in Dover Street where Joanna was visiting as usual. 'Have a lovely time, dear,' said Melanie and watched until the door of the house opened and Joanna was welcomed inside. The carriage then proceeded to Melanie's destination in Berkeley Square.

It was a large town house with steps leading to the front door that opened as Melanie trod up them and a footman bowed her inside. She was relieved of her cloak and there was the General and his lady welcoming her as she entered a tasteful and relaxing room furnished with comfortable chairs upholstered in soft blues and cream. A gentleman played a sonata on the harpsichord and the candles in the chandeliers created a warm glow over the colourful clothes of the people present, giving them the feeling of well being.

A servant presented a tray to Melanie, on which were glasses of sherry, but before she could take one, a large hand came forward, took one and handed it to her. She turned, her eyes lighting up as she faced Matthew.

'Oh, I didn't see you. Thank you,' she said as she took the glass from him. 'And why are you here, may I ask?'

Matthew's eyes twinkled naughtily but he answered seriously, 'Well, I saw the door was open so I came in. Why, have you done the same?'

'You know very well I haven't and neither have you,' she said tapping his arm with her fan. 'What I meant was how are you connected to the army?'

'Well, I have a brother who is fighting on the continent at the moment and I am connected to General Peabody-Brown as you know,' he said glibly.

'Oh, I see,' she said vaguely but somehow it didn't sound right to her ears. However she let it pass and said instead: 'I've just taken Joanna to her friend's house. There is a party, I believe, and she looked very pretty in a green and pink dress. I expect Hugh will find it charming.'

Matthew looked keenly at her but all he said was: 'I expect so.' He was sure Hugh had only mentioned a visit to his sister all that day.

Melanie cut in on his thoughts. 'You don't sound very interested,' she said with a gleam in her eyes.

'Should I be?'

'Of course. Joanna is your sister, after all.'

'Now what makes you think I should be interested in what my sister wears? If it was ...'

'I think we should circulate, don't you?' Melanie interrupted quickly.

'Everyone else seems to be engaged with someone, so I see no need,' Matthew replied. He looked round the room. It was true. Everyone seemed occupied in discussing the war as military men would, while their ladies gossiped about the latest on-dits and fashions. Some men wore their military coats with wigs sedately curled, whilst ladies dressed their hair elaborately but not as high as for a ball, of course. There was much laughter, sounds of "zounds" and "pshaw" and sneezing as too much snuff was inhaled and therefore the wafting of lace handkerchiefs was much in evidence.

Matthew had taken out his snuffbox of plain gold decorated only with his initials but after a few seconds' thought decided against it and replaced it in his pocket.

Melanie looked at him. 'Please take some if you wish. I do not mind, you know.'

'Do you take snuff, then?'

'Oh no. I did try once but it must have been the wrong kind as it put me off taking any more.'

Matthew laughed.

He was more than content to stay where he was, talking to Melanie. 'I wanted to ask you when you are free for a visit to the theatre and what would you like to see?'

'Oh, yes, that would be a very pleasant evening.' After a short discussion it was agreed that a Shakespearian play was in order and Mrs Dobie would be asked to accompany them.

'Perhaps you would care to dine with us first?' suggested Melanie sedately.

Matthew gave her one of his sweetest smiles that always made her blush. It seemed like a caress. 'Thank you, that would be delightful.'

Melanie was saved from replying as dinner was announced. General and Mrs Carew led the way into the dining room followed by their guests. She found herself seated between two gentlemen she hardly knew and Matthew was on the opposite side between two ladies who did their best to keep talking to him, only picking at their food. But Matthew was much practised in dealing with all kinds of situations and Melanie noticed that he would ask a question to which the ladies answered at length, giving him time to eat quite a large amount of food. Once or twice as she looked over at him he would wink at her, and then she would hurriedly converse with one of the gentlemen either side of her.

The dinner lasted for some time as most gentlemen had gargantuan appetites, which showed by the paunches under their waistcoats and the undoing of buttons as the meal progressed. Melanie noticed that although Matthew ate well he was not inclined to overeat as some, neither did he imbibe too much of the excellent wine. It certainly was easy to do so as a different wine was offered with each dish, these being of a rich nature. There was a rum soaked goose stuffed with chicken which in its turn was stuffed with herbs, a ragout of beef in a wine sauce, a roast saddle of venison and a whole stuffed pike. There were carrots, parsnips, potatoes, artichokes and onions; also jellies, creams, junkets and fruit.

Eventually the dinner was over and the ladies retired to chat while the men drank their brandy and talked about the war or old times and relieved themselves. No one knew that Matthew had been invited in Harry Anstruther's place as Harry said he had attended many such dinners before and as he was extremely busy, perhaps Matthew would like to go in his stead. If there was anything new to hear, Matthew would certainly pick it up. Also Harry, in his cunning way, had thought that Mrs Shaw might be invited too and that would please Matthew. Harry had a great regard for him and wished more were like him; also, he thought that Matthew and Mrs Shaw were a very suitable couple.

Melanie meanwhile went with the ladies, some of whom were keen to know if she had a *tendre* for the fair-haired giant amongst them. Melanie cleverly sidetracked their hopes for a romantic story by saying she had been asked by General Peabody-Brown to bring Mr Brooke's young sister to London with her for the season and that was why she knew him. Fortunately Mrs Carew came along and rescued her from the tittle-tattlers before there were any awkward questions asked.

The gentlemen after some forty minutes returned to join the ladies and all were entertained by a soprano and a tenor accompanied by the gentleman on the harpsichord. Melanie found, and she didn't know how he had managed it, that Matthew sat down beside her, but they were both conscious of the sideways glances of the tongue wagging ladies around them so said little to each other, though it was agreeable to sit near.

Two ladies in very ornate dresses of silk brocade with much trimming sat together on a chaise longue. One said softly behind her fan: 'Who is that young man? Is he in the army?'

The other one shook her head. 'I don't think so but he has *connections*, I believe.'

'Someone important.' They nodded their heads wisely. 'He is gorgeous, though, isn't he, with those unusual eyelashes?'

'Mm. Reliable and protective I should think. I wish I was younger.'

'Me too, dear.' They disappeared and tittered behind their fluttering fans.

If older ladies were remarking on Matthew, the older gentlemen were remarking on Melanie.

'Good looking woman, what?'

'Yes, and a widow. Should marry again. Interested?'

'Very, but I have a wife.'

'I know. So have I,' he finished with a sigh.

Melanie and Matthew could only murmur to each other in between the songs and the clapping, so when a short interval was announced and everyone began to circulate again, they decided to take their leave after thanking and complimenting their hosts on a very pleasant evening.

The time was nearly two o'clock and Matthew suggested that he saw Melanie to her door. She demurred at first, saying she would be perfectly safe as it was only a short distance away. But Matthew smiled and said that if it was only a short distance it wouldn't take long, would it? They left in Melanie's coach with Ned driving Matthew's behind them and proceeded to Curzon Street.

Although Matthew discussed the evening with Melanie on the short ride, he really wanted to see if his sister was safely back from her party. He couldn't say so, of course, but as the drive was only short, especially at this time in the morning when few carriages were around, it wasn't any hardship for him to spend a few more delectable minutes with Melanie.

All was quiet in Curzon Street. Melanie said goodnight to her driver while Ned nodded to Matthew, which meant he would wait. A weary footman opened the door as Melanie and Matthew entered.

'Everyone home?' asked Melanie. Then she saw a small figure sitting curled up on the couch and asleep in front of the hall fire which sadly was now nearly out. It was Tilly.

Melanie rushed up to her and laid her hand on the little figure. 'Tilly? Tilly?'

The little girl woke up with a start and saw her mistress. 'Oh, oh, ma'am, I'm—I'm sorry. I dozed off.' She struggled to her feet and attempted a little curtsey, nearly toppling over.

'Never mind that,' said Melanie. 'Why are you here? I'm not vexed, Tilly.'

'No—no, ma'am. I'm waiting for Miss Brooke. She's not home yet.'

Melanie turned pale. 'Are you sure? Would you go and see if she's in her bed, please? Perhaps you missed her coming in.'

Little Tilly went as quickly as her tired legs would take her to Joanna's bedchamber.

Melanie turned to Matthew, her eyes a mixture of worry and apology. 'I'm sorry, I thought she was going to her usual social evening when she is back around midnight.'

Matthew said nothing but nodded towards the stairs as Tilly came into view.

'She's not there, ma'am. She 'asn't come in yet.'

'All right, Tilly. You go to bed now and I'll see if she's still in Dover Street. I'll tell the housekeeper to excuse you being late up in the morning.' Tilly made her weary way to her bed while Melanie looked at Matthew. He hadn't said a word.

'Do you think Hugh and …?'

'No, I don't,' said Matthew curtly. 'As far as I know Hugh was visiting his sister yesterday.'

'Oh, goodness. Shall we go to Dover Street and see if she's still there?'

'A good place to start,' said Matthew. 'We will take my carriage. Ned is waiting.'

'I am so sorry, I haven't been very good at looking after Joanna, have I?'

Matthew put his arm around her to lift her into the carriage, at the same time giving her a squeeze. 'I defy anyone to look after Joanna all the time. She has a wayward streak, you know. I am not blaming you and you shouldn't blame yourself.' But they both worried quietly to themselves as Ned drove on to Dover Street.

CHAPTER 18

▼

Joanna entered the house in Dover Street and met her friends who were waiting. There was a lot of excitement in the air with much giggling and laughter and as Joanna was the last to arrive it was now time to call for the carriage. There was some last minute panic and cries of "has anyone seen my fan?" and "my handkerchief, I must have one" which added to the general mêlée. Eventually they were ready and climbed into the carriage that was on the small side for six young ladies. But they managed to push themselves in and cries of "you're sitting on my dress," and "I'm squashed," and "I shall fall off the seat in a minute," could be heard. It was all good-natured fun but Joanna wondered if her friends were being a little too loud voicing their complaints. She also wondered what state her dress would be in as it was certainly crushed. The others didn't seem bothered about their's.

It took a little while to travel to their destination which was number four Upper Wimpole Street but as there were many coaches and carriages on the streets at this time taking their occupants to various places of pleasure and entertainment, it was not surprising. Joanna was concerned at first but told herself she was with friends and they weren't worried in the slightest, so she relaxed ready to enjoy the evening.

Eventually they were set down outside a large house and as they tripped hurriedly to the front door, any shabbiness wasn't noticed or seen in the dark evening. The door was opened by a girl of about eighteen who introduced herself as Phoebe. All but Joanna knew her and before she could say anything more a group of other young ladies and young men had come to welcome the newcomers. There was a lot of laughter and noise as cloaks were removed. They entered a large room where the chairs had been pushed back to the walls to make a space in the centre for dancing. There was a table at one end of the room where a cloth covered some food but there was wine and lemonade for drinking at any time. There looked to be about two dozen young people present and Joanna was introduced to some of them but she was a little concerned that there didn't seem to be an older person present to keep an eye on the proceedings.

Joanna's eyes travelled round the room. She thought it looked shabby with dusty and faded curtains not fitting too well and the upholstery on the chairs was decidedly threadbare in some places. Everything seemed dull with no pictures on the walls or mirrors. She couldn't see the ceiling properly as it was in shadow. There was only one chandelier hanging in the centre. Was the rest of the house like this, she wondered, or was this a room specially put aside for holding parties for the young people so they wouldn't mess up the rest of the rooms? She couldn't really understand it at all. Surely the room could have been painted and the curtains washed?

Someone began to play a harpsichord and the dancing began. Joanna found the dances were different to what she had learnt but with a little pushing here and there she managed. They seemed more like jigs and country dancing. The boys' arms went round the girls' waists and there was a lot of laughing. The music could hardly be heard and it didn't help that a lot of notes didn't play, but no-one seemed to mind. There was no time to rest in between. It just seemed they all kept dancing until everyone was breathless. When they did change from one dance to another the boys just grabbed the nearest girl for their partner. When the next dance was over, Joanna decided to slip away quickly as she was very thirsty. She poured herself some lemonade and had just taken a sip when a hand was laid on her arm that jerked the glass, spilling the lemonade down her dress.

'Now look what you've done,' she said angrily. 'For goodness sake go away.' She began sponging down her dress with her handkerchief.

'You're to dance with me.' The boy's voice was slurred. Evidently too much wine all ready? He gave another pull on Joanna's arm.

Joanna, upset by her spoilt dress, which she had bought with her own money, and annoyed by the way she was being treated, told him to go away again in no uncertain terms. He turned ugly and grabbed both her arms. 'Dance,' he said.

But Joanna was made of sterner stuff. She managed to pull one arm away and hit his face with the flat of her hand in one almighty blow. 'Keep away from me,' she shouted.

By now others realised something was going on and everyone crowded round, grins on their faces. Some shouted: 'A firebrand!' And some were openly laughing which made Joanna furious.

Phoebe rushed to her. 'Why, whatever's the matter?'

'This—this person has just spilt lemonade down me and began pulling me about. I'm going home.'

'Oh—oh dear. Yes, I see. Come with me and we'll see what is to be done.' She looked at another boy. 'Take John away, Phil,' she said.

'Look,' said Phoebe when she had taken Joanna into the hall. 'I'm sorry about your dress but we don't put on our best dresses at these parties, someone should have told you. If you look at the other girls, they are wearing well worn dresses.'

'But why?' asked poor Joanna.

'Well, the boys can get a little rough. John was worse for drink, I think.'

'What, so soon? What will he be like later on, for goodness sake?'

'Difficult, I expect. The others will deal with him. Keep out of his way, if you can, but please don't go home yet. Try and forget about this and let's go and enjoy ourselves.'

Although Joanna did try, it had marred her evening. After the dancing, games were the order of the day. These were of a boisterous nature and Joanna tried to join in some of them but she began to long for Hugh and acknowledged to herself he had been right and she shouldn't have come.

However, they paused in their revelry to have refreshments that were now somewhat dry, being in a warm room albeit under a cloth. Evidently it had all been prepared beforehand and left, just as the young people had been left to do just as they pleased. It wasn't what Joanna liked or was used to and she felt betrayed by the girls who had befriended her. If this is what their parties were like she didn't want to know any more. Whatever would Papa or Matthew or …? She wouldn't think further. At the first opportunity she would leave.

At least everyone was a little more subdued now and seemed to have divided into two groups of boys and girls. Flashing eyes, little smiles and coy glances were aimed at the boys and eventually one came over and chose Phoebe. They left the room together. Then another boy chose a girl and then another.

'What's happening?' asked Joanna to the girl standing next to her.

She looked at Joanna as if she was speaking a foreign language. 'Why, don't you know?' Joanna shook her head. 'Each couple go and find a vacant room or cupboard and … oh!' She was pulled away from Joanna, and laughing she went out the door with her partner.

Joanna was horrified. The girl hadn't explained further but Joanna understood what she was going to say. No man had touched Joanna before and she wasn't going to be part of this now especially with these people. Even if Hugh had been here he wouldn't have behaved in this way. She would have to leave. But how? She just couldn't go out the door on her own, everyone would notice. Before she could think of anything, the boy called John came up and claimed her. The way he looked at her she could see he would be trouble. She began to shake. He grabbed her arm and pulled her out of the room into the hall accompanied by loud cheers.

In the hall all she could think of saying was: 'Where do we go?' John shrugged. He was certainly the worse for drink and not very steady on his feet. He still tried to hold on to her. Thinking desperately, Joanna said: 'Why don't you find somewhere upstairs for us to go while I find another handkerchief in my cloak pocket.'

Another couple came out, laughing and giggling. Joanna tore her imprisoned arm away and gave John a push. 'Go on,' she said 'or they'll find it before you.'

Muddled by the drink, John started up the stairs. The couple tried to hurry him along, with the result that the three of them were all mixed up and John fell. He managed to right himself and rushed upwards as best he could. Joanna didn't wait to see what happened. She found her cloak, opened the front door and was out into the street. With a great gulp of night air and a feeling of: 'thank God I've escaped,' she began to run down the street, not looking to right or left and not knowing or caring whether it was the right or wrong way. She was away from that dreadful house and that more than dreadful party.

CHAPTER 19

▼

The carriage stopped outside the house in Dover Street. 'Stay there,' Matthew said to Melanie as he jumped out. The house was in darkness so it was unlikely a party was still going on but Matthew hammered on the door anyway. It took three attempts before a servant, in nightcap and gown, opened the door.

'I'm Matthew Brooke. My sister came here to a party this evening.'

The man shook his head. 'There 'asn't been a party here, sir.'

'Are you sure? My sister joined her friends here, I know.'

'Ah! I believe they went to a party but it wasn't here sir.'

'Do you know the address where it was held?'

'Sorry sir, no I don't.'

'Very well. Sorry to have troubled you.' He gave the man a coin for his help. He had a word with Ned and joined Melanie inside the carriage.

'There was no party there and evidently it was just a meeting place.'

'Oh dear. But what are we to do and where are we going?' asked Melanie.

'We're going to visit Hugh to see if he knows.'

'We can't knock people up at this time in a morning.'

'Any better ideas?' asked Matthew.

Melanie shook her head. She felt it was all her fault. She should have checked more thoroughly but Joanna seemed such a sensible little thing and didn't need such close supervision. She felt she should apologise again but thought Mr Brooke would be annoyed. And things between them were going so well, too.

They were silent, each busy with their own thoughts until Ned stopped the carriage. Again Matthew jumped down and hammered on the door of Hugh's parents' house. It wasn't long before Hugh answered it himself. Although he wore a dressing gown Matthew could see he wasn't undressed completely.

'Is it Joanna?' Hugh asked immediately, when he saw Matthew standing there.

'Yes it is. What do you know, Hugh? She isn't home yet.'

'Oh dear, I told her not to go,' said Hugh. 'Wait. Let me dress. I won't be long and then I'll be with you.'

A few minutes later he joined Matthew and was surprised to see Melanie sitting in the carriage.

'We arrived home and Joanna wasn't there,' she said in way of explanation.

'Let's try number four Upper Wimpole Street,' said Hugh.

'I knew you'd have the answer,' smiled Matthew. He told Ned and they set off. Matthew went on: 'So you told Joanna not to go to this party.'

'Well, yes. I said it wasn't a nice area and she shouldn't go.'

'Oh, Hugh,' said Matthew with a smile, 'you have a lot to learn about women. If Joanna wanted to go and you wouldn't or couldn't take her and you told her not to go, she definitely would. The "see if I care" attitude.'

'It's my fault, is it?' said Hugh stiffly.

'No,' said Melanie, 'it isn't. I am responsible for her so it's my fault.'

'Oh, for goodness sake both of you,' broke in Matthew, 'it's Joanna herself who's at fault. She should know better. She needs a good spanking.' He looked at Hugh through his lashes as he said this and saw him purse his lips. 'Well?'

'I don't think that is the answer, sir.'

Matthew smiled.

There was silence until Upper Wimpole Street was reached. The houses were in darkness but they managed to find number four and Matthew knocked loudly on the door. After a long wait a servant came and in answer to Matthew's question said that, yes, there had been a party but everyone had left. He then shut the door in their faces.

Back in the carriage Melanie said: 'What do we do now?'

'Perhaps she is back in Curzon Street as we speak,' said Matthew.

'I think,' said Melanie, 'we should look for her. Could we drive around for a while and see if we can find her?' Matthew told Ned.

They looked through the windows as the carriage started forward to see if they could see a small solitary figure in cloak and hood. And then it began to rain.

Meanwhile, Joanna was beginning to have second thoughts. Yes, she had escaped from that horrible house and it was lovely to run out into the night, but now the first feelings of relief and freedom had disappeared to be replaced by sheer panic. Which way should she go? Dare she ask someone the way? Could she find a carriage to take her to Curzon Street? She looked round. All was quiet. There were no carriages or anyone walking near. She had no idea where she was or what direction she should go. The street she was in seemed long and there were no signs to tell her its name. All she could think of doing was to keep walking until she found someone she could ask. She realised she would be very tired and her slippers would be worn through but as long as she found her way eventually everything would be all right, she told herself as she turned a corner. She could hear voices. She thought perhaps there might be someone who would know the way but the voices were loud, and she might not be safe. She certainly shouldn't risk speaking to them so she hid against a gateway of a large house until she could decide if they were approachable or if she should let them pass. But she was pleased she had been cautious, as the men were definitely the worse for drink and therefore best left alone. She continued walking only after they were far away.

She went slower now as she was very tired and although she tried to think rationally she was very frightened. She had never been out in the early morning on her own before and she found it rather a scary experience. And then to depress her even further it started raining. She wanted to weep but knew it wasn't any use, as it wouldn't help one little bit.

Ned drove the carriage round one street and down the next, keeping his eyes open as far as he could in the rain for a little lady. Inside the carriage the occupants were doing the same, each of them anxious about a young green girl on her own walking the streets of London in the early hours of the morning. No one spoke but they sat silent in anxious concern. All of a sudden Ned stopped the carriage. Matthew immediately opened the door. 'Ned?'

'Figure ahead, sir, I think.'

Matthew started forward and in a loud voice shouted: 'Jo, Joanna!'

She turned and stood in the pouring rain, then realising it was her brother she began to run towards him. 'Oh, Matthew,' she cried as he enfolded her in his arms. He picked her up and bundled her into the carriage that was now on a level with them.

'Are you all right, dear?' asked Melanie.

'Oh, Melanie. Yes, yes. I think so, thank you. Hugh? S-sorry I'm very wet.'

'We've been looking for you,' said Matthew.

'Oh, well, I'm sorry but I'm pleased you did. I didn't know which way to go, you see, and I—I … you …' she burst into tears.

Matthew placed an arm round her. 'It's all right Jo. We found you and you'll soon be home.' She still went on weeping. 'You're very wet, aren't you? And now you're trying to make me very wet.' But Joanna still curled up against him crying. No one said anything more. They were so confined in the carriage and it was dark and no one could think of a sensible thing to say.

It wasn't long before Curzon Street was reached, however. The door was opened by a sleepy footman. Melanie said to Joanna: 'You must go to bed at once and get warm. Tilly placed a hot brick in for you. Shall I come with you and dry your hair?'

Poor Joanna just shook her head. 'N-no, I can manage. I—I'm sorry. Th-thank you for finding me. I'm—I'm sorry.' And she burst into tears again.

It was Hugh who stepped forward. 'Come on, Joanna, don't cry any more. You'll be wetter than ever, you know, if you do. You're safe now. I'll come later, shall I, to see you?' He took her cold little hands and tried to warm them. 'Look at me, Jo.' She managed to look up fleetingly. 'Would you like me to come, love?'

Joanna nodded. 'Please,' she managed to say.

'Right. You go up to bed now or you'll catch a chill and that will never do.'

Joanna nodded. In a small voice she whispered: 'You're not cross with me?'

'No, of course not.' He kissed her on the forehead and let her go.

Meanwhile Matthew had followed Melanie into the morning room so that Joanna could make her peace with Hugh.

'I'm so sorry,' she began.

'Don't let us have all that over again. Jo's safe now.'

But Melanie was distraught, as she had let this happen while Matthew's sister was under her roof. 'It's all right for you to say that but I feel …'

She was stopped from saying any more as Matthew took her into his arms and ruthlessly kissed her.

'W-w-what was that for?' she asked idiotically when she was able.

'I had to quieten that pretty mouth somehow, didn't I?' said Matthew reasonably.

'Well, of all the horrid things to …' She got no further as Matthew began kissing her again but this time he began more gently, then building up until longer and harder kisses were rained onto her lips until Melanie finally had to push him away as she gasped for breath. He held her for a few moments looking down at her.

'All right?' he asked softly. She nodded. 'Shall I come round tomorrow afternoon?'

'Yes, of course, if you would like.'

'What a silly thing to say,' said Matthew, back to his usual bantering style, 'of course I would like.' He smiled, kissed her on the forehead and said: 'Goodnight, my love,' and left.

'Well!' was all Melanie could gasp as she sat on the nearest chair.

Matthew found Hugh waiting in the hall. 'Joanna gone to bed?' he asked.

'Yes, poor little soul. I said I'd visit her tomorrow.'

'Good, I shall too. Come on, Ned will be in bed with influenza if we keep him waiting any longer in the rain.'

After delivering Hugh to his house they at last were back home. Matthew told Ned to go indoors and get dry. 'The horses need looking after first, sir,' said Ned.

'I'll see to them,' said Matthew, giving Ned a push. 'And Ned, find the brandy bottle.'

'Yes, sir,' said Ned with a grin.

CHAPTER 20

▼

The next day the only one partaking of breakfast in Curzon Street was Mrs Dobie. She had arrived home at the early hour of eleven o'clock when she went straight to her bedchamber, although she sat up for some while looking at her favourite fashion magazine. But she was asleep long before Melanie and Joanna arrived back from their social evenings so knew nothing of the turmoil that had happened. It was no worry to her that she breakfasted alone as she knew Melanie's habits of old and the kind of hours she kept and she was sure Joanna arrived home late but safe and sound and tired. She drew her shawl around her as she ate her freshly baked bread and preserve. It was decidedly chilly in spite of the fire and the rain from the previous night had now turned to sleet. Mrs Dobie thought it very likely that by nightfall it would be snowing.

By lunchtime her worst thoughts were confirmed and there was a steady fall of light snowflakes. When Melanie and Joanna joined her they were surprised at the white outlook. 'It's very pretty,' Joanna remarked absentmindedly, wondering whether she was glad it was snowing so that Hugh would be prevented from coming. She didn't know how she was going to face him again. True, he had been kind to her last night, or early this morning, but he might have had second thoughts about her and would be pleased to stay away. It was with a strained and pathetic little face that she sat down to lunch where she just picked at her food. Mrs Dobie, eyeing her knowledgeably, deduced something had gone wrong and wisely refrained from questioning her about her party. Melanie on the other hand sat eating thoughtfully, her mind faraway on something or someone else. Mrs Dobie addressed no fewer than three remarks about the food, weather and the previous evening to her, which Melanie had vaguely answered with a "yes" or a "no" and which didn't make sense at all. Mrs Dobie smiled. No doubt she would learn what went on the previous evening eventually and she looked forward to hearing what had occurred.

The two men, Matthew and Hugh had slept well and were also up late. Hugh had soon found sleep after thinking of his poor little Joanna but knew she was safe now and would see her later that day. Matthew and Ned had taken stiff drinks of brandy to bed with them and Matthew, stretching luxuriously, soon fell asleep with a smile on his face, feeling very pleased with himself.

By two o'clock that Sunday afternoon the snow had stopped and only a slight covering remained on the streets. Matthew, bearing in mind Ned's disabilities and his exertions the previous evening, told him he wasn't needed and he could walk to Curzon Street collecting Hugh on the way. Ned argued with him for a while but when he realised Matthew was adamant he thankfully retired to his chair near the fire in the kitchen to snooze the afternoon away before preparing a light supper in the evening.

Matthew, with boots on, a coat of dull red beneath his cloak and his tricorne pulled well onto his head strode out into the chilliness of the day and called at Hugh's house. He was similarly attired but in a coat of dark blue covered by a serviceable thick cloak. They strode along the street and Matthew thought more snow would be likely to fall later that evening by the look of the sky. Still, after all, it wouldn't be long before it was Christmas so snowfalls were to be expected. Large towns like London weren't affected as greatly as the country villages. He remembered when he was young how difficult it could be and how lucky they had been with large fires at the Rectory as opposed to the poorer cottages in his father's parish. He couldn't fault him for looking after his flock, and Matthew remembered hauling logs to burn on their fires. Sometimes he thought other people came first before the family. How his mother had coped with her hard work all her life he never knew. He thought he should write home. He had never done so apart from the occasional letter. Perhaps he could include a few lines in with a letter of Joanna's. But what would he tell them? He couldn't tell of the work he did for Harry, he wasn't allowed to and his father would certainly not be interested in his leisure pursuits such as dinners, balls, theatre visits and Jack's Academy, never mind about the 'fair sex'. No, all he could think of saying were the usual subjects of good health, happiness and to hope they had the same. He was brought back to reality by Hugh telling him to be careful of some slippery areas underfoot but otherwise they were enjoying the exercise in spite of the cold. They kept up a good pace and by the time their destination was reached Hugh was a little short of breath.

'You will have to join me at Jack's, you know, Hugh. A young man like you shouldn't be puffing.'

'I'm not puffing, sir. It's the cold.'

'Rubbish,' said Matthew, lifting the knocker. 'And no "sir" this afternoon.'

The door opened and Matthew enquired for Mrs Shaw. They entered and Bayliss appeared as they took off their hats and cloaks. 'The ladies are in the withdrawing room, sirs. Please follow me.' He announced them and Matthew and Hugh walked in to see three ladies rising from their chairs. Mrs Dobie gave a smile of welcome. Melanie blushed and although Joanna rose from the couch to curtsey she looked down at the floor. The men bowed.

Melanie pulled herself together. 'Please sit down. We didn't know whether you would come owing to the change in the weather.'

'We walked, didn't we, Hugh?' said Matthew. 'The exercise is good for us. How are you both after your ordeal last night?' He sat in a chair opposite the ladies while Hugh joined Joanna sitting on the sofa.

'We have recovered, thank you,' said Melanie. There was a short silence broken by Mrs Dobie, who said: 'I don't wish to pry, of course, but as I was home early and soon asleep I'm afraid I'm in the dark. Would anyone like to enlighten me or if not, shall we talk of something else?'

'I—I think I should tell you that everyone was home late because of me,' said Joanna in a small voice.

'Really?' said Mrs Dobie. 'Well, it's nice of you to say so, dear, but if it's all a secret, don't worry.'

Matthew interrupted. 'Well, Joanna, I think you should tell us all what happened, you know. I think you owe it to us and especially Hugh.'

No,' said Hugh, 'she doesn't owe me anything but I'm sure it is not so bad as you think it is, Joanna. And do you think you will feel better if you do tell us?' He took hold of her hand to give her confidence, which had the effect of making her smile and she even looked at him.

'Very well,' she began in a small voice. 'I joined my friends in Dover Street but I don't think I want to see them any more, Melanie, if you don't mind.'

'No, of course not, dear. It is for you to decide.'

Joanna nodded. 'Then we went in a carriage to Upper Wimpole Street. We were very squashed and my new dress became creased. When we arrived we went into a large room. It was very shabby.'

Mrs Dobie asked: 'And did you see any cobwebs and spiders and mice?'

'N-no, I expect they were there but the light wasn't good. Dancing began but the dances were very energetic and I didn't know them. And the harpsichord had some keys missing.' If she had looked at Matthew she would have seen his shoulders shake. Melanie did and glared at him. Joanna went on: 'There was lemonade on the table and as I was thirsty I went and poured myself a drink. Then this John, I think he had drunk too much wine, he grabbed my arm and spilt my lemonade down my new dress,' she finished disgustedly.

Matthew managed to hide a smile. It seemed to him that Joanna was more upset by her spoilt dress than anything else.

'Oh,' said Mrs Dobie, 'let me look at that, love, I think I know how to get the stain out if it's only lemonade.'

'Thank you,' smiled Joanna, beginning to feel better.

'So,' said Matthew, 'what did you do?'

'I slapped his face, of course,' she replied indignantly.

Matthew gave a hoot of laughter and Hugh joined in while Melanie and Mrs Dobie clapped. 'Well done,' said Matthew, 'I knew a sister of mine would have the answer.'

Now, Joanna, pleased with herself, was able to laugh a little. She continued: 'The others laughed and Phoebe, whose party it was took me outside and said she was sorry about my dress but I should have been told to wear an old one. I wasn't told, of course, and I think I should have been and th-then I'd have known it—it wasn't …'

Hugh squeezed her hand. 'Of course you would,' he said. 'Can you tell us who you slapped next?' His eyes laughed at her as he said it.

A smile appeared. 'Well, actually,' she said, 'I didn't but after dancing we had some games which were noisy and then it was time for refreshments. I didn't eat anything, as they didn't look very nice. They had just been under a cloth all evening, you know.'

'What happened next?' asked Matthew, looking steadily at her. Joanna looked across at him while Melanie, sensing something unpleasant, tried to intervene. But she should have known better, as Matthew interrupted her. 'Come on, Jo,' he said.

Joanna took a deep breath. 'Well, the—the boys began to choose a partner. I asked a girl what was happening. I—I was shocked and didn't know what to do.'

'What did you do?' asked Melanie before Matthew could get a word in.

'John came and grabbed hold of me. We went out the door. I—I told him to go and find a room while I found a handkerchief in my cloak. Then fortunately, another couple came out then and they and John became mixed up and John fell down the stairs.'

Everyone cheered. Joanna smiled. 'I didn't wait any longer. I grabbed my cloak and left and I ran the length of the street. I was so relieved to be away from that house, that was all I could think of for some time, but then it dawned on me that I didn't know the way back. So I just walked and then—then you found me. That's all.'

Before anyone could say anything, Hugh said to her: 'You did just the right thing, Joanna, and I'm proud of you.'

'Really?'

Melanie looked as though she would like to say something and Matthew just sat watching everyone's reactions and then said: 'Well done, Jo.'

'Indeed,' piped up Mrs Dobie. 'Shall we all drink to brave Joanna?'

'A good idea, Lily,' said Melanie. 'Ring for Bayliss, dear.'

While they waited for him to appear, Matthew asked Mrs Dobie if she would accompany Melanie and himself to the theatre and would she like to bring a friend? Of course, she was delighted to accept especially when she knew they were to see Hamlet by Shakespeare.

Matthew glanced over to Hugh and Joanna, lifting an eyebrow. 'I think,' said Hugh, taking his cue, 'that you and I are not wanted that evening. Shall we do something by ourselves?'

Joanna nodded. 'Yes, please. That would be lovely.'

Bayliss brought in and served the drinks before departing and Hugh stood up and said: 'A toast to Joanna for being a brave and resourceful young lady.'

Joanna was feeling much better now and nearly her usual self once more.

After that they chatted on various topics and when Bayliss appeared and asked if he should light the candles as the daylight was passing and more snow looked to be on the way, the men decided it was time to leave.

Melanie was able to speak to Matthew on the way out of the room to apologise for the type of girls Joanna had befriended. 'I really thought they were nice girls. I am sure their mothers don't realise what they do. I know them and they are perfectly respectable.'

'My dear girl,' said Matthew, 'you refine too much upon it. It has done Joanna good. She will be more careful in future and she will mind Hugh more, too. Now, are you going to kiss me goodbye or must I ...' With a finger under her chin he tilted up her face and suited the action to his words with a chaste kiss on her cheek. 'I expect that will have to do until next time,' he said.

Melanie smiled. 'I'm afraid so,' she answered demurely in return.

CHAPTER 21

▼

While Matthew was trying to interpret what was happening on the Continent, and keeping alert to all things around him during the day, he was able to relax, to some extent in the evenings and enjoy those spent with Melanie. Joanna, now that that wretched party had receded to the back of her mind, and encouraged by those around her, especially Hugh and Matthew, who told her she hadn't broken any of the ten commandments, was enjoying herself once again.

In Marlborough, life continued as usual or nearly as usual. Eliza's days formed a similar pattern as always, seeing that her husband ate well and was happy, supporting him in his parish work, running his household as he liked and entertaining General Peabody-Brown. The holiday that had been mentioned before Joanna had gone to London never materialised. Eliza hadn't been surprised and as it was now Advent and nearly Christmastime there was no hope of a break. In fact, life would be more hectic than ever if past years had been anything to go by. She missed Joanna, of course, and wished she could be home soon but knew that as she had gone to London "for the season", she wouldn't return until the spring unless Mrs Shaw decided otherwise. Joanna had written twice since she had been away and Eliza thought she was happy and she had mentioned her meeting with Matthew and that he was the same as ever he was. When Stephen read this, his comment had been one single "Hum".

Eliza would have liked to hear more from them both but she knew the post was expensive. She hadn't heard from Luke either and hoped he was well and alive, wherever he was. Not much news of the war reached them and the General never talked about it in her hearing. If he discussed it with Stephen at their chess sessions, she was never told. So she just hoped that all was well with her youngest son. Eliza felt that at least Mark was safe and happily married to Lavinia, and a small addition to the family was due early in the New Year which was something to look forward to. Perhaps she would be able to visit them for a brief spell when Joanna was home again so that she could look after her father. After all, Mark's living was near Exeter, so she wouldn't be travelling to the end of the world.

Now Eliza looked out of the window and sighed. To make life more difficult it had begun to snow. The fires had better be looked at and more logs brought in. She must find Ben and tell him. He would probably be in the kitchen with Cook at this time. Ben was the handyman who came in daily. He lived in a little cottage with his family not far away. As Eliza opened the kitchen door, Cook said: 'I've just made a hot drink, Mrs Brooke. You look as though you could do with one and it's your favourite.' After a few minutes she handed her a cup of what Cook called "her special". It was hot milk with honey, laced with brandy and topped with grated nutmeg. It was warming and sustaining.

'Thank you,' said Eliza as she thankfully sat down by the kitchen table. 'When you've had yours, Ben, could you bring in more logs? If the snow gets worse we shall need them.'

'Of course I can,' he said. 'Don't you worry about a thing. You just sit there and look after yourself for a change.'

Eliza smiled at him. 'I'm all right,' she said.

'That's what you'll say on your death bed,' said Ben.

Cook laughed. 'Go away Ben. Stop nagging.'

The clanging of the bell at the front door reverberated through the house. Eliza sighed. 'I wonder who …'

'Sit still,' said Ben. 'I'll answer it.'

He came back with a package. 'Post,' he said, 'and he needs paying.'

Eliza made to rise yet again but Cook forestalled her. 'I've some money here so sit still, Mrs Brooke, and you can make it right with me later.'

The package was addressed to the Reverend and Mrs Brooke. Eliza looked at it. Should she open it or would Stephen be annoyed if she did?

Cook, seeing her dilemma said: 'It might be urgent so I would open it if I were you. Mr Brooke will be out for some time, won't he?'

'Yes, oh yes. He's at a church conference and then I think he's visiting the General. I don't know whether he'll be home for lunch.' Then Eliza, needing no more encouragement, opened the package. 'Oh, look there's a letter from Joanna and, how lovely, there's one from Matthew too and this sheet says "for Mama only".

'Good thing you opened it then,' said Cook. 'Now you sip your drink and read your letters and enjoy yourself for a few moments while I get on.'

For once Eliza did as she was told.

First, she read Joanna's letter to her. It said:

Dearest Mama

Just to let you know that Matthew is very friendly with Mrs Shaw. In fact, he has taken her to the theatre twice! I know he visits here to see me, of course, but he has dined here many times and I really think they like each other a lot. I thought it would make you happy to hear this, as Melanie is a lovely person. Don't say anything to Papa as this is just between you and me. Any further developments and I'll try and let you know.

Love Joanna.

The other letter from Joanna to both her parents was about the visits to churches, art galleries and her comments on various buildings and people she had seen. Also that she had made some friends and that Mrs Shaw and Mrs Dobie were very kind to her. She didn't mention Hugh, of course.

Matthew's letter was shorter saying only that he was very busy but he had been able to keep an eye on Joanna and she was doing very well and that they were both in good health. They both sent their love and hoped Mama and Papa were well too.

By the time Eliza had read these letters twice and drank her milk she felt much happier and delighted for Matthew if Joanna had read the signs right. It was a cheerful Eliza who set about her usual household tasks once more.

Stephen returned halfway through the afternoon looking a little glum, Eliza thought, so she was delighted to cheer him up a little by telling him that two letters were awaiting him. He was pleased to hear from both his children, of course, but said: 'Joanna doesn't say when she'll be home, does she? I hoped it would be for Christmas.'

'No dear,' said Eliza, 'but she should be back in the spring. Travelling on the roads at this time of year is a little hazardous, isn't it?'

'I suppose so,' he said, giving her the letters. His mind was definitely elsewhere but as Eliza was used to this she said nothing and was only too pleased he hadn't objected to her opening the letters.

Stephen had called to see his friend, the General, on a serious matter indeed and something that was close to both their hearts, in other words "brandy". They both had expected barrels to be delivered before Christmas to stock up their cellars but there had not been the usual deliveries. Of course, the war with France perhaps had something to do with it. It was risky coming over the Channel at such a time and that was why the previous shipment had been more expensive. For years it had worked so well. The barrels of brandy brought out of France cleverly bypassed customs officials on both sides of the Channel, eventually to be sold on to the Free Traders who knew their customers. One of these was originally from Marlborough and a one-time friend of Ben's. There were quite a few "customers" in wealthy Marlborough so it was convenient, therefore, to bring the barrels along the river Kennet in the dead of night to a disused mill just outside the town. Here they would be stored where they would wait for collection by Ben for the General and Mr Brooke while others collected their share at various intervals for their respective buyers. The Free Traders would then collect payment and disappear into the darkness until next time.

'It's not as if we can go enquiring why our stocks have not been replenished,' laughed the General. 'I was talking to our Mayor the other day and he is in the same predicament as ourselves, and others. I know men in our position should lead blameless lives but I don't see that illicit brandy hurts anyone.'

'Except the government's coffers,' said Stephen dryly. 'Mind you, my parishioners enjoy it too, especially the older ones. It keeps them warm, especially in this weather.'

'Exactly,' said the General. 'And we have both fought for King and country well enough in the past. Also the men who deliver the stuff wouldn't have any other work perhaps if they didn't keep us all in brandy. They risk a lot, even death to bring it to us. So I don't suppose we can complain really.'

'No. I suppose all we have to do is wait. I can't see what else we can do,' murmured Stephen sadly as he departed.

But the General was made of sterner stuff and he now sat and cudgelled his brain as he had in past times when tactics and inventiveness were called for. After a while he nodded his head and a seraphic smile spread over his usual hard features.

CHAPTER 22

▼

Christmas came and went and the New Year brought cold and icy weather. Matthew and Melanie were still enjoying one another's company and life in general but occasionally Melanie mentioned that in a few weeks' time they would have to think of returning to Marlborough for Joanna and Chippenham for Melanie and Mrs Dobie. Matthew wondered if Melanie was waiting for a proposal of marriage from him before then but ever cautious to commit himself, Matthew thought about it but still held his peace. It wasn't that he didn't love her; he did, but wondered if it was a good idea to have a wife with the particular, dangerous work that he sometimes had to do.

Joanna had also enjoyed herself over the Christmas period with parties, dances and social evenings especially as Hugh had accompanied her everywhere. They enjoyed each other's company but Joanna knew that soon she would have to return home. What would happen then between Hugh and herself she didn't know. It wasn't as though Marlborough was only half an hour's ride away! She told herself something or someone would sort the problem out. After all, she had no say in the matter anyway and Papa had to approve of what she did. When Melanie departed she would have to go with her. She had wondered if Matthew would soon offer for Melanie but, of course, she couldn't ask him if he was going to. He was very good-natured where she was concerned but she didn't think he would like her poking her nose into any of his business. All she could do was bide her time and make the most of her opportunities while still in London.

At the office Matthew, Hugh and Arnold had a surprise one Monday morning in the form of an early visit from Harry Anstruther. He had something of import to tell them all, he said, so they gathered in Matthew's office as usual. He smiled. 'I hope you will be pleased with the news but I am sure you will be and it affects you all.' He looked at the faces in front of him, Hugh hanging on his every word, Matthew and Arnold mildly interested. Harry rubbed his hands together and said: 'We are closing this office and this department is to be moved into premises nearer to mine in Whitehall. It will be cleaner and, more importantly, safer for you. And being near will be easier for us all. The work will be the same, of course. Now, how do you feel about it?'

They sat quietly for a moment. 'It will certainly be much pleasanter,' said Arnold.

'Matthew?'

'Any particular reason for this move, sir? I mean just now? The area will be a great improvement, of course, but what about our contacts?'

'Something can be arranged, Matthew, don't worry about that. And you will all still want to be on the alert about your wellbeing. The area is more salubrious but always be on your guard. I've been hoping for this for a long time, you know, and when you were in danger recently, Matthew, from that Fox fellow, it helped to push the matter further with my superiors.'

'Well,' grinned Matthew, 'I know of one person who will be delighted at the news.'

'Who?'

'Ned, my servant. He will be able to send me out in respectable clothes and not these old decrepit ones I have to use here.'

'When do we move?' asked Hugh, eyeing all the files.

'As soon as possible.'

'As quick as that?' Arnold said, surprised.

'I have an assignment for Matthew while the move is taking place which I will tell him about privately in a moment. But, of course, when you are ready I will send security men over and extra help will be given you. I suggest you begin to organise papers and everything as soon as possible. That will fall to you, Hugh.'

'Yes, sir. I'll start straightaway.'

'I will help,' smiled Arnold.

They all discussed the move for a while and how it could be organised and then Hugh and Arnold left so that Harry could tell Matthew what was in store for him.

'I've had a letter from General Peabody-Brown,' said Harry when they were on their own. 'He says he has a problem that needs sorting out.'

Matthew groaned. 'I thought this was going to be important and involve a trip to France.'

'Well, no, not exactly. He mentions that it is to do with France and some contacts he has whom he hasn't heard from recently and he's worried.'

'What French contacts would they be?'

'I don't really know. You know the General, he likes to organise things to help the war. He thinks he's still in charge. And it did cross my mind that it might have some connection with Mrs Shaw's contact in France, you know, the one Oakley was going to. I don't suppose you've heard anything mentioned?'

'No, I haven't.'

'Mm, no, I don't suppose so or you would have said. Well, go home, Matthew. You haven't been for a long time, have you? Have a break and find out what it's all about, will you? If it's nothing, say so.' He looked again at the letter. 'Oh, the General says it will involve working at night and you are to take someone tough with you.'

Matthew sighed. He didn't really want to leave London just now but he supposed he'd have to do as he was told. And what was all this nonsense about taking someone with him? Who was he to take? The General had better come up with a very good reason for wanting him at this time. Not only would Harry be angry if it all turned out to be something trifling, Matthew would be too. Oh, damn the General!

He said the same to Ned that evening.

'Well, you can't have all good news at once,' Ned said. 'You're moving to a nice new office and not before time in my opinion and you'll be going home to see your parents. If you're not pleased to be doing that, at least your mother will be pleased to see you and ...'

'I know, I know. But for one thing I'd like to be moving my own files and I don't really want to leave London at the moment as you well know.' Matthew looked at Ned, a frown in his eyes.

'Ladies will wait,' said Ned. 'They get used to waiting for their men to return. Besides, it often makes them keener ...'

'Ned, shut up!'

Ned sniffed and turned away and went into the kitchen smiling to himself. The relationship with Mrs Shaw was serious then.

Matthew followed him. 'Sorry,' he said. Ned just nodded. 'And I have to take someone tough with me as something is going to happen at night. Whatever does it all mean, do you think?'

'Only one way to find out.'

'Yes, I know. Do you know someone tough, Ned, because I don't?'

'I will think upon the matter,' said Ned seriously. 'So what do you want me to pack and how will you travel, sir?'

'Oh, I don't know. Serviceable clothes, I suppose, I shan't be doing much socialising.'

'And when will you travel?'

'Today is Monday, so I had better make it Wednesday which gives us a day to organise everything. I'll go and see Jack in the morning for half an hour to see that I'm fit and ready for what's in store for me and …'

'There's your man, sir,' interrupted Ned.

'Where?'

Patiently, as to a child, Ned explained: 'From the Academy, sir. Take …'

'I can't take Jack with me but I grant you he'd be just the right one.'

'No, I know you can't. I was thinking about the black man, whatever his name is.'

'Silas? Mm.' Matthew frowned and thought about it. Then he laughed and clapped Ned on the back. 'Ned, you're a genius. If he can be spared he'd be just the man. And if we are working at night he won't be seen, will he?' Matthew continued to think about this and an unholy light came into his eyes.

Ned eyed him. 'And now what devilry are you thinking of? Sir,' he added for good measure.

'I was just wondering, Ned, how my Father will react to having a black man under his roof.'

'He's a clergyman, isn't he? He'll be pleased.'

'I wonder,' smiled Matthew.

Tuesday morning came and he visited Jack's Academy for a short session with Silas. Afterwards, he broached the matter of hiring Silas for the next two weeks to Jack, who after much thought eventually agreed if Silas was willing. The monetary side of the business was settled easily as Matthew knew that Harry Anstruther would pay all expenses on Matthew's return. Silas wanted to know what was involved and the work he had to do. Matthew told him he really didn't know until he arrived home, but he would travel with Matthew and stay at his home.

'There is no need to worry, you know. Once my mother is used to you she'll try and feed you all kinds of food.'

'Sounds good to me,' said Silas with a grin.

From there he went to organise the travelling. Like most professional gentlemen he went to hire a post-chaise at the nearest posting inn. These were painted yellow and known as "yellow bounders". There was enough room for two travellers and a reasonable amount of luggage. A postilion, also dressed in yellow, would accompany the carriage and he and the horses were changed at the next posting inn along the way. There was keen competition between the innkeepers to provide the best service they could so a high standard of comfort was maintained.

The next and last thing he had to do was to visit Curzon Street and bid Melanie and Joanna farewell and he wasn't looking forward to this. He left the visit until after lunch which he ate in near silence. Ned didn't interrupt. When he felt it safe to talk he asked if there was anything Matthew wanted doing while he was away.

'I don't think so, Ned. But it does cross my mind that you may be asked as to my whereabouts.'

'Probably, sir, but I shall look blankly at the enquirer and tell them that you don't confide in me.'

Matthew grinned. 'Thanks, Ned. I would like to have taken you with me, you know, but it would give rise to speculation. And I wouldn't like to subject you to this weather when you can keep warm here. I shall return as soon as possible.'

'Don't worry about me, sir, but I shall be pleased to see you back. Now do you go to visit the ladies?'

Matthew sighed. 'I suppose so.'

He decided to walk. There weren't many people about and those that travelled were inside carriages. They were sensible, Matthew supposed, as there was definitely a nip in the air. He could feel his nose and ears starting to turn numb with cold. The sooner he was indoors again the better. He turned the corner sharply into Curzon Street and nearly collided with the little figure who was hurrying along, a shawl over her head. There was no-one else around and when she saw the giant in front of her she shrank against the wall.

Matthew stopped. She looked at him, fear in her eyes.

'Tell me,' he said, 'I believe you work for Mrs Shaw?'

The girl nodded, clutching her shawl.

Matthew asked: 'Is she at home?'

'Yes, sir. All the ladies are.'

'Thank you. And your name is?'

'Tilly, sir.'

'Oh, yes, I remember now. You waited up for my sister, Miss Brooke, that night, didn't you?' He hunted in his pocket and brought out a coin. 'Here you are, Tilly, and there is no need to be afraid of me.'

'No sir.' Then, as she saw the coin, her eyes widened. 'All that? Oh, thank you sir, but I only said ...'

'You told me what I wanted to know so you earned it.'

Matthew smiled at her. Tilly saw the smile that was particularly sweet and gave him a sunny one in return. She was his slave!

Matthew was soon shown into the withdrawing room where the three ladies sat talking or reading by the fire. When Matthew was announced they looked up, surprised but pleased. As he sat Melanie said: 'This is a pleasant surprise and on a Tuesday afternoon too.'

'I thought you would be at your office,' piped up Joanna.

'I should be, of course,' said Matthew. 'But I've come specially to let you know that you will be deprived of my presence for a while.'

Joanna frowned. 'Why?'

'I am going away and before you ask any more questions, no, I can't tell you where.'

Melanie felt a queasy feeling in the pit of her stomach and she was aware of the blood draining from her face. This was a shock. It shouldn't have been, of course, but everything had been going so well, she thought, between herself and Matthew and now this news spoilt it all. She was now certain that Matthew's work was much more complex than he wanted her to believe and quite possibly dangerous at times. She should have known everything couldn't go along so happily, but when one was in love, as she was, one hoped the happier things went on forever. She had thought this before, a long time ago, but it seemed she hadn't learnt that good things didn't go on without end. She now pulled herself together and said: 'We shall miss you, of course. Will you be away for long and—and be all right?'

Noting her pale face, all Matthew was able to reply was: 'I shall return as soon as possible.'

'Yes, yes, of course.' Melanie smiled a little.

Matthew turned the conversation and asked them what they had been doing and what plans they had. But in the middle of the talk Joanna asked: 'Is Hugh going with you, Matt?'

'Not to my knowledge.' Then, seeing the look on Joanna's face said, with some amusement: 'And it's no use trying to find out anything from him, because he doesn't know.' Joanna pouted, then grinned at him. He knew her too well.

After a little more strained conversation Matthew decided he had had enough. If only he could take Melanie in his arms and tell her everything would be well and she wasn't to worry and when he came back he would ask her a very important question. But he couldn't. It wouldn't be fair. But what he did promise himself was that when he returned he would certainly tell her that he loved her.

CHAPTER 23

―――――――――▼―――――――――

It was a raw and cold day and Eliza and Cook dressed themselves in warm clothes to visit the shops and stalls in Marlborough that morning. As the weather could become worse they thought they would take the opportunity while the roads were passable to buy in extra food. They took the horse and cart as usual and just hoped that the animal could keep its feet over the icy patches. Fortunately, all went well and they were able to tether the horse not far away. Picking up their large baskets they hurriedly went to look in the shops to buy the best quality food they could. Other people were about, too, of course, all swathed in shawls and heavy cloaks, their breath steaming in the cold air. There was a stall offering hot soup and Eliza, ever soft hearted, bought three bowls for three poor, cold and hungry little girls standing sniffing nearby. Their grins of surprise and pleasure were thank you enough for Eliza. There were one or two other stalls in the High Street where the holders braved the elements to sell what produce they had. They stood on straw, stamping their feet in an effort to keep them warm. They blew on their fingers, their breath a pathetic substitute for hot coals. The man selling roasted chestnuts had a crowd round him, not only to purchase them but to steal warmth from his heated brazier and nearby, those that could afford it, sipped from small bowls of hot spiced wine.

Eliza needed more spices and herbs to supplement her stock that included peppermint and liquorice, powdered horehound and cowslip root. These were for coughs and colds. Many in the parish were ill this weather and herbs could give help to the children for their runny noses and to the old for their bronchitis. She and Cook bought meat, the bones of which could be stewed and made into stock for soups and they bought extra flour and cereals and other dried ingredients to keep in reserve. When they could shop no more and they had packed their purchases onto the cart, they thankfully drove home away from the drab cold streets.

'How about I make us a nice hot drink when we reach home?' said Cook.

'Not until we've unloaded,' said Eliza. 'I don't think I would be able to get up again if I sat and had a drink first.'

At last they were back at the Rectory and both ladies were only too thankful to have returned as their hands and feet were numb and their faces chilled. As Eliza descended from the cart, her little maid came running out. 'Oh, Mrs Brooke, there's two men and one's black.'

'Oh, where?'

'In the house. One said …'

She got no further as Eliza, looking up in concern was startled to see two large men, one white, one black, emerging from the house and coming towards her. Then her face was wreathed in smiles. 'Matthew, oh Matthew, is it really you?'

'Of course it is, love.' Matthew placed his arms around her, holding her close and kissing her cold cheek. 'How are you?'

'I'm well.' She looked up quickly, concern on her face. 'Are you and Joanna all right?'

'I left Jo enjoying herself and I'm fine.'

'Oh, good.' She let out a sigh of relief. What a wonderful surprise this was, to have Matthew home.

Turning, he said: 'Silas is a friend of mine. Please make him welcome.'

'Why, of course,' said Eliza, rubbing her watery eyes which she hoped they would think was because of the cold. She held out her hand and smiled, saying: 'You're very welcome, Silas.'

Silas, gently taking her hand and bowing over it, said simply with a flash of a white smile, 'Thank you.'

'Shall we help with the unloading?' asked Matthew.

It wasn't long afterwards, when the two strong men had transferred the shopping indoors and the horse had been led away, rubbed down and fed, that they all sat round the kitchen table with drinks in their hands.

'Now,' said Eliza, 'how long will you be staying? Shall we prepare your old room, Matthew, and the one next to it for Silas? We can light fires too so it will be warm and cosy.'

'Thank you, if it won't be too much trouble.'

'Of course not. I'm pleased to have you both and your Father will be too.'

Matthew made no comment.

Eliza asked more questions on how they had travelled and why they had come at such a time. Matthew had to be careful what he said as Silas and Cook were listening but he deflected most of the questions by asking where his father was.

'He is probably with the General. They like to play chess you know. He was going to make a few calls in the parish first, of course.'

'I see,' said Matthew. 'So, what do you do, Mama? Run around after my Father and all the parishioners as you always did?'

'Yes, well, you know I like to.'

'But when do you relax and enjoy yourself?'

'Well, do you know, I did just that when your letter and Joanna's came. I sat down and read these and Cook made me a drink. It was lovely.'

'Poor Mama,' was Matthew's only comment when she'd finished.

No more was said until they heard the front door open and shut and then a voice shouted: 'Eliza!'

Matthew instinctively placed a hand on his mother's arm. 'Stay there, I'll go.' He opened the kitchen door and saw his father standing looking at the bags that Matthew and Silas had brought with them and which had been left in the hallway.

'Good morning, Father,' said Matthew.

Stephen stood still. Then a smile crossed his face. 'Matthew, how are you?'

He advanced towards his eldest son and they shook hands. 'Come along into the study and tell me why you're here. You look well,' said Stephen, patting Matthew on the back. 'Are you staying long?'

'I don't know,' said Matthew, 'it depends.'

Stephen ignored this, telling Matthew to sit against the fire while he took a chair opposite. His father looked just the same as ever he did albeit a little greyer and a little plumper round the waist.

In his turn, Stephen looked his large son over too. 'You look well, Matthew. How are things with you? Is this a holiday or are you here for a reason? Joanna is behaving herself?'

'Thank you,' said Matthew deliberately. 'I am well and Joanna is being very good. You have no need to worry about her.'

'Good, good,' said Stephen, rubbing his hands together and holding them by the fire. For some reason he felt a little awkward with Matthew and wondered why. It was never like this before. Now, surreptitiously looking at him, Stephen had to concede to himself that Matthew was a fine figure and a good-looking young man. Had he himself looked like this when younger? Matthew broke in on his thoughts.

'And are you keeping well, sir? And how is the General?'

'We both are well. I've just been visiting him. Why are you visiting us at this time of year? I expect your Mother is delighted.'

'And you, sir?' asked Matthew bluntly.

'Of course I am pleased to see you, Matthew. I just wondered how you were able to leave your office at such a time.'

'Ah, there is a reason, of course. Has the General said anything to you?'

'No,' said Stephen slowly, with a frown.

'I shall have to see him first before I say anything more,' said Matthew.

Stephen made a noise in his throat, which could have meant anything.

There was a gentle knock on the door. It opened and Eliza put her head round. 'Just to let you know that Silas is helping to carry firewood and the baggage upstairs if you should need him, Matthew.'

'Silas? Who's Silas?' barked Stephen.

'Matthew's friend. He's helping me.'

'But he shouldn't do that,' said Stephen, somewhat bewildered. 'Whatever next! We have a visitor and you ask him to …'

'No dear,' interrupted Eliza, 'he offered and he's a nice strong young man, so …'

'Bring him in at once,' ordered Stephen.

Matthew winced. Did his father not consider his mother at all?

'Yes, dear, he'll be down in a moment. Ah, here he is. Silas, come and meet my husband.'

Matthew watched his father's face as Silas came through the door. It was a picture to behold. Pleasure, shock and blankness ran over it in quick succession. Matthew could have laughed out loud but instead took Silas by the arm and brought him forward. 'This is my friend who, as you can see, is a strong and pleasant person to have around, just as Mama said.'

Silas, used to many reactions to his colour in the past, just bowed and said politely: 'It is kind of you to let me stay here, sir.'

Stephen then managed to smile and held out his hand. 'You are welcome, Silas.'

The beautiful smile showed. 'Thank you,' Silas said. He turned to Eliza. 'Mrs Brooke, there are still things to carry upstairs. Would you like me to continue?'

'Oh, Silas, dear, would you? It would be such a help.'

Silas gave a small bow to Stephen and looked at Matthew who grinned back at him and nodded. Evidently his father felt it wasn't out of order for a black visitor to do these chores.

Outside the door, Eliza whispered to Silas: 'Don't worry about my husband. When he gets used to you, he will be all right.'

It wasn't until the following day that Matthew went to see the General. Before he had gone he had presented his father with a bottle of very expensive port wine and his mother with a pretty pink shawl, which she declared was just what she needed now the cold weather was upon them. Matthew had left Silas back at the Rectory. He was going to accompany Eliza and her shawl to Marlborough, after looking round the church with Stephen. As he was being shown the intricate carving of the figures on the Rood screen, Stephen asked him how he had become friendly with his son. Silas explained that he worked for Jack Broughton and Stephen nodded vaguely, having heard of the man from somewhere, but when Silas said that Mr Brooke attended the Academy for exercise and training, Stephen was more in the dark than ever. Why would Matthew want to do such a thing? He asked Silas if he was any good.

'Oh, yes, sir, he is very good.'

'So why has he brought you to visit us? It is very nice to have you, of course,' he finished hurriedly.

Silas shrugged. 'I don't really know, sir.'

Matthew by this time was paying his respects to General Peabody-Brown, who, of course, was very pleased to see him especially as he was presented with a bottle of port wine like Stephen. He asked Matthew how he was, the state of the roads and was his sister doing well. He went on to tell Matthew how he had persuaded his father to let her go to London with Mrs Shaw.

Matthew began to get bored. It seemed to him that the General was stalling for time. Why? Was it because the work he wanted him to do was particularly dangerous and he didn't know how to broach the subject? After a little more of the General's small talk Matthew said: 'Why do you wish to see me, sir? What can I do for you?'

'Ah, yes, Stephen should be here too. It involves him as well.'

'Really? Does he know?'

'Of course he knows,' said the General, surprised.

'He hasn't said anything to me,' said Matthew.

'I expect he thought it best left to me to explain.'

'I'm still in the dark. Are you going to tell me what the trouble is?'

'Yes, yes, of course. Did you bring someone with you, by the way, as I asked?'

'I did. I left him at the Rectory.'

'Good, good,' said the General, rubbing his hands. 'The fact of the matter is that many of us in Marlborough have not been receiving the orders we have placed with our retailers. We don't know whether the goods are being lost or stolen here in Marlborough before we receive them or if they haven't even reached here. We wondered, or I wondered, if you would be able to find out what is happening.' He looked keenly at Matthew under beetled brows.

'And what goods would they be?' asked Matthew.

'Does it matter?'

'Yes, I think it does. After all I have to know what I'm looking for.'

'Of course, of course. It's brandy.'

'Go on.'

'Well, you see, the barrels of brandy come over from France and they are brought along the Kennet and stored in the old mill. Perhaps you remember it? Then they are collected by certain individuals. Ben, who you may remember, collects ours. I did think perhaps the barrels were not reaching here at all and were being dropped off somewhere else completely different, but it did cross my mind that someone unknown is lying in wait for them at the mill.'

'So these barrels of brandy are brought from France across the Channel by whom?'

'How should I know?' asked the General.

'Do they go through customs?'

The General shrugged.

'Where do they go next?'

'Matthew, I don't know, do I? All I know is we have to collect them from the mill and the payment is made.'

'So what you are telling me, really,' said Matthew, 'is that the barrels of brandy are smuggled into Britain without duty being paid on them and then they are handed over to the Free Traders who bring some of them here which Ben collects for you and my Father and others collect theirs. And you give money to Ben to pay for them?'

'Well, yes, that's about it. But stocks are running low and I thought it all should be looked into.'

'By me,' said Matthew.

'You're the only one I could think of and whom we could trust.'

Matthew rested his chin on his steepled fingers and looked through his lashes at the General. 'How long have you been doing this with my Father?'

'Oh, years,' declared the General with a laugh.

'I think,' said Matthew standing up, 'that you and I had better go back to the Rectory so that my Father can join in this conversation.'

'Very well. How did you come?'

'I walked.'

'Then we had better take my carriage.'

Stephen was in his study trying to concentrate on Sunday's sermon. He had found Matthew and Silas's visit pleasant in one way but it had disrupted the usual day-to-day routine and now Eliza wasn't always where he expected her to be. Also he found himself thinking of his eldest son and found that he hardly knew him. He seemed to have a vast amount of confidence in himself and if he was as good at pugilism as Silas had said, Matthew was a force to be reckoned with. In one way, Stephen was delighted at the type of person he had become, but he found himself a little out of his depth in dealing with him. Was he getting old or just used to his parishioners, most of whom wanted his help or advice? He couldn't see Matthew doing that. It was while he was pondering these things that his son arrived, bringing the General with him. Stephen opened his study door and although he was pleased to see both men, he sighed for the sermon yet to materialise.

'Come in General. Shall we go into the library? I expect a fire is lit in there. What brings you here? Can I offer you a drink?'

The General declined and so did Matthew, who said as he sat down: 'The General has told me something of why Silas and I were told to come here. I thought you should join in the conversation, that is all.'

'I see,' said Stephen, sensing an atmosphere that wasn't entirely comfortable.

'What I understand is happening, and you must correct me if I'm wrong, is that smuggled brandy is left in the old mill by the Free Traders but you think that as there have been no shipments left there recently, someone is stealing them from the mill before you or Ben can get there.'

'Well, yes, that is it more or less but other people are involved like the Mayor and …'

Matthew held up his hand. 'That's not important. What is important, is that you are asking me to help you find your smuggled brandy.'

'I suppose so. Have you any ideas?'

'No,' said Matthew, 'and I don't want anything to do with it. These are dangerous men to deal with, as you well know. Do you realise that you are breaking the law? If you are found out, Father, you will be imprisoned with no church, parish or house. And what will my Mother do then, apart from break her heart?

You should practice what you preach. And added to that I should lose my job in aiding and abetting both of you.'

'Yes, Matthew,' said the General, 'we know all that but a lot of people do it and a lot of people benefit from it.'

'It doesn't matter,' said Matthew, 'the law is the law whether it's a good or bad one and I won't be part of all this. And I must say, at the risk of sounding discourteous, that both you gentlemen in your positions should know better. Excuse me.' Matthew stood up and left the room.

The General was the first to recover from the shock. He looked at Stephen, a rueful smile on his face. 'That told us, didn't it?'

'I can't believe he said all that,' said Stephen slowly, a dazed expression on his face. 'I must beg your pardon on his behalf, I …'

'There is no need. I admire the boy, I really do. But it doesn't get us any nearer in finding our brandy. There should be a delivery this Saturday night, too. Oh, well, if he won't help we'll have to think again.'

'Yes, yes,' said Stephen slowly, his mind in turmoil over Matthew's downright refusal, the thought of missing his brandy and the horror of what would happen if he was found out breaking the law. Now Matthew had pointed it out …! But no, he was overdoing it. If the General thought it all right it must be safe. But it left a small seed of doubt in Stephen's mind.

CHAPTER 24

▼

The next day was Saturday and Matthew and Silas went into Marlborough to find a post chaise to take them back to London the following Monday morning. They could have travelled back on the Saturday, of course, but Matthew thought it a little unkind to his mother who was so pleased to see him and had made Silas so welcome. Post chaises didn't run on a Sunday and anyway Matthew felt he'd like to visit the church of his childhood, which, he hoped, would please his father as well. He didn't know what to make of him though. How could he be so stupid as to let the General tell him what to do? He really couldn't understand him. If the words he, Matthew, had uttered had upset his father and pushed the rift wider between them than it was originally, then he was sorry for it; but something had to be said. He hadn't seen him yet this morning and it would be interesting to see how he behaved towards his son when next they met each other, probably at lunchtime. Deep down Matthew hoped he had been forgiven.

Silas enquired if he would be needed and Matthew said he thought he had sorted it all out without worrying him.

'It has been nice meeting your family, sir. Your mother is very kind, isn't she? She looks tired, though.'

'I know,' said Matthew, 'I shall have to talk to her.'

'Will it do any good?'

'I don't know but I hope so.'

As it was so cold, the rest of the day was spent indoors. Stephen wrote his sermon and at mealtimes he behaved as he usually did. Matthew had a chat to Eliza, which didn't do much good, as she said the cold always made her tired and she had to look after things in the home and those in the parish. She mentioned that she missed Joanna, as she was a great help. This worried Matthew as his parents shouldn't expect Joanna to stay home forever. If she and Hugh were planning on a further relationship they couldn't be prevented. As far as Matthew was concerned, they were just right for each other but he wouldn't interfere, neither would he mention anything to his parents. It wasn't his business. He wondered how the move to Whitehall had gone but no doubt Hugh would be competent in organising things. More importantly he wondered how Melanie was and he was sorry he couldn't tell her that he was only visiting at home. What a fiasco this had been. And all for nothing!

Evening came and Matthew spent time with his mother doing any jobs she wanted doing and making himself useful. They talked about local affairs too which his mother was interested in. Also they talked about Mark and Luke and Matthew did his best to stop Eliza worrying about the war. She seemed to worry about everything. Matthew tried to get her to talk about what she'd really like to do when the weather was warmer and where she would like to go for a holiday but she just said she couldn't think about it as Stephen was always busy. Eventually, she decided to go to bed and Stephen said he had some papers to look through for Sunday before he could retire and disappeared once more into his study. Matthew and Silas said "goodnight" and went up to their rooms. Matthew was more tired than he thought and after thinking of seeing Melanie again the following week quickly dropped off to sleep.

It was about three hours later when there was a light tap on the door that immediately woke him. It opened slowly and he heard his mother calling his name softly. 'What's the matter?' he asked, sitting up quickly.

Eliza shut the door quietly and went to sit on the edge of his bed. 'Stephen hasn't come to bed yet and I've been downstairs to look for him and he's not there either. Do you know where he might be?'

'No, I don't. Has he been called out by someone to a sick bedside, do you think?'

'Well, he usually leaves a note in the kitchen if he has. What do you think?'

'Go back to bed, love. I'll get up and see if I can find him and I'll let you know.'

'I'm so sorry, dear,' Eliza murmured as she left the room. Matthew dressed for outdoors with boots, cloak and hat. If his father had gone where he thought he might have, that is, the old mill, Matthew would really be angry with him. However, when he checked to see if the horse and carriage were in the stables and he found them missing, it confirmed his thoughts.

Matthew strode along the road towards the disused mill. It was dark with only a glimmer of moonlight and very slippery underfoot. Where there was a grass verge Matthew walked on this but for most of the time it was a rough track. The trees were dark, still and forbidding, so it was a good thing Matthew had no fear of the night or of whom the trees might be hiding. But he was alert at any small rustlings in the undergrowth and he stopped abruptly as a fox dashed across the road in front of him. Matthew continued his pace, eyes and ears alert. To the right of him beyond the trees the Kennet flowed, albeit sluggishly, and he listened for any movement or slight noise. As he neared the mill he saw a horse standing patiently with its carriage, which looked familiar. Matthew immediately placed a comforting hand over the horse's muzzle to stop it whinnying and listened. There were voices upraised in argument. Leaving the horse with a pat and a soft word, Matthew crept closer.

It was then that he heard shouting as tempers erupted and fighting began. He saw one man go down and Matthew hurried nearer. He could hear his father's voice shouting: 'There is no need for this,' and then he was knocked heavily to the ground.

Before Matthew could do anything, a dark figure emerged from nowhere and began fighting in earnest, keeping his body between his antagonists and the two men on the ground. Matthew recognised the fighting methods of Silas and quickly joined him, administering some choice punches. There were six men as far as Matthew could tell but they didn't stand a chance with two heavyweights like Matthew and Silas against them and they were soon beaten. In what state they were no one could see clearly but Matthew suspected there were some broken noses and jaws.

He turned. 'What the hell are you doing here?' he asked Silas. 'Did you know my Father was coming here and didn't think to tell me?'

'No, sir. You know I wouldn't do that. I heard some noise and I looked out the window and saw your Father and another man leading the horse and carriage carefully away. I don't know why but I thought something was wrong so I threw on some clothes and followed. They wouldn't see me, would they?' Silas grinned.

'They would if you smiled,' said Matthew, 'but thank you. I'm grateful and it was a bit of fun to fight on the same side for a change. I suppose we had better see what damage has been done?'

Stephen was still lying on the ground but now he was moaning, so obviously he was coming round. The other man was moving too and Matthew thought it was Ben who had gone with his father. Matthew and Silas stood looking down at them.

'Well,' said Matthew, 'are you both sound enough to get up now?'

'I'll fetch the carriage,' said Silas.

Matthew bent down to support his father. 'My head is swimming,' complained Stephen.

'I expect so,' said Matthew. Slowly and carefully, supporting his father, he helped him into the carriage where he sat clutching his head. Ben, being younger, seemed to recover quicker but he was helped inside too. 'I had better go and check on the others,' said Matthew. He found them as he had left them, lying on the ground. He decided to leave them alone as they began to groan. He also had a quick look inside the mill. He could only see two barrels. Evidently the others had been disposed of elsewhere.

They arrived back at the Rectory and Matthew and Silas helped the other two into the kitchen. Here they found Eliza. She had poked the fire so some heat could be felt after the damping down before bedtime. When she saw Stephen, his face swollen now from the hefty punch he had received, she gasped with distress for him and then found cloths to bathe him and ointments to sooth. Ben hadn't fared so badly and they managed to make him comfortable, after which Silas walked him home, supporting him. On the way back the horse was led to its stable for the rest of the night.

Matthew looked on while Eliza administered to his father. Whatever possessed him to go out just with Ben to confront such men? He began to wonder if his father was beginning to lose his faculties. He would certainly have to speak to him. And Matthew was annoyed that he had taken no notice whatsoever of what he had told him earlier. Did he think he knew these men better than he did or that his son was just talking rubbish? But all that would have to wait until the morrow.

At this moment Stephen looked battered and bruised. Eliza made him a hot herbal drink of vervain for a sedative nightcap and bathed his bruises with comfrey oil. After he had recovered a little Matthew suggested Stephen went to his bed. He looked at Matthew and rubbing his forehead said: 'I'm sorry I ...'

'Don't talk now. There'll be time in the morning. Let's get you to bed and sleep.' Matthew didn't leave him until he was comfortable and Eliza had placed an extra blanket over him and left a candle burning.

Matthew returned to his bed once more thinking he'd have to go and find another priest to take the Sunday services next day.

However, Eliza had organised it all, as there was a retired clergyman who they called on in an emergency, so Matthew had nothing to do but accompany his mother to the service. Anyone who asked as to Stephen's whereabouts was told that he had had a nasty fall which had shaken him but he would be perfectly fit after another day's rest.

To everyone's surprise Stephen decided to join them all for lunch. His body was still bruised and his face was sore and swollen but he managed to eat something and chat a little as Eliza told him about the service and that the congregation had wished him well. He just nodded. The previous evening's escapade wasn't mentioned.

Afterwards, Stephen asked Matthew to go with him into his study. As they sat down Stephen said: 'Thank you for rescuing Ben and me last night. I'm sorry to have been troublesome and I have decided to take your advice and not be involved in this brandy business ever again. I thought that …' (he waved his hand) 'but I see I was wrong and I admit it. You did right to show me where my duty lies and I should practice what I preach. I hope you feel that you can still bear to call me "your Father." I think sometimes I haven't treated you as I should, Matthew, but I still do love you like I do all my children. I—I hope you believe that.' He took out his handkerchief, blew his nose and surreptitiously wiped his eyes.

Matthew, listening to him, was filled with pleasure that at last his father appreciated him. He went and knelt down in front of him so that he was on a level with Stephen as he sat. 'I do believe what you say and I've always loved you, sir. But I am pleased that you will stay away from dangerous pursuits like last night. Those kind of men can be ruthless. Promise me to keep away from such people. The General can be a little too eager to play his "war games". Just keep friends with him and play chess but don't get involved in his mad schemes. I know what he's like.'

'Do you?' asked Stephen, diverted.

'Why did you think I came with Silas?'

'Was that the General's doing?'

'Yes. He wrote to my boss in terms that made it all sound important and that something had to be done.'

'Good gracious. And that is why you brought Silas, too.'

'Yes.'

'What work do you do, Matthew? I've never really known.'

'I'm not really at liberty to tell you. All I can say is that my office is now in Whitehall.'

'Gracious. Does that mean work to do with the war? And *your* office? Oh, yes, I see. Well, not really, but I understand.'

'Not a word to Mama. I don't want her to worry. And sir?'

'Yes, Matthew?'

'There is one thing you could do for me.'

'Anything, anything at all.'

'Please take Mama on a little holiday when the weather is warmer, possibly to the sea? It would do her so much good, you know. She works so hard and worries over us all.'

'Really? I never thought. But yes, I will, Matthew. It will do us both good. Am I such a failure as a parent and husband, do you think?'

'Certainly not. You are a very good Father, husband and priest. We are all weak at times, aren't we? We're only human.' Here Matthew grinned at his father, who held out his hand. Matthew took it in both his. 'It's been wonderful to see you again, sir.'

Matthew left him, feeling pleased at how everything had turned out. The first thing he would do when he went back to London was to order some bottles of good French brandy and send them to his father.

CHAPTER 25

▼

Ned was relieved to see Matthew back. He had arrived late on Monday evening after a reasonably good journey to London apart from some ice and snow on the road. Matthew had thanked Silas for his help to which he had replied that he had enjoyed it all; meeting Matthew's parents who had made him so welcome and also the fight they had had. 'It was fun,' he had said. He also realised this was not to be spoken of elsewhere, of course. Matthew had been thankful for Silas' help especially in saving his father from worse injuries.

He had been surprised that his father was led astray like that! He was the last person Matthew thought of as being weak. But there again, the General could be very persuasive. Some good had come out of it, though, and he and his father were now on better terms with each other and he had hopes that his mother would be considered more. Although it had been a waste of time going home in one way, Matthew had managed to make life safer for his father and hopefully, easier for his mother.

Ned said, as he helped Matthew take off his cloak: 'And did all go well, sir?'

'Yes and no, Ned. But it's good to see you, too. Any problems while I've been away?'

'No, sir, not that I know.'

Stretching in his bed a little later, Matthew switched his thoughts to the following day. It would be interesting to see the new office and hopefully all would be organised and all in the right places as he liked. But Hugh, no doubt, would see to that. He wondered what news of the war, if any, had reached them and if there had been any interesting developments to know about, but no doubt Harry Anstruther would bring him up to date on anything really important. Then, of course, his mind went to Melanie. He must meet her soon as he realised she and Joanna would be leaving London in the near future. He frowned, but before he could think further about such things, he fell asleep.

Ned woke him next morning with a cup of coffee and asked what clothes he would wear as befitted his new office. When the reply was a grumpy "anything", Ned sniffed but proceeded to lay out a serviceable coat and small clothes in a dark maroon. This was what a man of Mr Brooke's standing should wear, not those old, decrepit things that he wore at his previous dirty old office. However, Matthew wouldn't let him throw them out as he said that they could be of use sometime. Ned sniffed again, folded them up and hid them away in a dark corner cupboard.

Matthew was welcomed with a big grin from Hugh and a "welcome back" from Arnold. The office was much cleaner as it was in a more select part of the city and the windows could be opened to let in some air in the hot weather. They overlooked the main road, but as they were on the second floor, the noise from the carriages outside wasn't too loud. After Matthew had found the layout of everything, Hugh said that Harry wanted to see him at ten o'clock in his office.

'Why? Anything been going on that I should know about, important things?'

Hugh shook his head. 'I can't think of anything.'

'Nor I,' said Arnold.

Apart from asking how Matthew had fared there were no more questions.

At ten o'clock precisely, Matthew went to see Harry Anstruther. Harry asked him how his trip to Marlborough had gone to which Matthew said that he had sorted things out but there was no real connection with France and there was nothing to worry about, the General only using it as an excuse to sort out a private issue.

'Mm. I can guess,' said Harry. 'How's the new office? Better?'

'Yes, sir, not that I've seen much of it yet but it's a great improvement, thank you.'

'Good, good.' Harry fiddled with some papers and Matthew began to wonder what was wrong. Harry seemed to be having difficulty finding words, which was not like him at all.

'What's wrong, sir?' asked Matthew after a minute or two.

Harry looked up, a frown on his face. He cleared his throat. 'I've heard from Tim Oakley.'

'Really? Has he not joined the French after all?'

'It seems not. He's sent some other information that is useful to know. Perhaps we've wronged him but the next part is what I find difficult to tell you.'

'What is it?'

'He says: *'I have had my suspicions ever since I met her and now I know by living in her friend's house that Mrs Shaw is sending secret messages to the French to the detriment of England. I thought I should put you on your guard.'*

Harry looked at Matthew.

Matthew's immediate response was: 'Rubbish!'

'It may be rubbish but until we can prove to the contrary I'm afraid you'll have to refrain from seeing her, Matthew. I'm sure you haven't passed on any information you shouldn't, I know you better than that but perhaps a note in your pocket or something just mentioned in passing she would pick up and use.'

Matthew had gone white. His Melanie whom he loved, spying? No, no, a thousand times no! He sat with a frown on his face and tried to think logically about it all. Harry sat quietly watching him, giving him time to swallow the bitter pill. He was sorry about it all but he could not afford to risk anything and the direct accusation of one over in France, who was living with the enemy, could not be ignored.

'I'm sorry,' said Matthew firmly, 'I don't believe it.'

'I don't know as I do, Matthew, really, but you must realise I cannot afford to risk it.'

'Can't we ask her?'

'She'll just deny it anyway, won't she?'

'Yes, but I'd probably know ...'

'I don't think you would be a perfect judge, Matthew, you are biased.'

'What do I do? Refrain from seeing someone I have come to regard and admire?'

'Yes, for the time being. Keep away from her. I'm sorry but that is an order.'

'Which means if I meet her socially in someone's house I have to ignore her or leave the house or not go out at all?'

'I thought perhaps she would be leaving London soon, anyway.'

'True,' said Matthew, 'but remember that my sister is living with her. Am I to ignore her as well?'

'You must do what you think best, Matthew. I'm sorry. But I'll say it once more, "you don't see Mrs Shaw again." That's an order.'

Matthew sighed. 'Very well, sir. Understood.' He left Harry's office sometime later, his mind numb. He never expected anything like this to happen and couldn't really believe it to be true. But, he supposed it could be. It was possible she could still be attracted to him, as he knew she was, and at the same time spy for France. She could have plenty of contacts and she probably spoke French well enough. It was a dazed and puzzled Matthew that eventually returned to his new office and sat at his desk with his head in his hands.

Hugh, coming in and seeing Matthew thus sensed something was wrong and quietly beat a hasty retreat to his own room but kept an ear open and waited. He also put his head round the door of Arnold's room and told him not to bother Mr Brooke at the moment. Arnold nodded, not understanding but willing to obey.

It came, as Hugh knew it would, a loud thud accompanied by a string of oaths. Matthew had hurled some books at the wall! Evidently something was very wrong but Hugh risked having his head bitten off by taking in a glass of wine. He placed it on Matthew's desk and then picked up the mistreated books. He half expected to be shouted at but when he turned and looked at Mr Brooke he was sitting just staring into space, a saddened expression on his face. Hugh left him alone.

Later, when he decided to check if Mr Brooke was all right he took in some routine paperwork for him to sign. He found Matthew writing and working as usual and as if nothing was wrong.

'Ah, Hugh,' he said, 'where does one lunch round here?'

'There are the coffee houses if that's only what you want but I did find a small place in a back street. It didn't look wonderful but I thought the food reasonably good.'

'Shall we go now if Arnold doesn't mind? I need to talk to you.'

'Yes, yes, of course. I'll check with him, shall I?'

Hugh was worried. Was something wrong with his work and Harry had complained to Mr Brooke about it? It was in trepidation that Hugh accompanied Matthew to lunch.

The small tavern was reasonably clean and they were able to order a plate of meat and ale to drink. They sat at a small table in a corner and Matthew thought it a change to see other well-dressed gentlemen rather than the rough clientele they had been used to.

'Well, Hugh, how are things with you and Joanna?' asked Matthew.

'We've been out together quite a lot, sir. We enjoy each other's company.'

'Do you know when Mrs Shaw will be leaving London? I know it will be soon.'

'I haven't heard any date as yet but Joanna did say she was not looking forward to going home.'

Matthew smiled. 'And you?'

Hugh looked at his dinner plate, then up at Matthew. 'I'm not looking forward to it either, sir. I—we—I wondered if I should tell Joanna I loved her.' He said simply. 'Would it be too early to ask her, do you think?'

'I don't know, Hugh. You must do as you think fit but I'd not object if that information is any good to you.'

'Thank you. I would look after her well, you know. But ...'

'But?'

'You're upset, sir, I know. Is—is it anything to do with me? Because if it is, it wouldn't be right for me to tell Joanna ...'

'No, Hugh, it is most definitely nothing for you to be concerned about. But I think I shall have to ask you to help me.'

Relief showed in Hugh's face. Then he said: 'I to help you sir? Well, if you think I can ...'

'Let me explain this to you and this is all I can say. It is for your ears only and I don't want you to talk about it to Joanna or—er—anyone else. Understood?'

'Yes, of course, sir. You know you can trust me.'

'The first thing is do not tell Joanna or—or Mrs Shaw that I have returned. All she—they knew was that I had to go away. If they ask anything say I am still away and you don't know when I'll return.'

'Very well.' Hugh sat still a moment, thinking. 'What will happen if you are seen, though. You can't just ignore them and you're not small enough to disappear into a crowd,' he finished with a smile.

'I just have to hope for the best, I suppose,' said Matthew.

'Does that mean that you and Mrs Shaw ...'

'At the moment I just don't know what the hell it does mean.'

'No, sir,' was all Hugh said. He felt something must be wrong between him and Mrs Shaw. They had seemed so happy and Joanna had said she hoped they would marry each other. Now that didn't seem as though it would happen. If Joanna asked him anything he'd just have to say he didn't know, which, of course, he didn't. But it wasn't a comfortable thought.

Ned knew there was something wrong as soon as Matthew returned that evening but he wouldn't ask. He only said: 'How was the new office, sir? Better than the old one, I hope?'

'Yes, Ned, yes it is. Thank you.'

Ned could tell he was answering automatically and refrained from asking any more questions. He hoped Matthew would feel better after he'd eaten.

The food, as usual, was good. Matthew took comfort from it and consequently his spirits lifted slightly, so much so that he was able to smile albeit ruefully at Ned.

'Thank you Ned, that was good as usual. Sorry to be so miserable.'

'That's all right sir. Something's worrying you, perhaps?'

'Ned, what would you do if you'd been forbidden by your boss to see the lady you love?'

'Would that be Mrs Shaw, sir?'

'Yes.'

'We-ll, if I didn't want to lose my job I wouldn't be able to plant him a facer, so I expect I'd go along with what he said if he had a really good reason. Is that what's happened then?'

'It is.'

'I'm sorry, sir, I really am. She seems such a lovely lady. Not that I've seen much of her though. But she's been very kind too to your sister, hasn't she? Will your sister still stay with her?'

'Oh, yes. It is just that I'm forbidden to see Mrs Shaw or contact her. So if anyone is sent from them or from anywhere for that matter, asking about me, could you say I'm away, please? It won't be long before they leave and go home. I can resume my normal life, if I want to that is.'

'I see,' said Ned. 'And do you think that things could be resolved so that you and she will be happy again?'

'I don't know. I really don't. I would hope so but what would you think if you were her and had been ignored all of a sudden by someone she thought she loved? She'll think I'm the biggest rogue and villain in the world.'

'So you're worried what she thinks of you? Is that such a big thing compared with what is at stake if you are doing something for your country? I don't know what the trouble is as you're not allowed to say but however unpleasant it is, your affairs are unimportant, aren't they? Not to you, of course, but to everyone else they are.'

Getting up, Matthew sighed. 'You're right as usual, Ned. But I've just thought of something I can do.'

'Good. You'll see everything will be well eventually.'

Matthew shook his head but smiled once more. 'Thanks,' he said, and gave Ned a quick affectionate hug on his way past.

CHAPTER 26

▼

One morning at breakfast Melanie said: 'Ladies, I'm afraid that we must think of returning home next week.'

'Oh, no,' said Joanna, 'so soon?'

'I know,' smiled Melanie, 'but we have been here for our allotted time, you know. The lease on the house is up. I realise you don't want to leave Hugh, love, but no doubt something could be sorted out. I don't want to leave either but—but there's nothing I can do about it.'

'Have you heard from Mr Brooke, dear?' asked Mrs Dobie. 'Can he not even write to you?'

'I don't know what he's allowed to do or not in his job. I hoped he would try, somehow, to contact me. I—I don't suppose you've heard anything, Joanna?'

Joanna shook her head. 'I haven't seen him either,' she said.

'Could you ask Hugh if he knows where Matthew is or—or anything?'

'I can ask him, of course I can,' said Joanna, feeling sorry for her friend, 'but usually he says he doesn't know and if he did he's not allowed to say. Oh, he is calling round this evening. Would you like to ask him yourself?'

'Thank you,' Melanie smiled. No doubt Matthew would contact her even if she were back in Chippenham. He wouldn't just forget her, would he? She thought he was in love with her as she was with him and she had hoped … Then some important work had taken him away and she was just left high and dry.

She heard Mrs Dobie saying: 'We must start organising things here then, the carriages and our packing and remember to take all our little personal things with us and leave nothing behind.'

Melanie, of course, knew all about these things but Mrs Dobie said this for Joanna's benefit. They talked a little more but Mrs Dobie could see it wasn't much use as she was only answered in monosyllables, both young ladies being immersed in their own thoughts. It looked as though she would have to be the one to supervise the return journey but perhaps once away from London Melanie would recover a little and be her usual self.

For the rest of the day the ladies took a trip to the shops. It was Mrs Dobie's idea as she said there was nothing like a little shopping to lift the spirits. It helped but back in the house their gloom descended once more.

Joanna wasn't too unhappy, she just wished that the blissful state she was in could go on forever. She wasn't stupid, she realised she would have to go back home at some time but kept hoping something would occur to prolong her London visit. She would have to tell Hugh the news this evening. She hoped he would feel as devastated as she was!

Hugh called after they had dined. Unfortunately, he didn't arrive as early as Joanna had hoped. He told her he had to work late but the real reason was that he didn't want to get too embroiled in talk about Matthew. He was terrified that he would mention something he shouldn't. However, before leaving Hugh and Joanna alone, Melanie asked if he knew when Matthew would be back as they were travelling home on the following Monday. Hugh, of course, disclaimed all knowledge of Matthew's whereabouts but seeing Melanie's pale face and dark eyes, took pity on her. 'Would you like to write a note to him?' he asked gently. 'I could give it to him as soon as I see him again.' He thought, also, that would be true, as he would be giving it to Matthew the very next morning.

Melanie smiled. 'Thank you. Perhaps you will see Joanna later in the week before we leave and I could give it to you then?' And so it was agreed.

'Poor Melanie,' said Joanna after she had left the room.

'And poor us,' said Hugh with a smile, trying to move away from the thought of Matthew. 'So,' he went on, 'you are going home next Monday. Your parents will be pleased to see you again, no doubt.'

'Oh, yes,' said Joanna somewhat sadly, 'but I shall miss you, Hugh. It has been such fun.' She looked at him with tears in her eyes.

Hugh took her hand and pulled her down against him on the chaise longue. 'It has, hasn't it? And I shall miss you too. I love you, you know.'

'Oh, Hugh, and I love you.'

He took her into his arms then and holding her tight managed to kiss her eyes, the tip of her nose and finally her lips. All this took a long time and when he was finished Joanna was breathless. All she could do was cling to him. He stroked her hair and whispered endearments.

'I don't want to go home,' she whispered.

'And I don't want you to but,' he hastily placed a finger on her lips, 'this has to happen, sweetheart. Will you do something for me while you're at home?'

'What is it?'

'I want you to think really hard and sensibly if you would like to marry me. Could you do that?'

'Oh, Hugh, of course I can. I can tell you now.'

'No, not now. Think hard about it, yes? When you are on your own and away from me.'

'Very well. And then?'

'I will have to ask permission from your Papa, won't I?' he smiled at her.

'Oh, Hugh,' she sighed placing her arms round him. 'Will you tell Matthew?'

'When I see him but we have his blessing anyway.'

'Dear Matthew. And you will write to me, won't you?'

'If you write to me,' grinned Hugh.

Hugh visited for only a brief time the following Saturday. He didn't want to get too emotional before his leave taking. Melanie had a sealed envelope waiting for him and he promised he would give it to Matthew as soon as was possible. She nodded but somehow still looked worried.

After church on Sunday, checking and last minute packing took place so that when breakfast was over on the Monday all would be ready for the return journey.

Matthew saw Hugh on Monday morning. As he was supposed to be out of London he had kept a low profile and hoped the ladies hadn't seen him. Hugh informed him that the ladies were travelling home that day. In one way, Matthew felt relieved. Hugh gave him Melanie's letter and explained it was his suggestion that she wrote to him. He said she had looked so unhappy it was the only thing he could think of doing for her. Joanna, of course, had sent her love to him when Hugh saw him next. 'To tell you the truth, sir, I've never felt so uncomfortable. I couldn't even tell them where you were.'

'How do you think I feel?' asked Matthew.

'Bloody awful I should think.'

This made Matthew laugh. 'Hugh, I've never heard such language from you before.'

'I've never felt like this before, sir.'

Matthew looked at Hugh but said nothing. He could sympathise but as sympathy was no help to either of them at this moment he didn't attempt it.

'Well, I had better read my letter,' said Matthew and feeling, for some reason, reluctant, he opened it.

Hugh left the room.

Dear Matthew (Melanie had written)

I don't know when you will receive this as I do not know your movements or where you have gone. But I thought I must let you know that we have left London and Joanna will be home in Marlborough and I will be back in Chippenham.

If you wish to contact me at any time my address is as follows: (here she wrote her home address)

I do hope you will let me know that you are safe and well and I enjoyed our outings very much and being with you.

Melanie.

Matthew sat frowning over the letter, which he read twice. It was obvious she didn't know what to think and she hoped all was well between them but she couldn't say so outwardly. Evidently she didn't think too badly of him and wanted to keep in contact. If she really knew the situation perhaps she wouldn't be so keen to know him any more. He still didn't believe she was a spy. What a damnable job this was at times. He placed the letter in his pocket and left the building to see if Harry was in his office.

'Yes, Matthew, what is it?'

Matthew explained how he came to have Melanie's letter given to him. If he wasn't open and honest now and the letter was found later, questions might be asked as to why he didn't think to show it, especially if it was found that Melanie was working for France after all. Deep down Matthew was convinced she wasn't but that didn't prove anything. Matthew thought it advisable to keep nothing back from Harry. He was a sensible man and did an excellent job. Now he asked: 'May I see the letter? I am very discreet, you know.'

Matthew handed it over. 'There's nothing private in it, really.'

Harry read it quickly and handed it back. 'There's nothing there for me to worry about. Now to the other points Tim has raised. He tells us there will be skirmishes in various towns, which we expect and know about already. They are an inevitable part of war. He also says he thinks a large battle is yet to come. We expect this too and so do the Prussians who are fighting well. And we have an idea where it will be and we have men out there too. What he is telling us is true but nothing new. I have also heard from Hunt, the fellow I sent to follow Fox. You remember, the man whose jaw you broke? Hunt has tried to contact Tim. As you know we have others out there working for us and who tell us more than Tim does. I think, personally, that Tim is playing with us and is getting at you for some reason. What do you think?'

'I don't know. But I always thought Tim and I got on well enough.'

'That's as maybe and we shall see. We have to play a waiting game. At all events I suggest we carry on as usual and I'm afraid, at the moment, there is still to be no contact between yourself and Mrs Shaw.'

Matthew sighed. 'Very well.' He left, his heart heavy but by the time he was back in the office he thought that perhaps there was a glimmer of hope that all would be well.

CHAPTER 27

▼

The ladies' journey home to Wiltshire went without any problems. The hostelries were comfortable and accommodating in most ways. The only thing no-one could do was heal Melanie's and Joanna's broken hearts. Poor Mrs Dobie tried hard to lift their spirits but only succeeded in diverting them a little. Melanie and Joanna did their best to behave as usual but there were no giggles and amusing stories told, as when on the outward journey. Joanna did have the advantage of her friend inasmuch as she had someone to go home to and she looked forward to telling her mama and papa about some of the things she had seen and done. Also she could have long talks with her friend, Emily, for whom she had bought a small gift of perfume, and regale her with all the delights of London and, of course, Hugh.

They arrived in Marlborough on the Wednesday morning, having stayed overnight at the quieter Castle Inn in Speenhamland. In one way, Joanna thought Marlborough looked much smaller and somehow different. Melanie said it was because she had become used to the spaciousness of London with its parks and river. Joanna was set down outside the Rectory and while her baggage was being unloaded she set the doorbell pealing. Ben answered it and immediately called for Eliza, who came hurriedly to see who wanted her. When she saw Joanna her face beamed with happiness. 'Oh, Joanna, how lovely to see you. What a surprise,' and she placed her arms round her daughter and gave her a hug and a kiss.

'Mama,' laughed Joanna, 'how are you? Look, here is Melanie and Mrs Dobie.'

Eliza rushed to meet them. 'Come in, come in,' she said. 'How are you? Would you like some refreshment? Come in, do.'

Melanie smiled. 'Mrs Brooke, thank you, but we cannot stay as we have to travel further. But we have enjoyed having your daughter's company so much. Perhaps you will visit us sometime?'

Joanna said: 'Oh, Melanie, could we? And I will certainly let you know if there is any news.' She placed her arms round her friend and kissed her. 'I hope I hear something soon. Thank you for everything,' she whispered. Then Joanna gave Mrs Dobie a hug too, much to that lady's delight.

Joanna and her mother stood and waved to them until the carriage was out of sight.

Linking arms with her mother Joanna asked: 'Where's Papa?'

'He's out somewhere. What a nice surprise he'll have when he comes home. But let us ask Ben to help with your things and carry them to your room and you can tidy yourself and then come down to the parlour and we will have some tea and a natter before your Papa comes home.' And she hurriedly went into the kitchen to find some of Joanna's favourite sweetmeats.

Melanie, of course, had no one to welcome her home other than the house-keeper but she was thankful Mrs Dobie was with her. She had never felt like this since the death of Charles and although she told herself Matthew wasn't dead, or she hoped he wasn't, in one way she had lost him. Surely he could have let her know somehow that he would see her again or not. It would be only polite if nothing else. Hearing nothing she feared that he was tired of her. She had to get used to the loss of what might have been and get on with life again. It would be lovely to see little Joanna again sometime but not yet. She held too many memories.

And so Melanie picked up the strands of her social life in Chippenham once more and tried to forget a certain gentleman in London who had thrilled her so much. The trouble was other gentlemen who were charming, good looking and sometimes wealthy never seemed to measure up to that fair-haired giant. There was no teasing or a feeling of security with any of them, not like Matthew, but no doubt she would get used to it eventually and she would look upon that London sojourn with Joanna as just a pleasant episode. She would move on, she told herself. Therefore, she busied herself in the community attending Spring Fairs and having delightful social afternoons with her lady friends. She and Mrs Dobie went shopping in Bath and by the time the warmer weather arrived, she was nearly the usual Melanie, but not quite.

Meanwhile, Joanna told her mother about the house in Curzon Street, the shops and the little things she had bought and which she would show later. She told her about the parties, except one, and the social life she had led and the friends she had made. In the middle of all this the door opened and Stephen said: 'Is it true? Is Joanna home again?'

She ran over to him. 'It's quite true, Papa,' she said. For once in her life she was enveloped in his arms and he kissed her cheek, which was something he hadn't done for a long time.

Sitting down, he said: 'Tell me all your news. You wrote some very interesting letters and you look blooming. I think you must have enjoyed yourself.'

'Oh, yes, Papa, it was wonderful.' And she went on to tell him of some of the visits she had made. 'St Paul's and Westminster Abbey are so vast, you know. And we went to the Tower which was interesting but so grim.' And so she went on until Eliza said that she must see to the lunch and hoped to hear more later on.

The next day, Joanna began to pick up the threads of her life at the Rectory once more, helping her mother and father. She frowned to herself. Her father, somehow, was different. She had always thought him a trifle pompous and not always approachable. He was just the opposite now and she loved him all the more for it. He had asked if she had seen much of Matthew but she only said that he had visited and that he accompanied them to the theatre sometimes. But she never mentioned Hugh.

After that, the days came and went and Joanna became used to the Rectory routine once more. She accompanied her mother to Marlborough as she usually did and involved herself in the affairs of the parish. She had long visits and talks with Emily, which were fun. And the days became warmer. She still had time to think of Hugh and wished she could see him once more.

He must have thought about Joanna as sometime later a letter arrived for her from him. It had been given to her father with some other messages one morning at the breakfast table. 'What's this?' he had said. 'Oh, it's for you, Joanna, from London.' Stephen looked at her and noticed her flushed cheeks but he just passed the letter to her with the words: 'You had better read it. It may be important.'

As she eagerly opened it he glanced at Eliza and winked. She hurriedly looked down at her plate with a smile on her lips. 'Thank you, Papa.' Joanna knew that in the past Papa wouldn't have hesitated to have opened it, deeming it not right to have a stranger write to his young daughter. However Stephen now found Joanna had really grown up and felt that she should be allowed to open her letters, but he hoped he would be told from whom it had been sent.

The letter, of course, was from Hugh. He began by thanking her for her letter and was pleased she had reached home safely. Hugh went on to tell her how much he missed her and hoped that she soon would write to him. The rest was about where he'd been and how much he wished she had been with him. He finished by sending her all his love.

Joanna folded the letter, a smile on her face. Then she looked up and said: 'I should tell you, of course, that while I was in London I met Hugh Fenton. And this letter is from him.'

'How nice,' said Eliza. 'Can you tell us more about him and how long you've known him? What does he do?'

Joanna looked at her father who lifted an eyebrow, just like Matthew, she thought. 'Well, he is twenty-four and lives in London with his parents, at the moment. I met him when Matthew brought him along with him on our first theatre visit.'

'Oh, Matthew knows him then,' said Stephen.

'Yes, he works with him. I don't know what either of them do, exactly. They won't tell, you know. But Hugh is very nice and kind and—and he did say he would like to marry me.'

'Really?' said Stephen, while Eliza sat with her mouth open.

'Good gracious,' she said, 'It's a little soon for that, isn't it?'

'The separation for a while will give them both time to think seriously about it all,' said Stephen, looking at Eliza.

'That's what Hugh said,' said Joanna.

'Did he now? At all events he sounds a sensible fellow, then.'

'Oh, yes, Papa,' said Joanna. 'He's sometimes as serious as Matthew. But Matthew approves of him, you know. And I shouldn't think he would have introduced him to me, if he didn't know him well.'

'Did Matthew mention anything to you, dear, when he was here?' asked Eliza. Stephen shook his head.

'Matthew was here, Mama?' Joanna frowned. 'When was he here?'

'Oh, it was at the beginning of the year, wasn't it?' she asked Stephen. 'At all events the weather was cold.'

'But—but why? He didn't say anything to us,' said Joanna, frowning.

'I don't know why he came really, do you dear?'

Stephen nodded. 'Yes, it was something to do with the General but that is all I can say.'

'Oh,' said Joanna. Was this the reason Matthew had had to go away without telling them why? Joanna couldn't believe it. 'When did he leave?' she asked.

'He was only here about a week. He brought Silas with him,' said Eliza.

'Silas?' said Joanna, wrinkling her nose. 'Who's Silas?'

'A very nice young man. He was black, you know. I wonder if he had been a slave at one time. But he was so helpful. I missed him when he'd gone.'

Joanna sat trying to work things out. That must have been the time that Matthew had "to go away" he had said. Why had he not been in touch after he had returned to London?

'Did Matthew say where he was going after he left here?'

'No,' said Stephen. 'I assumed they went back to London. Oh, yes, I know they did as Matthew sent me a gift of brandy from there.'

Joanna sat still digesting everything. 'Oh dear,' she thought, 'had Matthew really tired of Melanie and just left her high and dry?' That is what it looked like but Joanna couldn't think Matthew would do that to anyone. There was only one thing she could do and that was to see her friend Melanie again and discuss it all with her. It was about time she renewed the acquaintance anyway.

One warm afternoon in June Joanna persuaded her mother to go with her to visit Melanie. They found the house easily enough just on the outskirts of Chippenham. It was large but more compact than the rectory, Eliza thought wistfully. Joanna wondered how she was going to have a tête-à-tête with her friend when her mother was with her. She didn't really know and hoped something would present itself. She need not have worried as Mrs Dobie was just about to go into the town and she wondered if Eliza would like to accompany her. Eliza was a little startled at first but Mrs Dobie said that perhaps she would prefer to look at some shops rather than listen to two young people tittle-tattling. After the initial shock Eliza thought it would be a pleasant change to look at something new and as Mrs Dobie said they'd only be about an hour the two ladies used Eliza's carriage to carry them into the little market town.

'How lovely to see you, Joanna,' said Melanie, kissing her friend. 'How are you and have you become used to Marlborough again?'

'Just about,' smiled Joanna. 'I had a wonderful time with you, Melanie, and I still think about what we did and where we went.'

'Come and sit down. Would you like a glass of wine?'

'No, no, I'm only here for a short while,' said Joanna, looking round the pretty pink parlour. 'Mrs Dobie invited Mama to go to the shops with her, otherwise she would be with me. I particularly wanted to speak to you alone.'

'Oh?'

'Oh, Melanie, I don't understand it at all but let me tell you. During conversation with Mama and Papa it appears that Matthew came to Marlborough and stayed at the Rectory the same time as he told us he was going away and couldn't say why. I don't know why he wouldn't say either and Mama said she didn't know. He took a black man called Silas with him. I've never heard of him before. However, they stayed only for a week and then returned to London. As far as I can see, and you must tell me if I am wrong, when you wrote a note for Matthew and Hugh took it and said he would keep it until he saw him, Matthew was at the office anyway. It is a puzzle, isn't it?'

Melanie frowned and went over in her mind what Joanna had told her, checking certain details. 'How did your Father know your—your brother had returned to London?'

'Oh, because he sent Papa some brandy. Also I had a sweet letter from Hugh but he didn't mention Matthew at all.'

Melanie thought a little more and said: 'It looks to me that Matthew, your brother, doesn't want to know me any more. But why he has to exclude you as well I don't understand.' She tried to smile at Joanna but it broke in the middle.

Joanna went to sit beside her and placed her arms around her friend. 'I don't understand it either and it's so unlike Matthew. He usually is so kind and honest about things.'

'I—I thought so too.'

'I'm sure there is something we don't know about,' said valiant Joanna.

'Like another woman?' whispered Melanie.

'No, I won't believe that of him.'

'You're a loyal sister. But I don't know what to believe. The best thing, I think, is for me to try and forget him.'

'Oh, Melanie, I am so sorry.'

'So am I,' whispered Melanie.

On the homeward journey Eliza asked if Joanna had a good chat with Melanie. 'I would have like to have talked to her longer other than just saying, "Good day",' she said. 'Especially as you said she and Matthew were very friendly.'

'That's just what we were talking about, Mama. I don't think Matthew is interested any more. I think you should forget the letter I wrote.'

'Oh, dear. Were you wrong, then?'

'At the time I didn't think so. But now I don't know what to think. You see he hasn't been in touch for a while and not even with me. It just isn't like Matt.

Hugh doesn't mention him, either. I think something is going on that we don't know about.'

'Like another woman?'

'That's what Melanie said.'

'Well, don't tell your Father,' was all Eliza said.

CHAPTER 28

▼

One morning in June Melanie's housekeeper opened the heavy oak front door in answer to the beating of an imperative *rat-a-tat*. She found a courier there with his sweating horse. He handed her a letter that she saw was for her mistress. She hurried to find Melanie who took it and nodded, at which the housekeeper returned and paid the man, asking him if he needed refreshment. He smiled and thanked her and she obliged with a tankard of foaming ale.

Melanie retired to the library, a small room but pleasant and cosy. She looked at the letter in her hand. On it besides her name and address was the word "URGENT". She frowned. The writing was familiar and yet it wasn't. She opened it and found out why. It was from her friend in Paris to whom she had written last year introducing Andre de Noyons, when she had used the schoolgirl names they had given themselves. Now "Adele" had written in a hand that looked as if it shook.

Dear Estelle

I am so sorry I have to write this but the man you sent to me saying he was your cousin has denounced me to the authorities for being an English spy. I don't know why. Please, please, do something I beg of you.

Your loving Adele.

Melanie sat, shock and concern for her friend showing on her face. She looked on the outside of the letter again. It had taken over a month to reach her. What must have happened to poor Adele? And where was her husband? And why had someone to whom she had shown kindness in recommending to her friend, who had no doubt looked after him, suddenly denounce her? She couldn't make sense of it at all. But she must do something to help Adele who evidently had written to her as a last resort. Melanie felt she was to blame and she shouldn't have been so accommodating to that Harry Anstruther, whoever he was, and written that letter. The only thing she could think of doing was to go over to Paris and rescue her friend somehow. She knew Paris reasonably well as they had been at finishing school there together, which was a little while ago now. England was at war with France but she spoke good enough French to manage, she was sure. As long as she kept away from anyone important and any authorities she should be all right. The best thing for her to do before that was to go and see the General and ask him how and where she should cross the Channel, also the best places to go before accomplishing this. She must also obtain papers necessary for travelling, when she was in London. She knew which Bank to go to for French currency as she remembered Charles going there when he went abroad. She would take the plainest clothes she had and serviceable shoes and only things she was able to carry in one bag. She would plan a story for herself as a French lady who lived somewhere in France and was travelling to Paris.

Melanie went to find Mrs Dobie and explained what she was about to do and why. It all sounded so easy and simple to her, but when Mrs Dobie heard her, she lifted up her hands in horror. 'You cannot go, Melanie. It is foolish. You will get yourself arrested and shot.'

'Does it matter as long as I do something for my friend? After all I seem to have made a mess of most things.'

'Rubbish, girl. I shall travel with you to see the General and see if he can talk some sense into you.'

That afternoon, the ladies, one dressed in the height of fashion, the other in a subdued serviceable grey dress under a light cloak, took the coach to Marlborough to visit the General. By good luck they found him at home. Of course, he was delighted to have visitors but eventually when he learned why, he looked at Melanie a long time with a frown in his eyes. Then he said: 'Do you realise what you are saying and the danger you will be in if you do go?'

Melanie shrugged. 'I have to go whatever anyone might say.'

'You could be arrested at any time, you know. And how about the travelling, a lovely lady like you, alone? I'm sorry to have to say this but you'll be raped by the first villain who sees you.'

Melanie paled but said stubbornly: 'That's not important. What is important is that I must save my friend. I placed her in danger and I must see she's safe.'

'But she wrote this a month ago.'

'I know, that is why I must hurry. I can go to London and stay with a friend and I can find the Bank Charles used to go to for some currency. I have to have papers to travel with so perhaps you can help me by telling me …'

'Oh, very well,' said the General abruptly. He had noted how determined she looked and doubted his ability to change her mind. 'If you're adamant about going, and I see you are, come and sit with me and I'll tell you what you must do. And give me the name and address of your friend in London in case I need to contact you.'

When everything was settled Melanie kissed the General and thanked him, kissed and said goodbye to a tearful Mrs Dobie and then left to climb back into the coach telling the coachman to "spring the horses".

'Oh, dear,' said Mrs Dobie, drawing a damp handkerchief through her fingers, 'she is so strong willed at times. I do hope nothing will happen to her.'

The General looked at Mrs Dobie and the tears. 'Don't worry,' he said kindly, 'I know what I can do. She won't go alone. I now have to write an urgent letter, so I'll send you home in my carriage. And do not worry,' he said again, 'she will be safe.' And poor Mrs Dobie had to be content with his assurance.

As Melanie had to stop overnight on the road, the General's letter, sent by special courier, was received well in advance of her arrival in London. As soon as Harry Anstruther had sat down at his desk the following morning it was waiting for him. He frowned as he recognised the writing but when he read the General's news he sent at once for Matthew and two other men. To the two he said to keep the house of Mrs Milton in Brunswick Square under surveillance and one was to let him know when Mrs Shaw arrived and to keep watch on her movements and follow her if necessary.

'You sent for me, sir? Something important?' Matthew had seen the other two men rushing down the stairs.

'Ah, Matthew, it looks like it. I've had an urgent letter from the General.'

Matthew groaned inwardly. What was he up to now? But when he had read the letter that he had sent, Matthew groaned aloud. 'Good God,' he said, 'must she add to my problems?'

'You think she's fooled the General? It may not be what it seems, you know,' warned Harry, seeing Matthew's stricken face. 'She might genuinely be going to rescue her friend. The General isn't usually a poor judge of character. I have sent those men to watch the house and one will follow Mrs Shaw while the other reports. At a suitable time we shall apprehend her and see what she can say for herself. I know it must look bad for her at the moment but until we have talked to her I'm keeping an open mind and I suggest you do too.'

'Of course,' Matthew nodded.

'Oh, you never know, you might have to go over to France. Be ready.'

'Yes sir.' Matthew left.

Later, Hugh found him deep in thought at his desk. 'Was it bad news, sir?' he asked.

'No, not yet. I might have to go to France at any time, though. If there's anything you wish to ask me about, do it soon.'

Melanie felt terrible. The journey to London had been a nightmare. The hostelries she had stayed knew her, of course, but as she had no maid or other companion with her she was looked at with suspicion. She hadn't slept well either, being worried about her friend and also, now she was alone, wondering how she would really manage. She would have to, of course, and although she tried not to think about the problems she could encounter in France, she was nervous and not the cool and composed young lady she was usually. She had dozed a little on the journey but what with the shaking of the coach because of the ruts in the road, the shouting and the blowing of tin by the coachman at the turnpikes, it was a dark eyed young lady who emerged from the coach outside Mrs Milton's house in Brunswick Square.

Caroline, her friend, was delighted to receive her as her husband was away visiting his elderly parents and she missed him. Melanie was much relieved at the welcome and felt like weeping. When Caroline heard what Melanie intended doing, though, she was horrified but knew that whatever she might say wouldn't be attended to, anyway. One thing Melanie was particularly pleased about was a delicious meal, and then a soft bed where she slept very well that night.

The next morning when she woke she was loath to leave her bed as she knew it was probably the last comfortable one she would occupy for a while. After breakfast she became more her usual self and could think of the places she had to visit before leaving for the coast and France. Caroline told her butler to arrange for transport for Melanie and he came back immediately and said, as luck would have it, a carriage was waiting at the door. Melanie stepped in and settled back on the seat going over in her mind where she had to go and who to see. The carriage stopped and Melanie became aware that she had been taken to the wrong place. As the door opened and the man let down the steps she said: 'I'm afraid there's a mistake. I wished to go …'

'There's no mistake, ma'am,' the man interrupted. 'Please come with me.'

'But I need to go …'

'Please, ma'am, there's nothing to be afraid of.' The man, although looking scruffy, smiled kindly at her and held out his hand to help her. Melanie had no alternative but to do as he said. As he walked beside her, another man walked a little way behind her. 'Do they think I shall run away?' she thought and on second thoughts perhaps it wouldn't be a bad idea. But by then they were inside the building and she was led up the stairs to a room above. The man knocked on the door and a voice answered. The man opened the door and ushered Melanie inside.

'Mrs Shaw, I am so sorry to bring you here, like this,' said Harry Anstruther, 'please sit down.' He indicated a chair.

'And why have you brought me here and who are you?'

'I'm Harry Anstruther and I'm sure you know who this is.'

Matthew stepped forward and bowed. He had stood behind the door as Melanie entered so she hadn't seen him. She gasped when she did see him but couldn't make out what he was thinking as he looked straight at her with a face devoid of expression. He drew out a chair and sat down.

Harry said: 'It has come to our ears that you are planning to go to France. Why?'

Melanie gasped. 'How do you know that?'

Harry and Matthew just sat and looked at her. Melanie licked her lips, wondering what this was all about. However, she said, rather severely: 'I had a letter from my friend in France, the friend who kindly gave somewhere to live to Andre de Noyons. She wrote that he had denounced her as a spy to the authorities. The letter was asking for my help and as I was the one who placed her in such a position, this is why I am going to France.' She glanced at Matthew. Did he smile?

Harry nodded. 'Do you have the letter and may we see it?'

Melanie shrugged and looked in her reticule. She drew out the letter and handed it to Harry. 'As you see it was dated over a month ago and that is why I'm in a hurry.'

Harry read the letter and handed it to Matthew. He spoke for the first time. 'And this is your friend's writing?'

Melanie nodded.

'Are you sure?' Matthew handed the note back to Harry.

'As far as I remember it is. Why?' No-one answered her.

Harry took out the letter that Tim had sent to them. 'This,' he said, 'is a note we received from the man you know as Andre de Noyons. I can't show you the letter as there is other important information enclosed, but he says: *"I have had my suspicions ever since I met her and now I know living in her friend's house that Mrs Shaw is sending secret messages to the French to the detriment of England. I thought I should put you on your guard."*

Melanie turned white and tried to speak but nothing came out. After what seemed an age she licked her lips and said in a breathless voice: 'I don't know why he should say such things about me. He doesn't know me. And it is not true. What would I pass on to the French that is detrimental to England? I don't know anything. I speak French, yes, like many who learnt it at school there but— but ...' Her voice gave out and she covered her face with her hands.

Harry signalled to Matthew, who poured some wine for her and took the glass to her. He touched her hand. 'Drink this,' he said kindly but as she took the glass she trembled so much some of the wine slopped on the floor. Matthew covered her hand with his, which was comforting so that she was able, with his help, to drink the rest of the wine that warmed her and soothed her parched throat. It helped her to survive this nightmare she was in. All she wanted at this moment was to melt into Matthew's arms and feel safe. But he wasn't on her side any more. Did they really believe she was a traitor? How ridiculous it all was.

Meanwhile Matthew was looking at the writing on the two notes together. 'I don't think they are the same hand,' he said.

Harry took the notes and looked at them. 'No, but I think they should be checked by the right department.' To Melanie he said as he held up her letter: 'This will be returned to you in due course. Meanwhile, you will go to visit your friend in France but ...' He paused as Melanie let out a gasp of relief, then continued: 'I will have papers and monies prepared for you. Also, Matthew will go with you.'

'No,' Melanie said, getting up, 'I can go by myself, thank you. And I need to go now or as soon as possible.'

'Matthew goes with you or you do not go at all,' said Harry. 'If there is more trouble in this respect, I shall have you detained at His Majesty's pleasure.'

Melanie gasped. 'You would put me in prison? Well!' She subsided angrily back on to her chair.

'You will find it more comfortable to have Matthew with you,' said Harry kindly. 'Stay with Mrs Milton until you hear from me please.'

Melanie sighed. She couldn't do any more. She would have to do as she was told. 'Very well,' she said. As she moved towards the door where Matthew waited to see her out, Harry said: 'Oh, and don't blame Matthew for not contacting you. He was under orders.'

She just nodded and left. The scruffy individual was waiting to take her back to Brunswick Square.

CHAPTER 29

▼

'Caroline, I'm sorry to embroil you in all this,' said Melanie to her friend the next day. 'I am forbidden to go to France on my own and if I make trouble they'll put me in prison, would you believe? So I have to waste precious time kicking my heels here until these men decide what I should do. It makes me so angry.'

'Well dear, I see it might but it will be better to have someone with you, and safer, you know. Why don't we make the most of our time together and you can eat and sleep well at least, while you're here.'

'Dear Caroline. You are so good to me. Thank you.'

'Who will go with you, do you know?'

'Yes, I know,' said Melanie quietly.

'Is he, I assume it's a "he", trustworthy?'

'I think so. I do know him and I had hoped, at one time, there was something deeper between us but I see now there isn't. He—he thinks the worst of me, I know, and how we shall get on together …' She finished with a shrug.

After a pause Caroline said brightly: 'Well, I predict you'll have a very interesting journey and when you return you must come and tell me all about it. Promise?'

Melanie smiled. 'Of course,' she said.

'At least you smiled,' Caroline laughed at her.

There was a tap on the door and the butler appeared. 'Excuse me, Madame, there is a note for Mrs Shaw. It has just come.'

Melanie quickly opened the envelope. It was from Harry Anstruther. It read:

Dear Mrs Shaw

Please be packed and ready for tomorrow morning at 10 am. A carriage will call for you. Please ask Mrs Milton to accompany you.

Yours etc
Harry Anstruther

'There's no reply,' said Melanie and the butler left.

'What's the news?' asked Caroline. Melanie read the note to her. 'How intriguing,' she said. 'I wonder why I have to be with you. I have no intention of going to France.'

'No indeed,' said Melanie frowning.

The following morning, having breakfasted, Melanie was ready to leave and waited for her friend. She appeared and said with a smile: 'Now let us find out why I am required.'

On the dot of ten o'clock a carriage arrived at their door. Matthew alighted and waited as the ladies tripped down the steps. He assisted them inside and then took his place and Melanie introduced him to Caroline, who didn't expect to see such a personable gentleman. Instead of snapping his head off as she intended, she smiled and said: 'And why do I have to be here?'

Matthew gave her a brief smile. 'We won't keep you long and you will be returned home soon.' With that he looked out of the window and said no more. The ladies made faces at one another.

The carriage wended its way slowly through the streets and to Melanie's surprise stopped outside a small jeweller's shop.

'Come,' Matthew said to Melanie as he opened the door.

'Why?' she asked. 'Where are we going?'

He just looked at her and held out his hand. 'Come,' he said again.

She gave an exasperated sigh and placed her hand in his. She was surprised to feel it squeezed slightly. As he closed the door he said to Caroline with a sweet smile: 'Please wait, we won't be long.' Caroline just nodded, wondering what was happening.

Melanie was taken into the shop where the jeweller was waiting. 'Wedding rings, sir?' he asked, whipping out a tray. Did he know they would come, wondered Melanie, as he was ready and waiting? It seemed like it.

'That's right,' Matthew was saying.

'No, no,' said Melanie, panic surfacing at the implication.

'We need a new ring,' said Matthew, gripping Melanie by the arm but speaking to the man behind the counter. 'Take that one off,' he ordered Melanie.

Melanie looked at the one Charles had given her. She stared at Matthew with tears in her eyes. Was he going to sell it to buy another for some reason? This was a nightmare.

'I know how to take it off carefully, madam,' said the jeweller kindly. 'It won't hurt.' He took her hand and rubbed a little sweet smelling grease onto her finger and carefully withdrew the ring. 'There, that was quite easy, wasn't it? Now I will wrap this one for you to take home, so. Now you can choose a new one.'

Melanie looked at Matthew. 'Why?' she whispered.

She was surprised at the softened expression on his face and he looked like the Matthew she used to know.

'It's all right, really it is,' he said.

A new ring was eventually decided upon and bought. The other one Matthew picked up and placed it carefully in his pocket. He thanked the jeweller and they left the shop. In the carriage Matthew handed Melanie's wrapped ring to Caroline. 'Please keep this safe for Mrs Shaw,' he said.

Caroline nodded and placed it in her reticule.

'Where are we going?' asked Melanie with deep foreboding.

'To church, of course,' said Matthew.

'No, no.' Melanie realised what it was all about now. She was to be married to Matthew without even being asked. Two months ago she would have been thrilled at the thought but now, in these circumstances, it was no, no, no. 'I won't,' said Melanie.

Matthew looked at her. 'If you wish to travel to France with me you will marry me,' said Matthew. 'It will be safer and your reputation will remain intact.' He said it without a trace of the lover as if he was explaining to a child. 'Your name will be Madame Marais while we are in France and it is shown on our papers.'

'But ...'

'That's enough,' Matthew cut in quickly as the carriage stopped outside the church of Saint Mary's.

Harry was already there and opened the door and let down the steps after Matthew had climbed out. 'Mrs Shaw, Mrs Milton,' he bowed. As Matthew took Melanie by the arm and into the church he said to Caroline: 'Thank you for coming. It is necessary to have a witness, you know. Please do not think you are doing something wrong. If Mrs Shaw is to keep her reputation she should be married before travelling over France with Mr Brooke. The marriage can be annulled on her return if she wishes.'

Caroline only nodded and followed the others into the church. She felt a pang of jealousy. She would have given her eyeteeth to marry and travel anywhere with such a gorgeous specimen of manhood as Mr Brooke. She sighed and thought of her own husband, dear, staid, Bertrand.

But Melanie felt she was in the middle of a nightmare. Surely the priest wouldn't marry them? He couldn't marry people just like that! Banns had to be read or a special licence had to be … Of course, that's what had happened, they had thought of everything. She saw the priest was ready and waiting for them and the short service began.

To Melanie it was soon over and she felt she was in a dream. She looked cold and felt it. She must have made the responses as she should, though, as no-one prompted her. She remembered Matthew's warm hand as he placed the ring on her finger and that was all.

They left the church, Harry finalised things with the priest and Caroline entered the carriage with Harry after she had kissed Melanie's cold cheek and wished her well. A travelling coach was waiting for Melanie and Matthew, which was comfortable and suitable for the long journey to Dover. Melanie sat in a reverie. Occasionally she shivered and rubbed her hands, feeling the strange ring on her finger. What had she done? Oh, God, what had she done?

Matthew, to begin with, sat and looked out of the window saying not a word. He was a little surprised that Melanie had taken it all so hard. This frightened woman was not the Melanie he knew. Was she after all not so tough as she had previously shown herself to be? He glanced at her now, pale, dark eyed, and nervous. He had to do something, so he moved slightly so he was opposite her and took both her cold hands into his warm ones. 'Look at me,' he said gently.

She raised her blue eyes warily.

'Look, love, there is nothing, and I mean nothing, for you to worry about. I know it was all carried out in a high-handed fashion but we are limited for time, as we have to arrive in Dover in time for the night crossing to Calais. Surely you know me well enough to trust me?'

Melanie licked her lips before answering. 'It—it is just that it's all so strange and—and I hadn't seen you for some time and I'm all mixed up inside. Besides, you believe I'm a traitor.'

'No, I don't, honestly, and neither does Harry, really, but you must realise we have to check everything and ignore nothing. Just let things flow over you and relax. When you want to ask me anything, you can. Does the ring fit all right?' Matthew had noticed she was fidgeting with it.

'Yes, it's just a little strange as it feels different. I could have kept the other one, you know.'

'No, it wouldn't have been right for me to use something as precious to you as that one.'

Melanie nodded. 'Thank you. That was thoughtful.' She moved her hands he was still holding.

'Better now?' he asked. She nodded and tried to smile. He released her. 'Good. We shall stop to change horses on the way and near Maidstone we can have some food.'

She hoped she would feel like eating it when the time came.

But by the time Maidstone was reached she was well and truly hungry. She had relaxed as Matthew said. She had thought it all through rationally and by the time she stepped down from the coach she was nearly her usual self again. Matthew had returned her friend's note to her, which pleased her. It was thought to be genuinely written by "Adele" but as Matthew said: 'We shall see.' He didn't explain further and she didn't ask him. He seemed to have everything well in hand so she wouldn't ask questions which no doubt he'd refuse to answer anyway.

As far as Matthew was concerned the first hurdle was over and Melanie had relaxed more but he felt he must keep alert at all times for both of them. Where he would take risks if he were by himself, he now had to look to the safety of a wife too, if only in name, so he had to be extra vigilant.

They ate well and Matthew kept the conversation going by asking Melanie about Joanna and Hugh and did she think anything had been arranged between them yet. Matthew knew more or less from Hugh what the situation was but Melanie was quite happy to talk about Joanna and how happy she seemed. With one conversation leading to another the meal was pleasant and companionable.

As they began the last part of the journey in England Matthew suggested they spoke French and he was pleased that Melanie was quite fluent after a little practice and that they understood each other. They arrived in Dover during the evening to the strident screams of the seagulls and Matthew immediately took Melanie into the small stone inn overlooking the sea for a light meal. The landlord, a fat jolly man, bowed low and welcomed them. Matthew had met him before when he had been on similar missions. They were led to a small private room to eat but Matthew said he would return soon as he wished to check something so the landlord's wife came to ask if Melanie would like to follow her upstairs to tidy herself. When she came down again Matthew was waiting, also two bowls of soup.

'Where did you go?' asked Melanie, seating herself at the table.

'To see that our trip is still possible.'

'And is it?'

Matthew nodded. 'From now on be careful what you say and when I speak French you do so too. Understood?'

Melanie nodded. Her heart seemed to leap. Suddenly the soup didn't taste so good. However, she managed something, encouraged by Matthew.

After taking their leave of the landlord and his wife it was time to find their ship and embark for France.

Matthew led the way down to the harbour where a small vessel was waiting. The crew as far as Melanie could see looked rough but she managed to climb down the steps, helping hands reaching up to assist her aboard. Fishing nets were apparent and there was a small makeshift covered area at one end of the deck where Melanie was told to sit and Matthew was close by. She was pleased she had a hood to her cloak and wished she had a blanket. But Matthew, seeing her huddled figure, moved nearer and placed an arm around her, drawing her close to which she made no demur. She snuggled against him, feeling his warmth, and slept.

All was quiet, only the movement of the sea against the sturdy ship could be heard. As they travelled further into the Channel there were larger craft patrolling the waters. Very few lights were seen, only enough to avoid accidents. The little craft Matthew and Melanie were in progressed slowly and carefully, the Union Jack prominently showing. Once they were hailed from a patrol boat but the skipper answered in English through a loud hailer. They were in mid-channel and if it had been daylight they might have seen the white cliffs of England and France!

After what seemed an age a little quiet activity began as the Union Jack was lowered and the French flag was raised. The men now spoke a kind of French patois which Melanie couldn't understand. Obviously they were now in French waters. All went smoothly apart from a light from a large ship shining on them but when they saw the flag they moved on. Eventually they sailed into quieter waters and subsequently into a cove that was hidden behind the cliffs. Dimmed lights appeared on the beach like large will o' the wisps. The men who held them rushed forward. Matthew and Melanie were assisted on to the beach and Matthew listened as the skipper gave him instructions. He nodded and he and Melanie moved away. She felt dazed but she kept moving, one foot in front of the other, where Matthew led, which was a rough pathway between the rocks. At last they were at the top, Melanie was breathing heavily, her mouth dry. 'Come,' said Matthew, taking her arm. It was beginning to be light and it wouldn't be long before sunrise and by then Matthew wanted to be away from the sea. He followed the path, as he had been told, and they found a cluster of small cottages with their patches of vegetables and chickens. The name of Dessin was on one of the gates and Matthew led Melanie up the path to the door. He knocked and it was soon opened. 'Monsieur Dessin?' asked Matthew. The man said he was and all was ready. By that he meant there was a room to rest and food to be supplied later.

The bed was rough and not too clean but Matthew did the best he could to make it comfortable. He told Melanie to take off her shoes and lie on it while he did the same. She made no protest. What with the crossing and the strenuous climb afterwards Melanie looked quite grey and tired. She wondered if Matthew felt the same. Together they stretched out under their cloaks and slept.

CHAPTER 30

▼

They woke later when the sun was up, the cockerels were crowing and there was the smell of new bread baking. Melanie began to shake out her dress and tidy her hair.

'We can get water from the pump outside to wash,' said Matthew.

Afterwards they sat down to fresh eggs, boiled bacon, bread and coffee. To both of them it tasted good and Melanie praised and thanked Madame Dessin. She was pleased and brought them more butter and some cheese.

Matthew asked about transport to Lille and evidently Monsieur Dessin could take them by horse and cart to the next village where they could catch the coach for St Omer. Matthew paid him much more than asked but as he said to Melanie later, he hoped he would stand their friend again if necessary.

They were surprised to find the road was good, being made of gravel which was much better than most of the French roads. The countryside was flat and rich like the Lincolnshire Fens, well cultivated and the land chiefly arable. They reached St Omer, the gates having been opened since four o'clock and they were surprised to see that it had a large square in the centre of the city and the streets were wider than many French towns. Matthew and Melanie concentrated on finding a carriage to take them to Lille and after some negotiations arrived there before six o'clock. They found a room in a reasonably clean hostelry where Matthew immediately sent for hot water for washing. Melanie looked out of the window while he performed his ablutions and wondered what would happen when it was her turn. She needn't have worried as Matthew said he would go and book two places on the diligence to Paris for the following day. Meanwhile she was to lock the door and only open it to let him in. He returned later, his mission accomplished, to a much tidier and happier Melanie.

'Shall we go out to eat?' he asked.

'Oh yes please. How long will it take us to reach Paris?'

'Two days if all goes well.'

'Everything has gone well up to now, hasn't it?' Melanie asked.

'Mm. The country people carry on as usual, there is little talk of the war but I think we shall find a difference when we reach Paris. They are a different kind of people. We shall have to keep our wits about us. Also we have to get through customs there. I ask you to keep your eyes and ears open. Don't forget, speak only in French. We can't afford to relax until we are out of Paris.'

'Oh, it will be as bad as that?'

'Maybe, but we shall see.'

'I—I don't think I could have managed it on my own very well, after all,' said Melanie. 'I—I'm pleased you are with me, Matthew.'

Matthew looked at her but just said: 'Thank you.' He didn't want Melanie to think he would take advantage of her now. She needed him and quite honestly, at the moment, he had enough on his mind without dealing with an emotional situation. He needed to keep his wits about him at all times. It had been easy up to now and the country people pleased to earn extra money but he felt things would be different in the future. He had to keep himself safe so that he could keep Melanie safe.

They boarded the diligence the next morning at an early hour. There were more people to join them. Matthew placed Melanie in a corner and sat next to her so that she didn't come into contact with the others. Apart from nodding to the other passengers at the start of the journey Matthew and Melanie just talked to each other or looked out of the window. The roads were good and no wheels came off, as sometimes they were wont to do. Short stops at small towns gave everyone a break and in particular Matthew was pleased to stretch himself. Halfway they stayed the night at the inn that was expecting them. The food was poor and expensive and one room was for everyone although Matthew managed to obtain a small room for the two of them for extra money. It wasn't very clean so they just took off their shoes and wrapped themselves in their cloaks but Melanie kept close to Matthew for added warmth.

They were off again early the next morning after a mean breakfast and Melanie felt hungry, tired and full of aches. She just sat and endured. Matthew felt the same but had been in similar positions before when on his travels. They arrived at the Paris gates by late afternoon. The diligence was escorted to the official office where their papers were perused and bags searched. The man looked at Matthew but said nothing. All the passengers were allowed through and Matthew hailed a fiacre, an open horse drawn carriage, to take them further into town. Matthew asked the driver if he knew of a small hotel where they could stay near to the Rue St Honore. The one they were taken to looked suitable. It wasn't luxurious but it was reasonably clean and in a quiet street. 'We shan't be here long, I hope, anyway,' Matthew had said.

Melanie was used to the routine by now and she had no fears that Matthew had designs on her body. He treated her, apart from seeing to her welfare, as he would another man and she decided to accept this and act accordingly. She inspected the large bed, which was the best they had had the whole journey, and the cupboards.

'Do you recognise this area of Paris, Melanie?'

'No, not really. Oh, but I do remember the building at the end of the street with the little turret in the corner but I don't know what it is.'

'Do you know where the Rue St Honore is from here?'

Melanie frowned and thought hard. 'I can't remember exactly as it was some time ago when I was here but I think it's further along that street there. I can't be sure, though.'

Matthew nodded.

'Matthew?'

'Mm?'

'Can I go shopping, do you think?'

'For what?'

'I could do with another change of clothes. Do you need anything?'

'No and neither do you. Come here.' He was sitting looking out of the window.

'Why?' Melanie objected to being ordered about.

For answer Matthew just held out his hand but kept his eyes fixed on the view. Melanie approached cautiously. As soon as she was near, he grabbed her and pulled her on to his knee. 'Matthew—really,' she began.

'Shush, be quiet and look.'

She looked to where he pointed. 'What do you see?'

'The buildings opposite, a few carriages, people.'

'And in particular?'

She looked harder. She saw a man leaning against the wall. He was small and poorly dressed with a battered tricorne pulled down low shadowing his eyes.

'Who—who is he?' asked Melanie.

'I don't know but I thought things were going too well.'

'What do you mean?' Melanie began to panic.

Matthew felt it and held her tight. 'The first part of our journey over the Channel was organised as we have used the same people before and I think up to Lille we were safe. But after that everything has gone too smoothly. We were watched and particularly at the Paris gates there should have been more questions and answers and the man there looked at me a little too long. So we are expected and they know we have arrived and where we are, as is proved by Johnnie standing over there.' He indicated the man lounging the other side the street.

'But what are we going to do?' Panic showed in Melanie's eyes.

'Nothing.'

'Nothing?'

'For the moment. But you can kiss me if you like.'

'Matthew, how can you think of—of such things at a time like this?' And determinedly she began to move off his knee, but he held her tight.

'I can think about kissing you anytime,' he smiled, 'and now, when I'm stressed is a good time to begin. And it might confuse the watchers.' He settled her in the crook of his arm and without further ado placed his lips on hers in a long, long kiss, stroking her throat and neck. When she began to fight for breath he kissed her eyelids and cheeks and then found her mouth once more. She felt limp by the time he had finished but managed to say breathlessly: 'Are you not stressed any more?'

'I'm much better, thank you, but perhaps …'

'No, no,' she pushed him away. 'Do you want me to look a complete fright?'

'Never, never could you be a complete fright.'

'But we shouldn't be doing this. We should think about my friend and …'

'How boring,' Matthew interrupted with a sigh as Melanie had turned away and was tidying her hair.

A knock sounded on the door. Matthew was on his feet in a second, placing a finger to his lips as he looked at Melanie, and went to open it. But it was only the landlord standing there asking if everything was well and would they like a meal. Matthew said they would and was told it would be on the table in half an hour.

The food was plain but good and the landlord pleasant. Only another couple were staying and apart from wishing them "a good evening" no more was said to each other. When Matthew and Melanie had finished they left unobtrusively. Matthew nodded to Melanie to go back upstairs while he had a quiet word with the landlord. He asked where the back entrance led and could he have a key. This was agreed at a price and the landlord thought what a shame that the lovely lady upstairs was to be left while her husband went out on the town. He went away shaking his head, but with extra coins in his pocket.

Matthew told Melanie to pull down the blind after he had departed and go to bed and keep the door locked until he came back, whenever it might be.

'But Matthew, where are you going? Shouldn't I be with you?'

'No.'

'But the landlord?'

'He is used to husbands leaving their wives to find extra fun elsewhere.'

Melanie opened her eyes wide. 'And is that where …?'

'Of course it isn't,' Matthew said irritably. 'I'm just going to reconnoitre and find 16 Rue St Honore, that is all.' He picked up his cloak and hat, felt that his sword and pistol were in place and left the room.

For a large man he moved quietly and no-one, apart from Melanie, knew that he had gone. He left by the back entrance so that their observer was not alerted, and light of foot he walked swiftly the way Melanie had told him earlier and hoped she was right. It took him a little while to find the street, and although she had been correct about the general direction, there were many small streets to cross before coming to the more inspiring one of St Honore. There was some moonlight and the occasional torch but Matthew kept to the shadows as much as possible. He heard footsteps but stood still until they had passed. Eventually he found the house he was looking for, a large and no doubt a beautiful one. All seemed quiet but Matthew moved round to find the back entrance. He thought he was nearly there but couldn't be sure. He stood pondering, his hand on the hilt of his sword. He was about to return to the front of the house again when he noticed someone emerging from the back of one of the houses. As Matthew was in shadow he wasn't seen, so when the small plump figure came abreast of him and Matthew murmured 'Good evening, my friend,' the poor little fellow nearly jumped out of his skin.

'What do you want?' the man asked.

Matthew stood in front of him no doubt looking like a giant. 'Just a little information, my friend. Where is the back way of number sixteen?'

'Why, sir?' The man's voice was shaky and he was either old or frightened or both.

'There is someone I wish to know about, that is all.'

'Who would that be then?'

'Madame de Marne, and her husband.'

'They are not here.'

'Where are they? Are they in trouble and need help?'

'Why, yes and no, sir. They are not here but at their country residence in Champagne. They are quite safe, sir.'

'Are you a servant?'

'A lowly one sir. I'm Old Paul who does the odd jobs.'

'Who is in the house apart from the servants?'

'A—a French fellow. He's important.'

'Is his name Andre de Noyons?'

'Yes sir. You're not a friend of his, are you sir? If so I'm sorry …'

'No, no, it's all right. What does this Andre de Noyons do?'

'I don't really know but he's very busy with the war and he's taken over the house which isn't right, sir, is it? It's not his. Monsieur and Madame are such lovely people and they're not allowed to live in their own home and …'

Matthew interrupted. 'Who else is in the house?'

'Besides the servants, you mean?'

'Yes.'

'He has his own servant and two armed men who give the orders.'

'I see. And where is everyone now, do you know?'

'Monsieur de Noyons is out, probably with the ladies, so are the two armed men. His servant is having a quiet night in and his room is at the top of the house.'

'And everyone else?'

'In bed, sir.'

'And where are you going, my friend?'

'For a walk, sir.'

'At this time of night?'

'It's the only time I can go, sir. You see I have an affliction and if I go out during daylight I have things thrown at me and …'

'I understand,' said Matthew. 'But could you let me into the house, do you think, instead?'

'But I don't know you, sir.'

'True. But if you want me to get rid of these people … You see my wife is Madame de Marne's friend.'

'Oh, well, that's different, I suppose. But I hope I'm doing right.'

'Oh, yes, you are,' said Matthew softly. 'To prove it, have this.'

Old Paul fingered the coin and thanked him and led the way into the back of 16 Rue St Honore.

CHAPTER 31

▼

Apart from a lantern near the door it was dark inside the house. Matthew followed Old Paul, closing the outer door behind him and treading as quietly as a cat.

'Which way do the two men come in?' he asked softly.

'This way, sir,' answered Old Paul just as softly. 'They're usually a bit noisy but they keep to the back stairs. The servants hear them as their rooms are down here, but they take no notice.'

'And which way does Monsieur de Noyons enter?'

'Oh, by the front door.'

'Can you take me there?'

'Yes, sir.' He led the way up the stairs and they came into the back of a large entrance hall. It was brighter here, with candles lit and a lantern so that whoever entered by the front door could see reasonably well.

Matthew saw the extent of Old Paul's affliction, a very bad cleft palate, poor fellow. 'And which room does Monsieur de Noyons use? Where does he work?'

'The one on the right near the door. It was Madame de Marne's morning room where she received ...'

'Is the door locked?'

'Yes, but I have a set of spare keys.' Old Paul disappeared down the back stairs once more while Matthew stood listening. All was quiet except for the creaks of the old house and the slow *tick-tock* of the long case clock in the hall. After a few moments Old Paul came back, fitted a key in the lock and opened the door. He carried a lantern and from it Matthew immediately lit more candles that were standing on the desk that dominated the room. It was a beautiful room with an

Aubusson carpet, gilt chairs and oil paintings of lovely children but Matthew hadn't time to admire it. Instead he went straight to the desk and sat down. Turning to Old Paul he said: 'Go back down stairs, find me some cord and stay down there. When the men come in keep hidden, I'll deal with them but I shall need cord.'

'Very good, sir.'

Matthew looked through the drawers of the desk. He found some paper headed Andre de Noyons and quickly wrote a short message on it, signing it with Noyons' name. He addressed the outside and sealed it with a wafer. Next he wrote another longer letter and addressed it to the French authorities denouncing Andre de Noyons as a triple agent. It might just be enough to discredit any information Tim had given to the French. He signed it with an undecipherable signature. He placed both letters in his pocket. Matthew was on his feet when he heard the two men arriving below. They sounded decidedly merry and Matthew had hoped he would have been by the door near the back stairs as they came in, but by the time he had moved into the hall they were noisily trying to negotiate the stairs. As the first one reached the top he was surprised to be seized by the throat, and a hammer blow from Matthew's fist sent him reeling back down the stairs he had just climbed, where he cannoned into his friend. Matthew followed them down and rained blows on them both. As they were unprepared and worse for drink they had no notion of fighting back. When they were finally knocked out, Matthew dragged them unceremoniously down the rest of the stairs to find Old Paul waiting with cord and a knife.

'Have you—have you killed them?' he asked tremulously.

'No, but they'll be sore tomorrow.' He took off their neck cloths and stuffed them into their mouths, then trussed them up securely. 'Where can I hide them? A cupboard or ...'

'In here,' said Old Paul, opening a door that housed fuel for the fires. Matthew said as he shut the door on the two sleeping men: 'Don't worry. Go to your room and stay there like you usually do and know nothing. I shall deal with Monsieur de Noyons but you don't want to know about it. I'm hoping Monsieur and Madame de Marne will return soon.'

'Thank you, sir. I won't say a word. Everyone thinks I'm stupid anyway.'

Matthew held out his large hand and clasped the small misshapen one that was placed in it. 'You are far from stupid, my friend. Thank you, I couldn't have managed without you.' Matthew placed some coins in his hand. 'Remember, say nothing. Oh, and you had better have the key back.' As he handed it over, Old Paul caught a glimpse of a sweet smile.

Matthew went to the morning room and lit another candle, the light of which would be seen from outside. He stood behind the heavy closed door and waited.

It was nearly half an hour later before he heard the key turn in the lock of the front door. He didn't move. There wasn't a sound. If Matthew knew Tim, he would be pushing the door open slowly with his sword. Matthew waited, holding his breath so that Tim couldn't hear him. The door stood wide, then slowly and carefully, one step at a time, Tim walked into the room. He wasn't quite clear of the door when, quick as a flash, Matthew rammed it as hard as he could, knocking Tim on the shoulder and head and making him stagger to one side but not to the floor. While Tim felt his head and tried to straighten up, Matthew closed the door.

'You never did have any finesse, did you, Matthew?' Tim complained, holding on to the back of a chair.

'Sit down,' said Matthew. 'You expected me, no doubt.'

Tim sat, still feeling dizzy. He said: 'Of course. As soon as I knew you were in Paris I expected you but not quite so soon. You don't waste any time, do you?'

'So who are you working for? The French?'

'Maybe, maybe not.'

'I assume you are as you have turned the de Marnes out of their house, accusing Madame of being a spy.'

'Don't you think that was clever of me? I like this house so I decided to stay and they are in their chateau in the country and I assume quite happy.'

'Are they, or are they in prison?' sneered Matthew.

'No, no, they're in the country, happy or not,' laughed Tim. 'If you don't believe me ask the servants. And how is Mrs Shaw? You know, how will it look if she goes back to London and it is known, as it will be, that she has been in your company, for how long?'

'What do you have against her? What has she done to you that you should accuse her of spying?'

'Nothing, I hardly know the woman, but you do, don't you, Matthew? I knew you wouldn't like it when she was thought to be working for the French. It was an opportunity too good to miss. It brought you and Mrs Shaw running though, didn't it, Matthew, old fellow?'

'Well, no, you have that wrong among other things. You see, she married me.'

'I don't believe it.'

'That's up to you, of course. You also constrained Madame de Marne to write that letter asking for help, too,' went on Matthew.

Tim just smiled but it looked a trifle forced.

'So, as far as I can see things, all these petty goings on of yours, no definite news, falsely declaring my wife a spy and all the rest is, for some reason, just to get at me.'

Tim shrugged. He slid his hand in to his pocket looking as nonchalant as possible. Was his pistol in it, Matthew wondered? 'And do I assume the man known as Fox was the contact you were having words with and that you hoped he would kill me while you were in France? Why?'

'Ah, yes. You broke the poor fellow's jaw, didn't you? Fortunately he was no more use to us, anyway.'

'And what about Hunt, the man following him?'

'He went the way of all flesh. Didn't you know?'

'So,' said Matthew, who was now sitting on the corner of the desk facing Tim in his chair, 'why me, Tim?'

Tim shrugged. 'You were always the blue-eyed boy, weren't you? You were always Harry's favourite. I never liked you.'

'I don't think he made any difference between us. I had to obey orders like you.'

'Well, that's how it seemed to me and I was tired of that office in that seedy area, expected to be on the alert, day and night whatever we may be doing. Life's better here, more fun and I am someone with much more money.'

'You hated me so much you wanted me dead and the woman I love dead too? Now what do I owe you for that, do you think?'

'But there is nothing you can do, you see. I have you covered,' said Tim, pleased with himself. He indicated the pistol pointing at Matthew and although it was still in his pocket a shot could kill.

'You'll kill me?' asked Matthew.

'Of course,' smiled Tim.

The words were hardly out of his mouth as Matthew dived at Tim, catching him unawares. Tim fired, hoping to hit Matthew but it went wide and Matthew was too quick anyway. Now he had his fingers round Tim's throat pressing hard on the jugular vein until he slumped into a heap. Looking at his one time partner and friend, now turned traitor and would-be killer, Matthew took out his sword and with the full force of his arms plunged it straight into Tim's heart. After a few moments, although the blade was finely honed, it took Matthew some effort to withdraw it. He automatically cleaned it on a nearby cloth, sheathed it, and bent to check that Tim was really dead. He took the letter that he had previously written to the French authorities out of his pocket and placed it on the desk. If they believed the note they would be pleased to have had the killing of a traitor done for them. With a heavy heart Matthew finally left the room.

Outside once more, Matthew stood a moment and took in a deep breath of some of the early morning air, after which he walked swiftly away.

He entered the hotel by the back way and climbed the stairs. He reached the room and scratched gently on the door. After a few seconds it opened slightly and then as Melanie saw it was Matthew, she opened it wider. She had a candle in her hand and her hair was all tangled and her eyes sleepy. Matthew would have liked to indulge himself by hugging her close and burying his face in those dark locks and weeping. But he had work to do, so instead he whispered: 'Hurry and dress, we must leave.'

She opened her eyes wide then. 'But—but it's the middle of the night. What's happened?'

'Hurry, we have to be at the eastern gates as they open.'

'Yes, yes,' poor Melanie muttered vaguely, not understanding a thing, but she proceeded to dress with fingers that felt like thumbs.

Matthew hurriedly packed his belongings and looked round the room to see nothing had been left behind. He placed money on the bed for the landlord, then left as quietly as they could. Outside Matthew carried both bags and led the way.

'What time is it, Matthew?'

'About three thirty. Don't talk, just move.'

So no more was said and Melanie concentrated on placing one foot in front of the other and keeping up with Matthew.

It seemed as though they had walked miles when the gates came into view. There were others waiting, mainly workers, so when the guards came out and opened the gates they all surged forward. Most of them were known and so the task of checking everyone wasn't difficult. But when Matthew and Melanie walked forward they both stood out from the others and, of course, were stopped. Matthew, with no hesitation, handed them the short note he had written in Monsieur de Marne's house. He had written as Andre de Noyons, as near to Tim's writing as he could manage, giving permission for Monsieur and Madame Marais to leave Paris. The guards, reading the note, nodded and Matthew and Melanie went through the open gate without a problem, much to their great relief.

They continued to walk for a while to make sure they were well and truly out of Paris, then Melanie asked: 'Can we—can we stop soon?' She was tired and out of breath as Matthew had set a fast pace. He had only spoken once and that was to tell her not to dawdle. To Melanie he seemed as though he thought the devil was after him. She had done her best to keep up and as it was bright daylight now she felt like nothing on earth, unwashed, untidy and desperately tired. At her words he had looked round at her. His face was hard and grey. Melanie thought he looked ill. But for all that he managed to smile a little. 'We have to go a little further. When I find a suitable place to stay we will stop, I promise.' And with that she had to be content.

After what seemed like hours to Melanie but in reality was only just over two, Matthew finally stopped. They had covered nearly another six miles and Matthew deemed it now safe to find some accommodation. 'Look,' he said and pointed.

She looked and saw the spire of a church and a few tiny houses. Men were working in the outlying fields and as they approached the hamlet they saw a tiny inn with a swinging board over the door. On it was printed "The Plough."

'Let's see what it has to offer.'

He found the landlord who immediately called for his wife. She was a buxom lady called Madame Joubert. She eyed Matthew and Melanie warily. Matthew asked if she could supply them with food and a bed and told her they had walked a long way as their transport had broken down and his wife was extremely tired. Madame noticed Melanie clutching her cloak around her and came to the wrong conclusion that she was expecting a baby. Because of this Madame's attitude thawed and said if they would like to see the room they were welcome. The room was plain but clean and the bed large. Melanie sat down thankfully. Madame nodded to Matthew and whispered that his wife in her condition should rest. Matthew, without a blink, agreed. 'Would you like some soup and fresh bread? We have some for the workers in the fields. They will be coming in later. But I could send some up to you now and some wine.'

Matthew thanked her and said: 'Good soup and a sleep would be wonderful.'

While they waited, water was brought for washing. Then the soup arrived and Melanie felt too tired to eat but Matthew kept talking to her until she had eaten sufficient. She said she felt terrible and that she just wanted to sleep and promptly cradled her head on her arms at the table.

'Wake up,' ordered Matthew.

There was no reply. He finished his soup then went round to Melanie and proceeded to undo her dress. 'Wake up,' he said loudly.

'Mmm?'

'Help me take your dress off.'

Melanie half-heartedly began to undo the bodice and the rest was easy. Matthew picked her up and tucked her into bed and she was asleep as soon as her head touched the pillow. He took off his outer garments and climbed in beside her. He lay for a while letting the events of the past night wash over him. He thought about Tim and decided he had done the only thing possible. Exhaustion eventually overcame him and Matthew slept.

Matthew woke up in the early afternoon feeling refreshed. He dressed and went to see if the landlord had a likely horse and cart that he could borrow to continue their journey. Monsieur Joubert was kind enough to say that he could drive them to the next large town, bearing in mind Madame's condition.

Back in their room, Matthew woke Melanie. He undid a few buttons at the waist of her dress.

'What—what are you doing?' she asked in alarm.

'Monsieur and Madame think you are "enceinte". Let's not disillusion them as we are being favoured because of it.'

Melanie blushed. 'Whatever gave them that idea? You didn't …' She looked accusingly at Matthew.

'Madame saw you looking tired and drew her own wrong conclusions. I had nothing to do with it. Unfortunately,' he muttered to himself.

'What did you say?' demanded Melanie.

'Nothing. Shall we go down?'

CHAPTER 32

▼

During that night Melanie awoke, weeping, as unpleasant dreams crowded her sleep. Matthew immediately placed his arms around her and cuddled her to him until she slept again. The act was instinctive, a desire to comfort and be comforted as Matthew had had the nightmares that were inevitable, considering his previous evening's exploits. He grieved inside for his one time friend and he felt he would be a long while recovering. In his mind he thought it all over again and again and eventually came to the conclusion he had done the only thing possible otherwise Tim would have killed him and where would that have left Melanie? He didn't like to think of it. For all that, he wished everything had turned out better, but he would have been expected to administer the final *coup de grace* as no one had compassion for traitors to their country.

Afterwards they continued their journey by wagons and carriages, and Matthew deliberately kept to the smaller roads as it was a possibility that the French authorities could be searching for them. They travelled east and stayed at places that were small, until they were over the border to the relative safety of Burgundy. Then they used the main roads and better carriages, making more speed, and turned to the north, intending to reach the coast of the Low Countries. It was tiring and Melanie was heartily fed up with it all and began to wish she had never come. This was a waste of time, of course, and then she would look at Matthew and see the set of his mouth showing his determination to get through it all and bring them both safely back home. Melanie decided to try and wear a brave face, at least when Matthew was talking to her. Sometimes he looked grim and drawn and this is when she kept a low profile. If he had bitten her head off she would have collapsed in a heap of tears, which wasn't any good to anyone.

She did manage on one occasion to ask him a question to which she wanted to know the answer. Whenever she thought of asking him it wasn't the right time but now even if it wasn't she thought she had a right to know. 'Matthew?'

'Mmm?'

'Before we travel any further will you tell me what happened to my friend and her husband? We have hurried through France and I've been wanting to ask you but you've been unapproachable, you know. Is there something wrong or something I should know about?'

Matthew looked at her. Her eyes were anxious, her face so worried.

'I'm sorry I forgot to say. Forgive me. Madame de Marne and her husband were turned out of their house but they have been staying in the country in Champagne. They are well and will be returning to Paris shortly.'

Melanie breathed a sigh of relief. 'How do you know this, though? Are you sure? What happened that last night in Paris?'

Matthew seemed to look through her rather than at her. 'What I've just said is true. That's all you need to know.'

Melanie felt slapped in the face. Surely she was entitled to know about her friend and Matthew wasn't telling her half of what happened, she was sure, and wondered why. She swallowed hard and tried again. 'Matthew, I have done my best and walked for miles without complaint. I have been in far from clean beds and rooms and have eaten, in some cases, very inferior food. I am extremely weary, and I know I look awful.' She had seen herself in a mirror and was surprised to see how pale and drawn she had become. She went on: 'Many times I—I wanted to weep and—and I still feel like it but I—I've refrained so as not to worry you. So surely I have a right to know what has been happening.' She ended with a gulp. She realised Matthew had looked after her as well as he could and although they had shared a bed she was still married to him in name only. She didn't think either of them could have coped with the emotional side of marriage and kept their minds alert and wits about them on the journey through France otherwise. But Melanie was heartily tired of all the travelling and in her heart of hearts just wished she could wave a magic wand and be back home in Chippenham.

Matthew at last turned to her. Could he tell her what he had done on that evening? Would she despise him for it and not want to know him any more? But before he could say anything Melanie went to him and placed a hand on his arm. 'There should be no secrets between a man and his wife,' she said.

'Perhaps not,' said Matthew, 'but this is something to do with my work and often it isn't pleasant.'

'And you don't trust me enough to tell me about it?'

Matthew looked at the worried blue eyes in the beautiful face before him and immediately his own eyes softened. He took the hand she had placed on his arm and carried it to his lips. 'Oh, my love, of course I trust you but I feel you won't want to know me if I tell you the truth.' Then, seeing her stricken face, he said hurriedly: 'But it is nothing to do with your friend. She and her husband are quite safe, I promise.'

Melanie nodded. 'Then please tell me what is upsetting you.'

Matthew sat down and drawing her on to his knee, told her simply and without embellishment why he had had to kill his one time friend.

Melanie felt shocked, but on the other hand, after she had thought about it further, couldn't see what else he could have done. She said: 'But Matthew, what would have become of me if you hadn't killed him and he had killed you? I would have been taken and—and … Oh, Matthew, don't you see you saved me by killing him. Thank you, oh, thank …' And the tears began to fall.

Matthew was relieved that Melanie had taken the news so well. He kissed her and she kissed him back as both their tears mingled.

The weather was hot and as the horse that pulled the cart they were travelling on wended its weary way they noticed regiments of soldiers marching along the road. They wore red knee length coats with black tricornes, which were decorated with wild roses picked from the hedgerows. They carried muskets and bayonets.

'Good gracious!' exclaimed Melanie, 'who are they and where are they going, do you think?'

Recognising the red coats, Matthew said: 'They look like British, with some Hanovarians probably. They must be marching to an engagement.'

They saw more along the road and some cavalry who wore blue coats. These would be British, Matthew thought, and wondered if his brother Luke was one of them. Some of the cavalry wore white and these again would be the Hanovarians. They disappeared into the distance as Matthew and Melanie stopped in a small town. After making enquiries, Matthew was told there would be a battle not too far away between the French, Prussians and British. He decided they should stay and they found a house where they were offered a room. Matthew looked at Melanie.

'What's the matter?' she asked.

'I think we should take a look at this battle.'

'I've seen battles before,' said Melanie. 'I followed the drum, you know. Charles expected it of me.'

'And did you enjoy following …?'

'No, but it was my duty. So why do we have to look at this battle?'

'I'm sorry but I think my brother Luke will be involved in it.'

'Are you sure?'

Matthew nodded, just watching her.

She sighed. 'Oh, well, perhaps we'd better wait until we know if he is safe. That is what you are worried about, I suppose.'

'Thank you. It will only mean a delay of another day or two.'

Melanie could have wept. She bit her lip. She was heartily fed up with it all and now a battle on top of everything else seemed the outside of enough. She looked up. Matthew was watching her.

'What?'

'I do realise the sacrifice you're making,' he said.

Melanie was mollified. 'Well, if anything were to happen to your brother and we hadn't bothered about him, we wouldn't be able to live with ourselves, would we?' She managed a little smile and then found herself in Matthew's arms being kissed.

'Thank you,' he whispered in between the little kisses he rained gently all over her cheeks to finish with a long hungry kiss on her lips. 'There is no need for you to accompany me,' he said.

'Oh, Matthew,' she said as she came up for breath, 'please don't. It takes away all my energy and I need it …'

'Good,' said Matthew and continued kissing her until with a supreme effort Melanie pushed him away.

'No,' she said, 'not now. You—you must find out more about your brother and as I have said, I have watched battles before.'

'Yes, you said. And as you are "enceinte" you had better rest,' he finished with a grin. He left the room quickly before something was thrown at the door. Matthew was nearly back to his usual self again.

Shortly after, he headed towards the town of Minden.

The battle began there early in the morning on the first of August. Matthew found himself a key position on higher ground where he could view most of the fighting. Many other people from the surrounding area were there too, among them French and Prussians, who mixed together without animosity. Their only worry was to find a vantage point so that they could watch the spectacle. Matthew sat next to an older Frenchman who quite happily shared his spyglass with him.

Matthew could see the red coats of the British foot soldiers beyond a woodland and in the distance a glimpse of the River Bastau. He saw what he was particularly anxious to see and that was the British cavalry and prayed that Luke would be safe. They looked proud and focussed, sitting very straight in the saddle with swords at the ready whilst holding their horses still. Lord Sackville, who was in charge of them, was in the front. Matthew saw the French and Prussian armies ready. All was comparatively still and quiet waiting for Marshal the Marquis de Contades, who commanded the French troops, to give the signal to attack. He lifted his sword and yelled an order and all hell broke loose.

The battle was fierce and soon the sky was obliterated by smoke as gunfire blasted the air. The boom of cannons and explosions were temporarily deafening, covering the cries of the wounded and the neighing of frightened horses.

Prince Ferdinand of Brunswick not only commanded forces for his King, Frederick of Prussia but also for his Britannic Majesty, King George the Second. As Matthew looked he couldn't believe his eyes when he saw British foot soldiers attacking the French cavalry and looking successful. What brave fellows they were, but he expected Contades didn't think so. During the cannon fire Matthew noticed a horseman sent by Prince Ferdinand, riding towards the British cavalry. He spoke to Lord Sackville, no doubt giving him orders to charge. Nothing happened. Matthew could see the men had swords at the ready and they were holding their horses back with difficulty. The messenger rode back to Prince Ferdinand and nothing happened. The messenger came again and again and still Lord Sackville wouldn't obey orders. His deputy in command, the Earl of Granby, tried to lead them forward after being requested to charge for the fourth time but again was halted by Lord Sackville. What was the man playing at, Matthew wondered. The fighting went on with men charging, attacking and counter attacking and at last Matthew saw the cavalry surge forward. At the end of the day it was over with Prince Ferdinand the victor.

The noise stopped, apart from the moans and shouting of the wounded, and the sickening smell of the dead assailed the nostrils. Many valiant soldiers who had survived tried to help their wounded comrades. Makeshift areas were found where doctors with their instruments did their best to keep the wounded alive, after amputating limbs before gangrene set in. People from nearby villages came to help with rags to bind the wounds and staunch the blood.

Matthew looked for his brother among the wounded in the place where he last saw the cavalry engaged, and found a group of cavalry men and hoped Luke was one of them. He wasn't but when he asked if they knew anything about his brother they pointed to a group of men who lay on the field being attended to by local people. He found Luke propped up against a hillock with a hand pressed to his left shoulder. His eyes were closed and his face was grey with pain.

Matthew took out a bottle from his pocket and held it to his lips. 'Come on, Luke, drink,' he commanded.

'Mmm what?' Luke drank some of the brandy and managed to open his eyes. 'Matt? It can't be,' he muttered.

'But it is. Let's see if I can make you more comfortable.'

'How?'

'Just be quiet and help me.' Matthew gradually peeled Luke's coat away. Luke was on the verge of fainting but eventually Matthew managed to bare his shoulder where a musket ball was lodged. He took off his own shirt and ripped it up. He made a pad from some of it and bound it in place with strips. After pouring more brandy down Luke's throat, he heaved him to his feet and carried him along. Fortunately Luke favoured his mother and was of lighter and smaller build than Matthew and his father. As he passed them, Matthew called to the group of men he had spoken to before and asked them to tell Luke's commanding officer that he had taken his brother. Back on the road again, Matthew, with Luke up in his arms, carried him like a baby back to the house where they were staying.

There was much concern for Luke, not only from Melanie, but from the owners of the house. They were kind enough to send for a doctor who, with difficulty, managed at last to dig out the musket ball from Luke's shoulder. The wound was washed and bound and a sleeping draught administered. Matthew and Melanie took it in turns to sit with him through the night.

For some days Luke was weak with the loss of blood but he was kept quiet, fed small amounts of digestible food frequently and was watched over at all times by Melanie and Matthew who, of course, took the lion's share. Bit by bit, Luke recovered and eventually he was on his feet again although feeling weak. His left shoulder was still bound and his arm in a sling to keep it still and to stop the wound bleeding.

'You know,' Luke said, 'I wouldn't have had this if we had charged when we were expected to. If Sackville had obeyed orders and not been so bloody minded we could have overthrown the French army and the whole battle would have been over quicker.'

'So what will happen to him?' asked Melanie.

'Well, he'll be tried, of course, but knowing him he'll probably change his name and fight somewhere else.'

At last the doctor pronounced Luke well enough to travel so they made for the Low Countries and the coast where after a while they were able to board a ship to take them across the North Sea. They landed on the Lincolnshire coast and were thankful to be back in England once again.

After three more days they finally reached London and Matthew took Luke to his London home with him. Ned, of course, was delighted to see Matthew back again safe and sound and he was a great help in nursing Luke back to health in the days that followed. Also he was able to keep an eye on Luke when Matthew was at work. Matthew lost no time in letting the authorities know about Luke's whereabouts as he wanted to return to his regiment, his friends and his horse as soon as possible.

Melanie was delivered safe and sound back to her friend's house in Brunswick Square. Matthew told her gently that his time would be taken up for a while with Harry Anstruther and he thought it would be good for them to be apart for a time. For one thing, he said he hoped Melanie would rest and recuperate from the strenuous time she had had. He asked her, when she was finally back home in Chippenham, to think long and hard whether she still wished to stay married to him or not. He said when Harry could let him have some time off he would take Luke home to his mother for some tender loving care and then he would visit Melanie and she could tell him what she had decided to do. He thanked her for her help with Luke and she thanked him for bringing her home safely. Matthew quickly kissed her on her cheek and she hurried indoors to seek refuge once more with Caroline.

Matthew went into the office two days later. Hugh was delighted to see him, but thought he looked tired. Word was sent to Harry that Matthew had returned and he was immediately sent for. Matthew made his report.

'It seems you were right, sir. It was a personal thing against me but for the life of me I don't know why. I didn't realise he hated me so much.'

'Jealousy can create many problems.'

'He was definitely working for the French,' went on Matthew, 'and had taken over the de Marne's house. They should return soon, however.'

Harry looked at Matthew. 'So what happened to Tim?' he asked softly.

'I killed him,' said Matthew, and as he looked up, Harry could see the pain in his eyes. But there was no room for sentiment.

'Quite right, it was the only thing you could have done,' he said and squeezed Matthew's shoulder as he passed.

CHAPTER 33

▼

Joanna sat at the kitchen table supposedly helping Cook by peeling the carrots, but as she had spent the last twenty minutes on one particular carrot it didn't look too hopeful that they would be ready for the midday meal.

Cook said: 'Miss Joanna, is something wrong with that carrot that you are mutilating it so?'

'Mmm? Oh, no, I don't think so. Why?'

'Well, considering it has taken you forever to peel it …'

Joanna looked down. 'I'm sorry, I'm not being very helpful, am I?' She seemed about to weep so Cook said no more and as Eliza bustled in, just nodded slightly in Joanna's direction.

'Shall I help, dear?' said Eliza. 'Would you rather do something else or go and see Emily?'

Joanna heaved a sigh. 'No, Mama, I'm sorry.' Her lower lip quivered.

'Now, you're getting yourself upset for nothing, you know,' chided her mother. 'No news is good news.'

'But I haven't heard from Hugh for ages now or Matthew for that matter. And when I went to see Melanie some weeks ago she wasn't there and Mrs Dobie wouldn't tell me anything. I feel everyone is against me.'

'Well, we're not,' said Eliza, 'and neither is that poor carrot.'

Joanna managed a smile.

What she didn't know was that Hugh hadn't written as he had been deluged with paperwork at the office. As Matthew was on the Continent it meant more work for Hugh and longer hours. By the time he was home and had eaten, the evenings were advanced and he was too tired to do anything more. Even if he had made an effort to write to Joanna he couldn't mention Matthew. He supposed he could tell her he loved her but he felt that she already knew that and there was no need to keep saying it. Matthew would have told him otherwise, of course, but then he was more experienced with the ladies. Hugh continued to go to work every day hoping Matthew would return soon as it was now the beginning of September.

On this particular morning Joanna felt no one wanted her and she sat with her head propped up by her hand, staring into space, carrots long forgotten. Cook and Eliza just left her alone and carried on as usual. They were interrupted by the jangling of the front door bell. Joanna, startled, looked up. 'Do you think it's a letter?'

Eliza, already on her feet, said she'd go, and picked up her purse so that she could pay the courier. She opened the door. No courier stood there but Matthew.

'Hello, Mama,' he grinned at her, 'look who I've brought home with me.'

'Matthew,' she held her face up to be kissed, then looking past him, saw Luke. She opened her eyes wide. 'Oh, my Luke! How wonderful to see you! Are you all right? But of course you're not, you have your arm in a sling. Come in, come in.'

Luke bent to kiss his mother's cheek. 'Mama, it is good to see you but I'm sorry to look so pathetic.'

'Never mind, you're here.'

Joanna, hearing voices, rushed out. 'Matthew, Matthew how wonderful and—and Luke? Gracious, how did you come to be here? Oh, my goodness, you're hurt! Poor Luke, come along in and tell us all about it.'

All this time Eliza had been leading them into the parlour and fussing over them saying how lovely to have them.

Matthew said: 'I've brought Luke home for some tender, loving care, Mama. Oh, Jo, be a love and fetch my bag in, will you?'

Joanna looked at Matthew and was about to say something cutting but she changed her mind, seeing how pleased she was to see both brothers. She opened the front door again and saw someone handling the baggage. Then she went nearer. 'Hugh!' she screamed, 'Hugh, it *is* you, isn't it?' And she rushed forward. Hugh turned just in time to receive Joanna's lithe young body into his arms. 'Oh, Hugh, Hugh, I've been wanting you so badly!' she said.

'And I, you, my love.'

'I've been so miserable and I hadn't heard and I've done nothing but mutilate the carrots this morning and …'

Hugh held her tight and kissed her. 'You've had a wretched time, haven't you, but I can explain a little to you later. But what I have to do with carrots I can't work out.'

'Well,' said Joanna, 'I'll tell you later but do come in and meet Mama. Papa is out at the moment.' It was a radiant Joanna who joined the rest saying: 'Mama, here is Hugh as well!'

'Oh, my goodness! Hugh, you are very welcome. It is lovely to meet you. Dear oh dear, I don't know whether I'm on my head or my heels. Rooms must be organised and Cook …'

'I'll tell Cook we have three extra to feed,' said Joanna.

Extra food was cooked, rooms and beds prepared and baggage sorted out. In the middle of all the mayhem Stephen walked in accompanied by the General. 'Why, whatever is going on?' he said.

'Papa.' Luke stood in the doorway. Stephen stared at him, not believing his eyes.

'Luke, how wonderful—but you're hurt. Is it bad …?'

'No, no. Good morning General.'

'Let us go inside and you can tell us how you came …' Stephen began.

'Papa,' Joanna ran forward. 'Oh, Papa, come and meet Hugh.'

She led the way back into the parlour where Eliza was talking to Matthew and Hugh. 'Here's Papa and the General,' announced Joanna.

Introductions had to be made, of course, and eventually in the midst of all the talking, lunch was announced. In spite of all the extra people, Cook had managed to make a tasty meal.

After it was all eaten and conversation had lapsed, Matthew cleared his throat and said: 'As we are all together I would like to explain some things to you all. I can only tell you certain things, so please don't ask anything more of me. Then I shall leave you for a while to go to Chippenham.' He paused, then resumed: 'Mrs Shaw had to visit urgently someone in France. I also had work to do there. I was asked by Harry Anstruther, the man in charge of these things, to take Mrs Shaw with me and bring her back safely. Careful plans had to be made as we are at war with France, as you all know. Also, so that Mrs Shaw's reputation wasn't ruined by travelling alone with me, we were married by special licence in London before we left.'

Reaction to this announcement was mixed. Joanna clapped her hands and said, 'Oh, how lovely.' Eliza looked stunned and Stephen looked aghast.

Matthew waited and looked ruefully at their faces in front of him. 'It was understood, between us, that the marriage could be annulled afterwards if necessary. Our particular work in France was accomplished but we had to leave quickly because of certain circumstances, which can't be disclosed. We made our way through Prussia instead of returning over the Channel. But it was as well as we found out about the battle at Minden and I went to find Luke. It was fortunate that I did as he had a musket ball in his shoulder. I managed to find a doctor other than the field surgeon, so he was attended to quicker. When he was well enough we travelled across to the coast and so came home. I sent my—my wife home as I had much to do at the office. Hugh had worked extra hard while I was away, too, and both of us have been promoted.'

Everyone clapped and Eliza said: 'Oh my goodness, you've all been in so much danger, too.'

Matthew smiled. 'But it's all right, Mama, if you know what to do. Now will you excuse me while I go and see if I'm still to keep my wife.'

'But you *do* want to, Matthew, don't you?' piped up Joanna.

Matthew looked at her with a softened expression on his face. 'Yes, Jo, I do.'

Before anyone else could say anything he murmured another "Excuse me" and left the room.

A silence descended on those sitting round the table. 'I don't like the sound of all that,' said Stephen bitterly.

'Melanie is very nice, Papa,' said Joanna. 'Isn't she, Hugh?'

Hugh nodded. 'I thought so,' he said.

'She kindly helped to look after me on the journey home,' put in Luke.

'I find her charming,' said the General, with a wink at Eliza.

'She looked after Joanna well when she was in London,' she said.

Stephen sighed. 'We'll see, won't we?'

All the way to Chippenham, Matthew wondered if he was to be made the happiest man in the world or the most devastated. He hoped Melanie would be at home to receive him. What would he do if she wasn't? And so he proposed all kinds of questions and answers after which he mentally shook himself and thought that compared to this, any problems Harry asked him to solve were easy. But by the time he drove up to Melanie's house he was looking cool and calm as usual.

A groom came to take the horse while Matthew knocked on the door, which was opened by a servant and after giving his name Matthew was shown into a room overlooking the garden at the rear of the house. Through the window he noticed a figure sweeping leaves. It was Melanie. The servant went out to tell her she had a visitor. No sooner had she heard what he had to say she dropped the broom and ran, at the same time untying her apron, which she let drop to the ground. A few minutes later, not wanting to tidy herself further, she entered the room and uttered one word: 'Matthew.' Then stopped.

Matthew thought that as she had rushed in to see him it boded well and so he turned with the smile that she remembered. 'Hello, my love, how are you?' he said. They were ordinary words but they sounded wonderful to Melanie.

'I'm well, thank you. And you?'

Matthew solemnly shook his head. 'Not very,' he said.

'Oh, dear,' Melanie looked concerned. 'Can you tell me about it?' She patted the sofa next to her as she sat down. Matthew sat where she indicated. 'I'm feeling better, now,' he said.

She looked at him, a frown in her eyes. 'Are you teasing me?'

'No. I was feeling quite ill but I'm improving by the minute,' he said seriously.

'You have a twinkle in your eye for all that seriousness. I don't believe you're ill at all.'

'My heart is very sick,' said Matthew sadly.

'Would it make it better if I said …'

'Yes?' prompted Matthew, hopefully.

'I said you are making it all up,' she finished severely.

'Now I'm feeling ill again,' he complained.

Melanie hid a smile. 'Would you be better if I—if I—I said …?' She looked at him hoping he would help her.

He did. 'Please be my wife, Melanie,' Matthew asked her softly.

'Do you really mean it?' Matthew nodded. 'Oh, my love, yes please. I've waited and hoped you felt the same.'

'Of course I do.' And Matthew took her into his arms for some long, long kisses. 'Mmm,' he said, coming up for air, 'you smell of fresh air and autumn.'

'How are you feeling now?'

'I'm nearly recovered but not quite.'

'Lily is out. Would—would you like to see my—my bedchamber? Or …'

'What a good idea! I think I shall be quite recovered afterwards, you know.'

Hand in hand they mounted the stairs.

As they all sat against the fire at the Rectory after their meal, Stephen and the General excused themselves. This gave Joanna an opportunity to ask her mother why her father didn't like the idea of Matthew marrying Melanie.

'Well, if you remember, I was the only one to meet her when you went to London. Your Father had to visit someone who was sick. I didn't think he needed to know how young Melanie was. In fact, he assumed she was an older person otherwise he wouldn't have been happy to let you go to London at all. So I—er—I forgot to tell him.'

'Mama!' exclaimed Joanna with a giggle. But she placed her arms round Eliza and kissed her. 'You're the best Mama, ever,' she said.

It wasn't until much later that Matthew and Melanie arrived with Mrs Dobie as well. Melanie had changed her dress to a rich blue silk which wasn't cut too low. Matthew brought her into the room where they all were and said simply: 'I've brought my wife home with me.'

Joanna, of course, rushed to her and kissed her. 'It's lovely to see you again and I have lots to tell you. Oh, here's Hugh.'

'It's lovely to see you both,' said Melanie. She looked round for Eliza. 'Mrs Brooke, please be glad to hear our news.'

'I am, oh, I am, my dear,' said Eliza and kissed her.

Stephen and the General came in, hearing the noise. Melanie saw Stephen and went straight to him, gave him a curtsey and with a lovely smile said: 'Mr Brooke, we haven't met before but I'm so pleased to do so at last. I hope you are happy with Matthew and I as there is something we would love you to do for us if you would.'

Stephen stared in astonishment. He had never imagined such a lovely looking lady. All he could do was to smile at the anxious young face turned up to him. 'What is it you wish me to do?' he asked indulgently.

'Would you be so kind as to let us take our wedding vows again in your church, with you officiating? We had such a hurried marriage, you know, although it was quite legal. But it would be more like a wedding with the family around, too.'

Stephen found himself smiling. 'Well, do you know I would be delighted to arrange a service for you. Perhaps we can discuss it later?'

'Thank you,' and Melanie stood on tiptoe and kissed his cheek.

'Hey,' said a voice, 'What about me?' It was the General, of course.

While Melanie gave him a kiss, too, Stephen beamed round at all those present. Even a clergyman was allowed to puff out his chest in pride sometimes, wasn't he? His children had done very well for themselves. And Eliza? He saw her smiling happily at everyone and fondly at her two sons and daughter. She was such a good wife and mother. Stephen decided there and then that he would take her to see Mark and his wife and baby Saul as soon as possible. She deserved it.

And next year he would certainly take her on that long awaited journey by the sea.

END

978-0-595-50463-3
0-595-50463-9

Printed in Great Britain
by Amazon